MR. MAYFAIR

LOUISE BAY

Published by Louise Bay 2016

ISBN – 978-1-80456-990-0

The Doctors Series

Dr. Off Limits

Dr. Perfect

The Mister Series

Mr. Mayfair

Mr. Knightsbridge

Mr. Smithfield

Mr. Park Lane

Mr. Bloomsbury

Mr. Notting Hill

The Christmas Collection

The 14 Days of Christmas

The Player Series

International Player

Private Player

Standalones

Hollywood Scandal

Love Unexpected

Hopeful

The Empire State Series

<u>Gentleman Series</u>

The Ruthless Gentleman

The Wrong Gentleman

<u>The Royals Series</u>

King of Wall Street

Park Avenue Prince

Duke of Manhattan

The British Knight

The Earl of London

<u>The Nights Series</u>

Parisian Nights

Promised Nights

Indigo Nights

Faithful

Sign up to the Louise Bay mailing list at
www.louisebay/mailinglist

Read more at www.louisebay.com

ONE

Beck

"Kevin Bacon is full of shit," I said as I thwacked the small, black rubber ball with my racket.

Dexter lurched away as the ball ricocheted toward his bollocks. "What did he ever do to you?"

"The six degrees of separation thing—it's bullshit."

"What?" Dexter asked, panting. I was kicking his arse, and I knew that had to hurt his delicate ego. No doubt he'd chalk up his losing to that skiing injury he still complained about. As far as I was concerned anyone who skied deserved every injury they got—hurtling downhill with metal flippers on your feet could end only one way.

"You know, the idea that everyone on the planet is just six people removed. So, a friend of a friend of—"

"You can't blame that on Kevin Bacon. It's not like he invented it," Dexter said before serving.

"Okay then, if you're going to be pedantic, Frigyes Karinthy is full of shit."

"I can't tell if you're swearing at me or speaking Ukrainian."

"Hungarian," I replied, wiping my forehead with my sleeve. I measured exercise not on calories burned or time spent in the gym but on the amount I sweated. Someone needed to develop a machine to measure perspiration—I'd pay good money for it. As far as I was concerned it was effort that always earned the best results. "He developed the bullshit theory. I looked it up on Wikipedia."

"Fuck," he spat as the ball hit the plaster below the red line, giving me the victory I'd expected since we got onto the court. Dexter only lost at squash when he had business trouble, so I wasn't going to crow about my win.

"Yeah, I get it. What's the problem?"

I bent and scooped up the out-of-play ball as it trickled toward me. "The theory is flawed. I have dredged every single one of my contacts and I can't get an introduction to Henry Dawnay."

"You're still trying to get a meeting with that old billionaire?" Dexter grinned, as if my failure in business was going to make up for his shitty performance on the squash court. "You might have to give it up."

"Henry Dawnay is not just some old billionaire. He's *the* old billionaire standing between me and nine-point-four million quid. And I'm not about to give up on that kind of money. I've plowed every contact I have and come up empty. I thought one of you lot would have some kind of connection to him. What's the point in having rich, successful friends if they're no use to me?"

"Us lot? You mean your five closest friends who'd walk through fire for you?"

He knew I was joking as sure as I knew United were going to win the league. The fact that the guys I'd forged bonds with as a teenager were rich and successful was simply circumstance. Their jobs weren't important. They were the best men I knew outside my own dad. And I'd walk through fire for them just as I knew they would for me. But that didn't mean I couldn't complain about the fact that none of them had been able to score me a meeting with Henry Dawnay, even if it did make me sound like the moody git Dexter always accused me of being.

I rolled my eyes and nodded toward the changing rooms. I needed a shower and then I needed a plan. "I don't need anyone to walk through fire for me. I need someone to introduce me to the man who owns the property standing between me and ten million quid."

"You said nine point four."

"Have I told you how annoying you are?"

"A couple of times," Dexter said, pushing through the door to the changing room. "Look, if you can't get an intro from someone you know, why don't you track him down, bump into him, and introduce yourself."

I fixed him with a thanks-for-the-advice-mum look. "I did. Last month in the lobby of the Dorchester. He shook my hand and swooped right out without stopping to get my name."

Dexter winced, and he was right to. It'd been embarrassing. I'd felt like a nine-year-old boy meeting Cristiano Ronaldo.

I opened my locker door and pulled out my phone to check my messages. Two more missed calls from Danielle. *Shit.* Another thing I had to deal with. "I've managed to get access to his calendar so—"

"How the hell have you managed that?"

"Don't ask. You need plausible deniability so you don't end up in prison." From what I understood, I'd broken several British laws and a couple of international ones by getting that information. I hoped it was worth it.

"Well, I hope you and Joshua end up in jail."

I ignored his assumption that another member of our brothers-in-arms, Joshua, was involved. It was an obvious assumption—Joshua liked to hack into government agencies to unwind. The rest of us played squash. "I'm well connected—some would say powerful in real estate circles. I've got money and resources. For Christ's sake, I know the brand of loo paper this guy uses. But apparently, it's not enough to get a meeting." Things would be very different if my birth certificate had carried my biological father's name.

"You need to calm down and figure it the fuck out."

"Great advice," I mumbled as I scrolled through my emails. One was from Joshua with Henry's itinerary and schedule for the next couple of months. I slumped onto the bench and opened the attachment, hoping to find he'd finally arranged a lunch or a meeting with someone I knew.

But no. Nothing. Although there was an entire week blocked out. Perhaps he was going on holiday?

"This is the guy who you want to buy the building in Mayfair from, right?"

"Yeah, I own every other piece of property in the row except that one—the most run-down of the lot of them, and he's done nothing with it. It's standing empty and prime for redevelopment. It's prime for *me* redeveloping it." It was a building I'd been obsessed with since I could remember.

"Look, worst case, you just work around it."

I shook my head. "I don't work around things. I take a wrecking ball to them." I'd crunched the numbers. I wouldn't make a profit if I didn't have Henry's building. And I didn't take losses. And anyway, it wasn't just the money.

It was the building my mother lived in when she found out she was pregnant with me.

It was the building my mother was evicted from as soon as her boyfriend, the owner of the building and my biological father, found out she was pregnant.

When he died, it had been inherited by a distant cousin, and since my mother told me the story when I was a teenager, I'd been laser-focused on buying that building. Maybe I thought if I owned it—owned what I should have inherited—wrongs would be righted.

Then I could tear it down and start again.

I'd rewrite history.

I studied the document Joshua had sent. Why had Henry blocked out an entire week? The man didn't take holidays. I looked closer. The only reference in the entire week was M&K. I typed it into the search engine on my phone. What could M&K stand for? As I scrolled through the results, I couldn't see how a furniture shop in Wigan or an American DJ could be relevant. Henry wasn't just old money, he was titled—an earl or something, although he didn't seem to use it. I was pretty sure he wasn't shopping in Wigan or entertaining DJs.

I switched screens, and just as I was about to call Joshua to try to get more information, another email flashed up with an attachment. When I opened it, the dates of the M&K week were the first thing I saw. It was a glossy, electronic wedding invitation. Apparently Joshua had been just as curious as I had. A wedding that lasted an entire week? Did these people and their guests not have jobs? M stood for Matthew and K for Karen. The bride and groom. I plugged their names into Google. They were no one I knew. But there was no surprise there. They looked like the type to have met on a croquet field—Matthew was all sports jackets and straw boaters. I didn't know how old-Etonians and people with inherited wealth looked different from most normal human beings, but they did. It must be the floppy hair or the air of entitlement they wore.

A society wedding would be a perfect place to approach Henry. He'd be relaxed and in a good mood as he spent time with his people.

But his people weren't my people.

My money was as new as the dawn and that left me on the outside of the wedding party, peering inside, at the end of unreturned phone calls and unable to meet with Henry Dawnay.

"Speaking of wrecking balls, how's Danielle? Managed to destroy that relationship yet?" Dexter asked, pulling me out of my Henry obsession.

I glanced up from my phone. "What? She's fine." I wasn't sure she was exactly fine. I'd pissed her off. Again. The last conversation we had over dinner, she'd started to talk about taking things to a deeper level. But I liked the shallows—dinner a couple of times a week followed by a sleepover. I didn't have time for anything else. The rest of the time I was working—figuring out the next deal, scoping out new opportunities, firefighting issues on current sites. It didn't leave time for much else in my life other than for my five closest friends. As much as it might make me a dick, women were important in the generic sense. But a particular woman wasn't. So the last few months it had been Danielle. Before that it had been Juliet and by the end of the summer, it was likely to be someone else. But I should return Danielle's calls. I'd been busy and this Henry thing was getting to me.

"When's the last time you took her to dinner? Or even had a conversation with her outside the bedroom?"

"Jesus, are you my therapist now?" Guilt prickled beneath my skin, and I kept my eyes on my phone. I'd cancelled dinner this Saturday. Again. She'd been pissed off, so I'd given her some space. But it was Thursday. *Shit.* I should have called her back by now. If I confessed to Dexter, he'd tell me I was a dick. But it wasn't like I planned it that way. I was just wrapped up in everything else I had going on, and somehow Danielle had fallen off the bottom of my call sheet. I switched screens and dialed my messages to check her tone of voice and see if I was still in the dog box.

I deleted the three "Call me back" voicemails. The fourth escalated into "Where are you?" The fifth another "Call me back." She sounded calmer, more relaxed. Perfect. Just as I'd hoped. But the sixth voicemail was one I hadn't been expecting. Or maybe it was. I listened as she dumped me—her tone resigned, her words cutting.

"You okay?" Dexter asked, studying my expression.

I ended the call. "Yeah. I'm a selfish, piece-of-shit workaholic. And Danielle Fisher's ex-boyfriend."

For the second time this morning, I got a well-deserved wince from Dexter.

I shrugged—as if it couldn't be helped. As if it wasn't entirely my fault. "I should have called her back sooner."

Dexter nodded as he fixed a towel around his waist. "Yeah, you should have. But at the same time, if she was the right woman for you, you wouldn't forget to ring her. Or avoid her calls. You'd want to speak to her."

"And what the fuck do you know about dating the right woman?"

"I know," he said.

"But it's not Stacey," I said, referring to the woman he was currently sharing a bed with.

"Stacey's not . . . Just because I fucked up with the right woman doesn't mean you have to. Learn from my mistakes."

I rolled my eyes and went back to the email from Joshua. "I'll be sure to mention to Stacey she's in an interim role next time I see her."

"Don't be a dick."

"You first," I replied. I was being a dick. Danielle had sounded kinda resigned, like I'd lived down to her expectations, which stung. It was the tone my form teacher had used when I'd told her I had no intention of going to university. My grades had been good, but I wasn't interested in more studying. I didn't belong in that world. I wanted to be out in the world earning money. I doubt she'd use that tone with me if I ran into her now. She'd thought I was being lazy except it was the exact opposite. University was good for people like Henry and whoever this Matthew and Karen were—I had better things to do. I needed to earn my fortune.

But no matter how rich I got, I still didn't mix in the circles that Henry Dawnay did.

Well, that needed to change. I had to figure out a way to score an invite to the society wedding of the year.

TWO

Beck

I traced my finger down the guest list for a second time. I must have missed something. Some*one.*

"I checked it three times, sir," my assistant, Roy, said from the other side of my desk. "I even searched against contacts of your contacts."

By the time I was out of the shower and back at my desk, Joshua had sent me the guest list from the wedding Henry was attending, and I'd been determined to find my way in. The groom's father was well known in the City—a partner in one of the oldest investment banks in London. I knew the type—hated it when clubs in London were forced to let women in, longed for the days when no one expected you back in the office after lunch. I should be grateful—they were the men who left meat on the bone that I came along and gobbled off. The bride's father was a landowner, so he didn't do a lot except drive about in a Land Rover dressed in tweed. If I just knew someone who would be going. Then I could get them to speak to Henry at the wedding and talk me up, explain how I was good for my word and easy to trust—maybe even mention how I had a business proposition for him. I'd have to be careful who it was. Dexter and I goaded each other, but if he was going to that wedding, Henry would think I was his fairy godmother by the time Dexter was done—any of the six of us would do the same for each other. We were brothers in all but name. But anyone else? I wasn't sure I'd trust someone outside our circle with something so important. It would be better if I was a guest at the wedding myself. Then Henry would be a captive audience and I was sure I could convince him to sign on the dotted line.

"And you're sure that I don't know *anyone?*" I might not have been to the right schools or grown up in the right circles, but I'd been successful for years. I was earning more money than most of London put together, and I dealt with lawyers and people in business all day, every day. But I didn't know a single person who would be at this three-hundred-fifty guest wedding.

"As sure as I can be. I've cross-referenced against your contacts and your LinkedIn page. And I checked the last five years' Christmas card lists to see if I'd missed anyone."

It wasn't so surprising. We might all be British and living in the same city, but I still existed on a different planet to these people.

"I don't suppose there are any single women on the list?" There must be someone going without a boyfriend. I was single. So I'd track them down, seduce them, and be available as a plus one for weddings and bar mitzvahs. No, that was a shitty plan. I needed to be sure I was getting into this wedding—I wasn't going to leave it to chance. I wanted some kind of guarantee or contract or something.

"The ones invited with an un-named plus one are at the

bottom of the list," Roy said. I turned the page to find one male name and three female names.

"Do you have their ages?" Or photographs.

"No, sir. I can find that out for you though."

I needed to know exactly who these three people were.

Candice Gould

Suzie Dougherty

Stella London

Three single women—it had to be my way in. As invitees to M&K's wedding, they had something I needed more than oxygen. I might not be able to guarantee a plus one by seducing them, but everyone wanted *something*. And I had considerable means at my disposal. I just needed to figure out what they wanted and then do a swap—a plus one for a pony or a week on a yacht or whatever it was people who didn't work wanted in life. I just needed to track them down and make them an offer they wouldn't want to refuse.

One of these women was the key to the Dawnay building.

THREE

Stella

Another day, another dollar, so the phrase goes. But for me another day meant another twelve hours at my crappy office with the crappiest boss who ever lived. Placing people I didn't know into jobs they didn't want was the worst. It might have only been two months into the role, but I'd never get used to being a recruitment consultant.

My mobile buzzed on my desk beside me and I glanced over my shoulder toward my boss's empty office. She hated people taking personal calls. If breathing took time out of the day, she'd ban that too.

It was Florence. She never called me at work. Taking my life in my hands, I swiped to accept the call. "Hey," I whispered.

"Are you in front of your computer?" she asked.

"Of course I am. I'm chained to it, what—"

"I'm five minutes away. Whatever you do, don't check your emails. Get your coat and meet me downstairs."

Florence must be crazy. I was constantly checking my emails. "I'm staring at my inbox, Florence."

"I mean your personal emails. Promise me. Log off and meet me downstairs or I'm going to march into your office and haul you out."

"It's only just gone six. I can't just leave. What's the problem?" It sounded serious. "Are you and Gordy okay?" She and Gordy were the perfect couple. If there was trouble in paradise, then anything was possible.

"I've just turned into Monmouth Street. Have you got your jacket on?"

Oh God. She didn't say that they were okay. Florence needed me. And she trumped the wrath of my boss. "I'm coming," I said, wedging the phone between my shoulder and my chin as I logged out.

I pulled my jacket off the back of my chair and headed to the exit, ignoring my boss's assistant's pointed look at the clock as she saw me leave.

I saw Florence as soon as I stepped out of the lift. She was facing me from the other side of the glass doors of the office, her shoulders slumped, her forehead furrowed, and her face as pale as a corpse. It was clear something catastrophic had happened.

I was going to kill Gordy.

"I'm so sorry, Florence," I said, and I opened my arms and pulled her into a hug.

She held me so tight, I struggled to breathe. She must be devastated. We all thought Gordy was one of the good guys.

"I wanted you to hear this from me," Florence said as she pulled away and snuck her arm around my shoulder.

"Of course. I'm here for you," I replied as I grabbed her hand. "I'll help you bury the body if you want me to."

She frowned as if she was surprised by my offer, but

how could she be? There wasn't anything I wouldn't do for Florence. For either of my two best friends.

We crossed the street and found an outside table at the bar opposite my office on Monmouth Street. One of the few positives about my job was that it was based in the West End and surrounded by bars and restaurants. "We're going to need wine," I said.

We were going to need a shovel. If she didn't kill Gordy, I would.

We ordered a bottle of wine and took a seat. "So you saw?" Florence said. "You seem very calm."

"Saw what?" I asked. "Oh," I said, pulling out my phone. "You said there was something in my personal email."

"You didn't see?" Florence asked.

"What?"

She pulled my phone from my grasp and grabbed my hands. "What body are you helping me bury?" she asked.

"Gordy's, of course. Tell me what he's done."

She shook her head. "It's not Gordy. It's Matt."

My stomach dropped straight through the seat of my chair and I froze. If Florence had raced over here from where she worked in the City at six on a Wednesday, it couldn't be good news. Had he been in an accident? Had his dad died?

"He's getting married," she said, squeezing my hands.

I pulled away from her as I tried to understand what she was saying. "Of course he's not getting married. We've only been apart two months." I didn't like to say we'd split up because it wasn't an accurate description of what was happening. We were just apart right now. It was just a temporary thing. He was just freaked out that all our friends were getting married and people kept asking us when we were next. He was just doing that guy thing where, just before they pop the question, they have a man meltdown. Just look at Prince William and Kate Middleton. They had a three-month break before William proposed.

"I'm so sorry, Stella."

Florence looked up at me, her eyes filled with tears, and my heart began to gallop. She was serious. "What do you mean? Who to? How do you know?"

"The invitation was delivered to Gordy's office. And then there was the email follow-up with the schedule. Never mind."

I tried to swallow but my throat was too tight. I reached for the glass of wine that Florence was hastily pouring. "I don't get it. There must be some mistake." How could Matt be getting married? He hadn't proposed to me, and we'd been going out for seven years. We'd been living together for six. It wasn't possible. Florence must have it wrong.

Florence shook her head. "It gets worse. I really don't know how to say this, but he's marrying Karen."

I shivered as my body turned cold.

I couldn't speak.

I couldn't breathe.

I couldn't think.

Florence slid a white card in front of me.

I traced the embossed writing with my fingertip as my stomach churned slowly and relentlessly, like it was mixing concrete. It was the invitation I would have picked out for my own wedding—thick white card, a thin gold surround, and an elegant black font. Simple. Classic. Refined.

Apparently stealing the love of my life wasn't enough. My best friend had to have my taste in wedding invitations, too.

"Karen and Matt?" I searched Florence's face, looking for answers. "*My* Matt? *My* Karen?"

Florence tilted her head to the side. "For some reason, they've invited you. I had no idea they were even a thing. Neither did Gordy."

They sent me an invitation? I suppose I was the common denominator between them. "How long have they . . .?" Was this the real reason Matt left me? His excuses when he left seemed so lacking, looking back—

I'm not sure we were meant to be together forever.

We don't want the same things in life.

I'd assumed he was just getting jittery as we approached the time for weddings and babies.

Apparently, I was wrong.

"Karen swears it's since you two split up but . . ."

"You spoke to her?" Now that I thought about it, I hadn't had an actual conversation with Karen or an in-person catch-up for . . . Well, I couldn't remember how long. We messaged each other. All the time. Most days. But I hadn't seen her or spoken to her in weeks.

"Called her as soon as Gordy called me when he got the invite. It was delivered to his office. Which was weird. It wasn't like I wasn't going to find out."

I was only taking in half of the words that Florence was speaking. "What did she say?"

"Just that . . ." Florence paused and drew breath. "She and Matt had realized they had feelings for each other and it was serious, and she didn't really say anything more. As soon as I mentioned you, she made up some excuse about another call and rang off."

So my boyfriend was getting married. Ex-boyfriend. Potaytoes Potahtoes. The man I'd shared a bed with for seven years up until two months ago was getting married.

On any other day, that would have been the worst thing that could have possibly happened. But to my best friend?

Why?

"Is she pregnant?"

Florence sat back in her chair. "You think that's why?"

Why was any of this happening?

Why was Matt getting married to someone else when he was supposed to be marrying me?

Why was my best friend getting married and hadn't told me?

Why were they marrying each other?

"I'm not sure any explanation would really be an answer," I said. "But if they'd shagged and she'd got knocked up that might be some kind of logical reason for a quick wedding." It was certainly easier to understand than my best friend catching feelings for my boyfriend because that led to questions—how long had they had feelings for each other? Had Matt always wanted Karen when he was with me? Had they been having an affair? For a few months? Years? Since the beginning of our relationship?

"I don't understand why she didn't tell me," I said. "It wasn't like I wouldn't find out. She was going to let me find out by opening my invitation."

"I don't have an answer to that, other than she's a total bitch."

That would have to do. For now. "I guess that's why she invited me. To announce the news. Because she was too much of a traitorous coward to tell me to my face that she'd stolen my boyfriend."

"Do you think they were having an affair while you two were still living together?"

"That's at the top of my list of questions I have for them both." Had I seen any signs? Since we'd moved to London,

Matt had worked late a lot. But we'd come down from Manchester because he was offered his dream job. Of course he was going to put body and soul into it.

When had he had time for an affair?

We were at the stage where I bought Matt's underpants and he reminded me that I'd not called my brother for three weeks.

We were a team.

We were in love.

We were going to spend the rest of our lives together.

Or so I'd thought.

I should be crying, but for some reason the tears hadn't arrived. Perhaps I didn't believe it was true. Perhaps the fizzle of anger I was beginning to feel had dried them out.

Karen had been a part of my life since the day we'd both started school. I always felt slightly unkempt next to her. Even then. At five, her knee-high white socks never fell down, wrinkling at the ankles like mine did. At thirteen she never suffered with acne and wrestled with cover-up, and in our twenties, I'd never seen her with a single clump of mascara or eyeliner that was smudged.

Karen had known Matt since before we were a couple. She'd come up to visit me in Manchester, during our first term at university, twirling in, making the boys drool and swapping make-up tips with the girls in my block. She'd been struggling to fit in at Exeter, which made no sense to me. All my friends loved her.

When Matt pulled me onto the dance floor during the summer ball, told me I brought out the best in him, and he liked my boobs, I was thrilled Karen had already met him so she could help me overanalyze every part of our relationship.

Seven years later, Karen knew Matt almost as well as I did.

"Maybe you should go to the wedding and when they do that bit about impediments, you can stand up and ask that question," Florence suggested. "But obviously, you can't go."

"Of course, I can't go," I replied. Despite the invitation, I was almost certainly the last person Karen wanted at her wedding. It wasn't as if seeing my ex-boyfriend—the man I'd thought I was going to spend the rest of my life with— marrying my ex-best friend was top of my list of things to do this summer.

"Are you going to go?" I loved Florence like a sister, and if Karen was capable of sleeping with my boyfriend, what could she do to Florence?

"Of course not," she replied.

"But Gordy will want to go. And he won't want to go without you. If more time had passed and I was married or at least dating someone, I'd definitely go." If nothing else, I'd love to see Karen's face when she got my RSVP.

"There was a schedule that came with the invitation," Florence said.

I frowned. I'd been so focused on the white card that looked so much like the one I would have chosen, I'd forgotten about the email.

"It's like a week-long thing up in Scotland."

I slumped back in my chair, grateful that my jacket covered the mole-hill sized goosebumps that popped up all over my arms. "His uncle's castle?" I asked.

Florence nodded and the dull churning in my stomach kicked up a gear like an idling car put into drive.

"That's where he always said he wanted to get married." We'd visited last summer and hiked, ridden horses, slept under the stars. It had been amazing. Magical even.

"He's a ginormous wanker," Florence said.

Matt Gordon was having the life he and I had always planned—with someone else.

FOUR

Stella

I stared into the glass of wine Florence had put in front of me. She'd found an excuse to be passing by my office every day since she'd told me about Matt and Karen, which meant I wasn't drinking alone.

The same bar. A fresh glass of wine.

The last three weeks had been like being stuck in a fog where I couldn't see anything, think about anything other than Karen and Matt. It was the fog of betrayal.

I'd been going into the office, but I didn't remember doing anything other than logging on at the beginning of the day and logging off at the end of the day.

I still didn't have the answers to any of the endless questions I had.

"You two should go and then you can report back on how awful it is and how tasteless her dress is," I said. Poor Florence. Doubtless she was bored of my endless rumination about what had happened. I *wanted* to snap out of it. To think about something else. But I was just stuck in this awful no-man's-land where I tortured myself with a thousand imagined scenes of Matt and Karen over and over.

Creeping around behind my back.

Laughing about how stupid I was for not realizing it was her he loved. Not me.

Hunched over a calendar trying to find the perfect Saturday to get married.

Putting together a wedding list.

Choosing wedding invitations.

Kissing.

Fucking.

I grabbed my glass of wine and gulped down a mouthful, hoping it would dull my imagination.

"Maybe you should go with a hired hot, sexy stud—like in that film," Florence said. "The one with the woman from Will and Grace."

"*The Wedding Date?*"

She nodded enthusiastically. "Seriously. There must be an agency in London. You could even pretend you're engaged. That way you get to ruin Karen's big day by shaming her. First for stealing your boyfriend and second for inviting you."

"What did they put in that wine?" I asked. Florence was an accountant and always dreaming up alternate, more exciting realities for herself. "You know I couldn't do that."

"But you should. Karen's stolen your boyfriend and you don't want to embarrass her? You need to start putting yourself first. You're always so focused on everyone else; you need to put your needs at the top of the list."

"I'm pretty sure Dermot Mulroney isn't for hire, and that film didn't take social media into account. People would just look up a hired boyfriend. Find out he charges by the hour, and I'll look like a total idiot. So really, I *am* thinking about myself."

"Yeah, maybe. He needs to be some hotshot international businessman or Hollywood actor or—"

"At least know how to wear a suit," I said.

"Speaking of," Florence said, staring over my shoulder.

I turned and saw what Florence was fixated on. Or more accurately, who. He wasn't her usual type. Tall, yes, but Florence usually went for blonds. Thick, dark hair, olive skin, and the square jaw was more *my* type. In theory, anyway.

In practice . . . Well, Matt hadn't been short exactly, but we were the same height when I wore heels. He was hand-some—to me anyway. But he wasn't the kind of guy you'd particularly notice.

But *this* guy wasn't a man anyone could ignore.

He caught me staring and grinned. Instinctively, I smiled back. I turned to Florence as the man swept past our table and up the stone steps flanked with bay trees and into the bar.

"You need to be dating someone like that and take *him* to the wedding," Florence said.

"That guy is either married or gay. And if by some miracle he's neither, then he's a psychopath. Men are a no-go zone for me. I don't trust myself. If I've been wrong about the man I've been sharing a bed with for the last seven years, then I'm no doubt wrong about a lot of other stuff and everything to do with people with penises."

"Ladies." A waiter approached our table with an ice bucket and two champagne glasses.

"We didn't order this," I said, eyeing the bottle of Dom and wishing we had.

"It's from the gentleman at the bar," he replied, nodding toward the window.

Turning, I locked eyes with the dark-haired stranger who had knocked me out of my wallowing for just a few seconds.

"We can't accept this," I said as the waiter poured the champagne into glasses. Something about the way my smile had come so easily made me uneasy. If he could coax a smile from me with the mood I was in, he definitely couldn't be trusted.

"Of course we can," Florence said, raising her full glass at the stranger.

I rolled my eyes and took a sip, determined not to look at him again. "So, you think I should ignore the invitation or RSVP no?"

"I think you should RSVP with a letter bomb or say nothing at all," Florence replied.

"It would be nice if I had an exciting reason to say no, other than the obvious," I said.

"Just don't reply. Or make up a reason. Say you're in the Maldives for work."

"Yeah, no one's going to believe I flew to the Maldives for work. I'm a recruitment consultant, not a supermodel." The only travel I'd done since I started two months ago was to our head office in Wiltshire, and I wasn't sure a day trip to Swindon was going to make anyone jealous.

"I guess. But at least you can talk about your promotion."

"Again, head of professional services at a recruitment consultancy isn't going to get anyone's attention." My quick promotion had been welcome, but it hadn't filled my heart or satisfied my soul. It had paid the mortgage.

"Have you totally given up on the interior design thing?"

Florence's question *should* have had an easy answer. When Matt had moved out, I'd been building up my business, but I wasn't making any money and I had bills to pay, so I'd had to be sensible and take the first job that came along. I still wasn't convinced it had been the right thing to do, but I'd clung to the flat we'd shared, insisting I stay in it, so he'd signed it over to me—mortgage and all. At the back of my mind, I'd thought he'd come back—come home to me. "Recruitment provides a steady income I need to pay the mortgage."

"I can't believe you gave up your business and moved to London for him, then he turned around and did this to you."

"I didn't move to London *for* him." That made me sound weak, and I might have been cheated on and betrayed, but I *refused* to become a victim.

"You'd still be in Manchester if he hadn't had that job opportunity."

"I know, but we were a couple, a team, and it was his dream job." My interior design business had been thriving. I'd started getting repeat business, and every job I got led to another. Matt's job offer had been his dream—and a once-in-a-lifetime opportunity. "He was the man I was going to spend the rest of my life with. I wanted him to have the job he always wanted."

"So you put him first, like you always do."

"I chose our relationship—I chose the dream of a future together. I thought I'd be able to build an interior design business in London." The first few months had been spent settling in and establishing contacts. But when Matt had left me, I'd had no clients to speak of and a mortgage to pay.

I'd done the only thing I could do—applied for everything I could find whether or not it was design related.

"But you hate recruitment. You said it was just temporary, and that you'd do it while you were building your client list."

"Yeah, but then life happens." Recruitment was long hours. Since I started the job, I didn't feel like my life was my own. My boss seemed to think she owned me. Last Wednesday she'd called me at ten-thirty at night. I'd been in bed with my iPad, watching *The Chilling Adventures of Sabrina*, hoping to stumble across a spell to turn my life around. She didn't even mention the time, as if it was totally reasonable to call and ask whether the interviews for one of our big clients had gone well. "The only way I could go back to interior design would be if I landed a single client who could keep me busy for, say, six months. That way, I'd have guaranteed money *and* an up-to-date portfolio that would lead to more work."

"Can't you get a job at an interior design business? At least you'd be doing what you loved."

"There just aren't many jobs and when they do come up, the pay is terrible because it's full of trust-fund kids. They don't need the money."

"Excuse me." The very deep, male voice made the soles of my feet vibrate and my skin pebble with goosebumps.

I looked up into the sunshine and found the hot suit who had bought us champagne standing by our table. My smile overtook me as if elbowing my brain, which knew better, out of the way. "Erm, thank you for the champagne," I mumbled.

"I couldn't help but notice you as I passed by, and I wanted to get your attention."

I didn't say that he'd managed that just by walking by.

"It's a welcome treat after a shitty day," I replied. He smiled, and for a split second it was as if a ten-foot wall had appeared, surrounding us, blocking out the rest of the world, leaving just the two of us staring at each other.

"I'm sorry to hear that you've had a bad day, but I'm pleased I could improve it," he said, flashing me a smile that I felt in my knees. His broad shoulders, the warmth that bubbled beneath my skin when he spoke, a cupid's bow so sharply drawn I'd like to follow its curve with my tongue all said the same thing—this guy was all man.

"Please, join us," Florence said, and I wanted to kill her. She knew I was now sworn to a life of celibacy. I didn't need Sex-God Suit waving temptation in my face. Plus I was wearing a splash of the miso soup I'd had for lunch—more proof I wasn't ready to flirt. Date. *Interact* with men.

"You two have fun," I said, bending to pick up my bag. "I'm going to head off."

I knew Florence was scowling at me without even looking at her. But I didn't care. Okay, so men didn't hit on me all the time, but today wasn't the day. I wanted to go home, get into my pajamas, watch *Made in Chelsea*, and eat my body weight in frozen yogurt.

As I stood, Hot Suit put his hand on my shoulder.

"Five minutes of your time? I have a proposal for you, Stella."

I froze, a chill running down my spine as I tried to figure out how the hell he knew my name.

FIVE

Beck

"How do you know my name?" she asked, flashing me a suspicious look.

"May I join you? I'll explain." She frowned but didn't say no, so I pulled a chair from a neighboring table and took a seat. Stella London was the only single woman going to this wedding. The other two possible names were elderly aunts: one who was completely bedbound, the other based in Florida and no longer able to fly. Both were clearly invited just to be polite.

Stella was my last chance. I had to make this work.

I'd headed to Stella's office to try to meet her. The situation was too complicated to explain in an email—I'd end up sounding like I was one of those Nigerian lawyers promising you a cool hundred mil if you just sent him three hundred quid for admin. I'd decided the best thing to do was to turn up at her office and ask for a meeting—it was a business proposition I was suggesting, after all. As I passed her in the street, she'd looked familiar and beautiful, but I thought nothing more than that as I'd headed into the bar to go to the loo before heading up to her office. While I had my dick in my hand, I'd realized who she was. I wasn't about to pass up an opportunity to approach her. There was too much at stake.

"I understand you're a recruitment consultant," I said. "And an ambitious one from what I can tell. You've been promoted since you joined Foster and Associates, and you've only been with them a couple of months." I paused. I needed to slow down. Take my time. I couldn't blow this.

I sat back and regarded her. The social media photographs I'd found didn't do her justice. Her hair was longer and fell in soft, blonde waves to her shoulders and what I'd thought were blue eyes were almost purple and entirely distracting. She had full lips that bore no trace of make-up, and a beauty spot on her left cheekbone that a fifties Hollywood bombshell would have been proud of.

She looked at me and frowned. "Why do you know how long I've been in my job? Never mind, I need to be going."

"I know this is a little odd." I sat forward. "Just give me a couple of minutes to explain. I'm here to make you a busi-ness proposition. One that I believe you'll find very interesting."

I'd done my research on this woman as I always did when entering into a new business relationship. The worst thing in development was to be surprised after work started. It was the easiest way to overspend. Much easier to spend the effort up front—understand what things were going to cost you and put it into your budget.

From my research, I'd seen that Stella had progressed quickly in her job since coming to London. She'd had a career change, but she was clearly ambitious and driven. She'd given an interview in a trade magazine last month talking about how much she loved the firm she worked for and how she hoped to be partner. I needed to make sure she said yes to my proposal, so it made sense that I would offer her something she really wanted—a further step up, a chance to realize her ambitions. I didn't have time to waste negotiating. I needed Stella to agree.

I was going to make her an offer she couldn't refuse.

"I'm a real estate developer, and I'm about to start a new project. I thought you might want to work on recruiting the team."

"You want to use Foster and Associates?" Instead of looking excited, she looked confused. It was the same look Joshua had gotten when I'd asked him if he was going to Vegas for Gabriel's stag party—as if my question didn't make sense.

"I think we'd be a great fit. I'll need to recruit over a hundred people, and I could take the proposition to the partners in your firm and make my business contingent on you getting junior partnership." She can't have ever had that many appointments just fall into her lap. No question of negotiating the fee or it being a non-exclusive contract—Stella had the business. Plus working for Wilde Developments would be a feather in her cap. We were a brand people talked about.

"Why would you do that?"

"Lots of reasons. Like I said, I think we'd work well together and from what I hear, you're good at your job."

She rolled her eyes as if I were some lecherous old weasel who had just asked her to come upstairs and see his etchings rather than someone who was offering her a once-in-a-lifetime opportunity. I'd expected her to be a little more enthusiastic. "Then I suggest you call the office. I don't deal with real estate."

Perhaps she'd misheard me. There's no way she'd be so dismissive if she'd heard me properly. "I'm offering to help you make partner."

She burst out laughing. Was this girl drunk? This was not going how I'd planned. "As if I care."

I fisted my hands as my palms started to sweat. *Fuck.* I'd thought that Stella London was career driven and ambitious. Had I got it wrong?

"You don't want to be partner?" I asked, trying to keep my voice steady.

"Why do you care? Who are you?"

"I need a great recruitment consultant," I said, my brain whirring, trying to get ahead of this conversation.

"Well, I'm not one." She exhaled and turned to her friend. "I'm not cut out for it."

If she didn't care about recruitment then she could just name her price. I was an idiot; I should have had a backup plan. From the article I'd read, I'd clearly made assumptions I shouldn't have. "I need your help, Stella." How had I ended up in a place where the goal I'd been working toward my entire life was dependent on whether a stranger wanted a promotion? If this was any other real estate deal, I would have walked away months ago. But I couldn't give up on this one.

"Seriously, anyone in the office would be glad of the work. Call Sheila. She's in charge of real estate recruitment."

Any recruitment consultant wasn't what I needed. I had to level with her or I was going to lose her. "Yeah, but she doesn't have what I need."

She turned toward me. "Which is what? I'm not sleeping with you because you have a staffing crisis."

I couldn't help myself—I laughed. "No, that's not what I mean. I want to talk to you about Matthew and Karen's wedding."

She turned the color of freshly fallen snow. "What about it?"

"I was hoping I could go as your guest."

"Well, you're fresh out of luck. Because there's no way I'll be there and even if I was—you're a perfect stranger."

I was jinxed when it came to this deal. "I just need you to hear me out. Give me five minutes."

She glanced at her friend. "You're right. I'm not good at putting myself first. I should leave, right?"

Her friend shrugged. "You can always walk away when you've heard him out."

Stella sighed and collapsed back on her chair. "Okay, then be straight with me. Who the hell are you, how do you know me, and what on planet Earth do you want?"

She was clearly out of patience. I normally found that when my back was against the wall, straightforward honesty was the way to go.

"I'm Beck Wilde. I'm a real estate developer. A man called Henry Dawnay holds my future in his hands. He owns a building that I need to buy."

When I was doing up bedsits in Hackney, before Hackney was popular, exhausted from twenty-hour days and filthy from pulling up floorboards and knocking down walls, every now and then I'd take the tube to Bond Street and wander around Mayfair in the middle of the night to stare at the Dawnay building. It had become an obsession.

I wanted that building. I wanted to buy it so I could

demolish it. Rebuild it from the ground up so it was new and better. I wanted to conquer it. Conquer my past.

I would stop at nothing to buy that property.

But Stella London was my last hope.

"Karen's godfather?" she asked.

I had to hold myself back from pinning her to the chair and asking her whether she had met him. This could work out even better than I'd hoped. "You know him?"

"A bit. He was always around for her birthdays, and we went to his place in the Bahamas when we were seventeen, but I don't see why you need to go to a wedding to buy a building. How do you know me and what—"

"On planet Earth do I want?" I finished for her. "I've been trying and failing to get a meeting with Henry for months. That wedding will provide an opportunity to speak to him, to convince him to sell his Mayfair property."

"I don't get what that's got to do with me."

"I did my research. I know you were invited—I want to go as your plus one."

She laughed. "Yeah, well, like I said, I'm not going, so you need to find someone else."

I hadn't counted on her refusing the invitation just like I hadn't expected her to laugh in my face when I offered to help make her partner. I never fucked up like this. Every sign I got was telling me to walk away from this deal. But I couldn't. This building was a symbol of bad luck for my family. It just made me more committed to buying it and making it mine. "I would make it worth your while." She could have the entire nine-point-four million in profit I was projected to make for all I cared. Well maybe not the entire profit.

"Like I said, I'm not going to the wedding and I don't care about getting Foster and Associates new work." She stood again. "And this time, I'm really leaving. Florence, I'll call you later, and man with the Dom—Beck, whatever—thanks for the champagne."

Christ, I was losing her. Maybe I'd come on too strong. I should give her space. Try again on a different day when she'd had time to think about it. I pulled out a business card. "You don't care about getting Foster and Associates new business," I said. "I get it. But consider what it is you do want. Even if it's just a check. I need to get into that wedding."

"A check? No amount of money could convince me to celebrate the marriage of Matt and Karen."

Why couldn't I catch a break, have a stroke of good luck? It was like someone was deliberately trying to sabotage this project. I was used to my hard work paying off. I'd never put so much time and effort into securing a property and yet I was stuck—making no progress. It was as if the development was punching me invisibly and in slow motion over and over.

"If not a check, maybe I can do you a favor," I said. "I know a lot of people. If you wanted to move jobs, I might be able to help. Or maybe you want a holiday of a lifetime. Have a think."

"I'm not interested," Stella said. "Going to that wedding would be like a holiday in hell. Worse."

"Stella," her friend said. "Take his business card."

Stella shot her friend a look that could kill. "I'm not going to that wedding. I don't care about getting a shitty promotion. Or a holiday. Nothing is worth enduring that for."

"I know. But there are things you do care about," her friend said. "You don't lose anything by taking the guy's business card. That way if you think of something you want that's worth going to that wedding, you can call him."

I wanted to write Stella's friend a check right there.

She grabbed my business card out of my hand like a child resignedly eating its carrots. "This day is out of control. I need it to be over."

I knew that feeling.

SIX

Stella

"Think about it as if he's the genie." Florence's voice crackled out from the speakerphone as I finished up brushing my teeth.

I took a sip of water from my glass, rinsed my mouth, and spat it out. "Have you been drinking?"

"I'm serious. Hot Suit's the genie."

"What? And I'm the lamp? Well, he's not getting inside me."

"No, you crazy pervert. You're Aladdin."

I rolled my eyes. "And he's going to grant me three wishes?"

"Exactly. He said to think about what you want. You might not be going for partnership at your recruitment consultancy, but maybe he can help you get a different job."

"Have you forgotten the price the genie's asking me to pay? You can't think that it's a good idea for me to go to that wedding. I'd rather stab myself through the hand with a rusty knife over and over."

What was Florence thinking? She didn't even want to go to the wedding. A wedding was about celebrating two people in love, not watching two people who had lied and betrayed you in the worst way possible start their lives together.

"Of course, going to the wedding would be horrific," Florence said.

"Well, we both agree on that."

"But . . ."

What was she thinking with her *buts*? There were no acceptable *buts* in this situation. There was no way I was going to that wedding.

"You really want your business back. Your life back. Right?"

"Of course." I wanted to rewind to back when Matt loved me, and we were happy together. But I didn't know when that had been. Had he and Karen been sneaking around my back while we were in Manchester? Was the reason we'd come to London so they could be together? I took another swig of water.

"If Beck can give you that, then maybe a few days at the wedding would be worth it."

Had Karen got to her? Had someone convinced Florence that what Karen and Matt had done wasn't so bad? "Beck can't rewind time. He can't stop Matt and Karen getting married."

"If he can't undo your past, he might be able to make your future better."

I couldn't think about the future. I was still stuck in the fog, trying to figure out which way was up. The two months before the invitations arrived, I'd gone about my business, thinking that ultimately Matt would come back to me. I hadn't actually thought we were done for good. I hadn't started planning for life without him.

"I know it would be awful," Florence continued. "But think of it this way—they sent you that invitation because they were cowards, because they wanted to hurt you. Who knows? But, if you were to go? It's the last thing they're expecting. You take some control back. You'd make them feel really uncomfortable."

"Making them feel uncomfortable isn't worth making myself miserable."

"Agreed. But it's more than making them feel uncomfortable. It's about putting yourself first for once." As I went to interrupt her, she continued. "Just hear me out. If, in theory, this guy, Beck, could give you something that would make going to this wedding worth it, then you should do it. Agreed?"

Florence was like a dog with a bone. I didn't understand why she wouldn't drop this. "There isn't anything I could want from Beck. Nothing would be worth going to that wedding for."

"I'm not sure that's true," she said. "He says he's a property developer, right?"

"Yes," I said. "He wants to buy some property that Henry Dawnay owns in Mayfair." I grabbed the latest issue of *Elle Decoration* from my bedside table. I'd let Florence keep talking—she clearly needed to get this out of her system—but there was no way I was going to that wedding.

"Right. So, I've been looking him up. Because, what else is there to do on the bus but research strangers on your phone? I've been known to nab shots of people who look interesting when they get on and run them through facial recognition software."

"You're kidding me."

"Nope. Knowing more about someone than they know about me is powerful. Anyway, Google Wilde Developments."

There was no point arguing. I was just going to have to placate Florence. I pulled my laptop from the end of the bed and did as she asked.

"First, everything he said seems to be true. He's in real estate and has made a lot of money developing boutique, high-end residential units in central London. Can you see them?"

As I brought up the sleek, image-heavy website, my heart began to flutter as if it were being brought back to life. The projects displayed were breathtaking. Spacious, airy, with incredible views. The finishes used were expensive—Italian marble, Murano glass, and beautiful porcelain tiles. As a designer, I'd love to work with this kind of budget. And I loved the unusual spaces that had been carved out of the old buildings. Modern classic was my personal style, not that anyone would know if they came to my home, despite me being an interior designer. Matt had been very particular with our flat. When I was in the business, my portfolio had been much more traditional because that was what my clients had wanted. The stuff Wilde Developments was doing was much more what I liked to work with. "I wonder who his designer is," I said, scrolling through the pages. "They have great taste."

"So do you," Florence said.

"With a budget like this, there's a lot I could do." I missed transforming spaces from shabby and unloved to fresh and exciting. I felt like a fairy godmother, making people's lives a little better by improving their homes—providing a space they loved they could retreat to when they needed comfort or show-off when they wanted to impress friends. The way I saw it, I was like a doctor or a therapist—I produced medicine for the soul.

"That's exactly my point. You can ask Beck to give you that opportunity."

"What? A check so I can redesign my flat? No way—I'm not taking money from a stranger in return for a date."

"No!" she yelped. "He's going to redevelop the Mayfair property, right?"

"Right." Had I missed something?

"So, tell him you want to be the lead designer on the development."

I snorted. "Don't be ridiculous. I haven't worked in six months. I have no portfolio. And I've never done anything on this scale. Or in this style."

"Use your portfolio from your Manchester business," Florence said.

"The clients want a very different look in Manchester—it's not as cutting edge and the clients aren't international. And I never did any new build stuff. You can do a lot more with a blank canvas."

"Well it doesn't matter anyway, because you don't have to interview. You know you can do it. Can't you? That would be worth going up to Scotland for."

Florence was being ridiculous. I couldn't just demand a job from a stranger. He'd laugh in my face. I couldn't even convince my boyfriend that I was good at my job. What hope did I have that I could convince a high-end real estate developer? "Well, of course I could do it, but I have no proof to offer him. There's no way—" Designing the interiors of one of these buildings was stuff my dreams were made of. All I had on my CV recently was recruitment. Even when I had been interior designing, I'd never taken on a project like the ones Wilde Developments did. I wouldn't impress Beck with the interior spaces I'd done in Manchester.

"Beck said to consider what it is you want. And you keep telling me you hate your job. Sounds like a perfect solution."

"What, resort to blackmail?"

"It's not blackmail—it's a business deal. He's got something you want—you've got something he wants. It's an exchange."

"You could say the same thing about a prostitute and her client."

"I'm not saying sleep with the guy—although I'm sure it will be tempting as all hell. He asked you to name your price to take you to a wedding. A job like that would be worth a week of pain, wouldn't it? This is a chance to get your career back, your life back. Is a lifetime's happiness worth a week watching your shit-for-brains ex marry a girl you thought was a friend?"

A job for a company like Wilde Developments would last for months and build my portfolio so I could go back to doing what I loved.

"In theory. But I'm not sure I'm capable of witnessing Karen and Matt together, of watching them get married." The words stuck in my throat. Karen had known I'd wanted Matt to propose. I'd talked to her about it. She'd offered her advice, told me to give him an ultimatum. Were they together then? Had her advice been designed to break us apart rather than move us forward? Every conversation I'd ever had with her had a shadow cast over it. I'd thought she'd bury a body for me. But, now I knew that mine was the body she wanted to bury—so she could marry my boyfriend.

"Do you think it's actually physically possible for me to

go to that wedding? I think I'd throw up constantly or start uncontrollably screaming through the speeches or something. I don't trust myself not to do something terrible."

"If you go, I'll come with you," Florence said. "As moral support. And you never know, you might gain strength from knowing that you were using their wedding to get what you wanted. It's an opportunity for you to take the power back. It's the chance for closure."

Powerlessness . . . Yes, that was a good description of what I'd felt over the last few weeks. My future had been snatched from me and I could do nothing about it.

I hated Karen. And I hated that I hated her. I didn't want to be someone filled with bitterness and hate. I wanted to move on. I wanted that closure Florence promised.

Something to aim for would give me a focus rather than constantly ruminating over the two people I didn't want to think about at all.

"And if you needed more icing on the cake, you get to go to the wedding with the hottest guy I've ever seen. People will assume you're a couple—in fact you can make him Dermot Mulroney. Get him to pretend to be your boyfriend —you'll be winning at life."

Florence made it sound like the deal was done. "So, you want me to convince Beck to make me the lead designer on a multi-billion-pound property development *and* pretend to be my boyfriend, and at the end of the week, I'll have closure and be over my ex bff and ex-boyfriend betraying me?" Florence's positivity was endearing but she was clearly drunk or crazy.

"Are you telling me you'd still refuse to go to the wedding if Genie-Beck made that deal?"

Of course, there was no way I could refuse the deal Florence was describing. She was right, I'd been making decisions and compromises as one half of a couple for a long time. I'd put Matt and my relationship before anything. But Matt and I weren't in a relationship anymore. We weren't just on a break. I was on my own. And I had to start thinking about my future. The recruitment consultancy job was going to be a temporary measure that turned permanent if I didn't take decisive action.

Was it possible that Beck Wilde was my winning lottery ticket? My dose of medicine that would help me heal, help me get over the way Matt and Karen had betrayed me, and hand me a career-making job opportunity at the same time? "There's no way he'd agree."

"You won't know if you don't ask. What have you got to lose?"

It felt as if I'd already lost everything I'd ever had—my career, my relationship—but going to the wedding just might take my pride.

And it might just give me it back.

All I had to do was convince Beck I had the ability to take on a project like his with no track record, no proof whatsoever, then show up to the wedding of my ex-boyfriend and ex-best friend.

Should be easy, right?

SEVEN

Beck

Normally, I was all about finding creative solutions to impossible problems. That was what real estate development was all about, but *normal* was not the situation I was in.

A shit-storm—that was the situation I was currently in.

"Look, Beck, I've done as much as I can. Your time is up." Craig's voice rang out from the speakerphone on my shiny glass desk.

Chills ran down my body. There had to be more I could do. I couldn't just walk away from the Mayfair project. I spun my chair to the side, so I got a view of St Paul's dome towering above me. The sight through the windows was a reminder to me of how far I'd come. "It's not as simple as putting it behind me. The market's changed. No one can hold property for a few months without developing it and come out with a profit."

I'd lose ten million pounds.

At least.

And if it was *just* ten million pounds, it would be easier to walk away. But this development offered me more than money could buy.

Craig wasn't the one who'd have to swallow the loss and he certainly wasn't going to lose sleep over me walking away from a lifetime's ambition.

"So, you'll make a loss. It's a sunk cost. Move on."

I shook my head. That wasn't going to happen. I hadn't given up on Henry. If I could just get five minutes, I was sure I could convince him to sell.

"I know it's not what you want to hear, but the bank can't extend terms anymore. We're going to have to pull the funding. You'll get an official notice by courier later today setting out that you have thirty days to either start works, or we'll step in and put the property on the market if you still refuse to."

I sat back in my chair, running a finger around the collar of my shirt, as if trying to loosen the noose I felt tightening around my throat. The words had been said. Craig had dressed it up but effectively I'd be in default of my loan if I didn't make progress within the month. I'd lose money, my dream, and my reputation was going to take a kicking.

I was down for the count. I had to stumble to my feet somehow—find the energy from somewhere.

There was no way I could let the bank step in. If the development failed, there would be whispers in the industry about whether I'd lost my edge. It might even put off future lenders funding other projects. I couldn't go backward. I'd come a long way from developing one-off flats in the East End.

Stella *bloody* London.

I'd thought she'd be the answer to everything. But I hadn't given up on her.

I had to think creatively. But at the moment I was out of ideas, my brain was blank, and hope was the only thing left.

"I'm not going to default," I told Craig. "I'll have the signatures on the Dawnay building, believe me."

"I hope so, but like I said, you get thirty days to get that transfer to happen or we take steps to recover the loan."

A knock on my office door interrupted my quick comeback. "I'll keep you updated," I said, and turned to see the door open and the receptionist enter. "I have to go, my next meeting's arrived." I didn't have a meeting for a couple of hours, but there was no point in rehashing old ground with Craig. I understood him loud and clear. He'd lowered the sword of Damocles a couple of centimeters more.

"Sorry to interrupt, sir," Gina said, "but I have a Stella London in reception who insists that you'll want to see her."

The pressure around my ribs abated a little, allowing me to take a breath and register the grin that was nudging at the corners of my mouth.

Just when I thought my arse was about to hit the floor, lady luck smiled on me and brought me Stella London. There was only one reason she'd be here—to make a deal.

Right about now, I'd say yes to anything she wanted to get me into that wedding.

I asked Gina to bring her in, then dragged my fingers through my hair.

Stella entered the room, her blonde hair swept back from her face, her red skirt clinging to her perfect hourglass figure. The hairs on the back of my neck stood to attention as if about to be inspected by a sergeant major. Perhaps it was because she'd been sitting when I'd met her, but I hadn't remembered her as being quite so attractive.

"Thanks for coming in," I said. "Can I offer you something to drink? Tea, coffee?"

"I'll take a sparkling water. No ice."

I glanced at Gina who nodded and shut the door on her way out.

"It's nice to see you again." Attractive women were always nice to see, but I was hoping I was going to like what she had to say even better than I liked looking at her. And I liked looking at her a lot.

"Now I've done some research about you so I'm not so much on the back foot," she said.

If she'd looked me up, she must be interested in whether I could be trusted. And that meant she was definitely interested in making a deal. Now she knew I wasn't a charlatan or a conman, we could get on with business. "Please, have a seat," I said, indicating the chair opposite my desk. "And you must tell me what you found out."

She glanced around my office as she sat. "A lot." She narrowed her eyes at me as I took a seat opposite her. "Some good things. Some . . ." She blushed, clearly not wanting to tell me what she was thinking, which made me want to know all the more. "Lots of things."

"Tell me," I said, and I couldn't help but grin. Christ, the blush began to spread down her neck, and I wanted to pull open the buttons of her blouse and trace it down as far as it went.

"Never mind," she snapped. Her sharp words made my cock twitch, and I cleared my throat, trying to focus my attention on the business she was here to do. "But I do know that you need an introduction to Henry, which I can provide you with."

"So, I'll accompany you to the wedding?" My heart knocked on my ribs as if it were trying to get my attention. Was it that easy? "For the entire week," I added. I had thirty days, and by the time the wedding rolled around, I'd have a week left. I'd need all the time I could get with Henry. It wasn't just a question of convincing him to do the deal in principle. I needed his signature on the paperwork.

"If you agree to my terms."

She just had to name them. There was nothing I wouldn't do to go to this wedding. After that call with Craig, I had no time to lose. It was like I was standing, looking at the summit of Everest just a few steps away, and being told I couldn't make it. I hadn't come all this way just to walk away from achieving everything I ever wanted.

"Go on," I said, trying not to look too eager to hear what she had to say.

"You've been holding the Mayfair properties next to Henry's a while now and it must be costing you a lot of money."

I wanted her to get to the point. She wasn't telling me anything I didn't know.

"What are your terms, Stella?"

"I've had a look at your work." She paused as if deciding what to say next. "I want to be the designer on the building —kitchens, bathrooms, floors, joinery, finishes, then I'll decorate and dress an apartment for public viewings." She crossed her long legs in front of her, and I had to fight to keep focused on what she was saying.

I let her words sink in and tried to reorder them in my brain in a way that made sense. "You're a recruitment consultant," I said, trying to think back to the research I'd had done on her. She'd moved to London about six months ago from Manchester and started at the recruitment firm. Had she had a background in design? Surely she didn't think anyone off the street could become a designer overnight.

"I trained in interior design," she said. "Had my own

business up until six months ago. This kind of project is right up my street."

Her gaze flitted from my shoulder to my hand and then out of the window. She was lying about something. I just wasn't sure which bit. I remember that she'd had her own business in a completely unrelated field when she'd been in Manchester. I must have been so fixated on being able to give work to the recruitment consultancy that I'd skimmed over the fact that it was an interior design business. *Shit*, I was so hungry for a win, I was missing details. "I have someone for that project already." How serious was she about this? Could I persuade her just to take a check? That would be a lot easier.

She pushed out her chair and went to stand as if the conversation was over, but there was no way I'd let her leave. "Talk to me about your experience. You're in recruitment now, why do you want to go back?"

"I changed jobs because of a personal situation, but designing is what I want to do," she said. "I love great design but more than that, I like to create homes that people love to live in—places people can imagine themselves. Places people raise a family, celebrate their successes, and recover from their failures. It's my passion, my calling if you like, and I'm really good at it." She cleared her throat as if she were nervous. "You asked me for my terms—I'm telling you what they are."

At least she was prepared to make a deal. "Do you have a portfolio that I can look at?" Rather than just dismiss her conditions, hopefully I could point out, as charmingly as possible, why her suggestion was ludicrous, and I could get her to accept something else—something I was able to give her.

"This isn't a job interview. If you don't want to go to this wedding, then fine." She stood and had her hand on my office door handle by the time I got to her.

"Stella, come on. Let's discuss this," I said, inhaling a strain of rose petals. I brushed up against the silk of her blouse. I was entirely too close to her, and I took a step back. I put my hands in my pockets, stopping myself from pushing her hair off her face so I could see those eyes better. "You can understand that the kind of properties I work on require a designer with a track record working at the cutting edge of design. I'm just trying to protect us both."

"Sounds to me like you want to have your cake and eat it, too. You asked me to name my terms."

I needed to think fast. I wasn't a man who liked being held at gunpoint but that was what Stella was doing. But the alternative was the bank blowing my brains out. I had to get to Henry. I'd do whatever it took. Maybe she could work alongside the designer I already had on board for the project.

"I know this isn't an interview," I said. "But humor me." She held my gaze and didn't flounce out, so I continued. "Say I agreed to have you work on the Mayfair project. What's your vision?"

She sighed but began to speak. "I'd say you're trying to appeal to wealthy people who have their main home in the country and just want a *pied-à-terre* or childless singles and couples. And you're selling to an international market— we'd have to consider that. I think the style of your last development in Fitzrovia works well, but potential buyers are going to expect a little more luxury, more exclusivity with the same classic style. I'd suggest we have each unit have something unique about it. That's not unusual in these high-end developments but most of them go modern—I suggest we go vintage. We could use antique glass in the bedrooms, inset some reclaimed marble into one of the walls in the bathroom with glass shelving in front. A theatre close to my office is being refurbished. We could buy the stage off them, restore it, and use it as the floors in a master bedroom. Or I can source light fixtures from stately homes. We don't want to overdo anything—just one or two things in each apartment that no one else has that has a history that we can use as part of the story of what's so appealing about the flat. It's beautiful. But it's marketing."

I liked her ideas. And she understood I was aiming to sell the apartments, not just make them look pretty. I took a deep breath. She had me by the balls. If I said no, I'd say goodbye to my best chance of getting the Dawnay building. "I've got to have the right to pull you from the development if things aren't working out." Maybe I could get her to take me to the wedding and then renegotiate—give her a one-off flat to design and then use my normal designer on the Mayfair project. Worst-case scenario, I'd just have to gut the place after she was done.

She pulled out her folio case from where it was tucked under her arm and produced some paperwork. "You can fire me if I miss the deadlines set out in the project plan or if I overspend by more than seven percent. It's set out there in clause ten."

I flicked through the contract for services she'd handed me.

"It's all standard stuff," she said. "Just sign on the last page."

Without a contract, I had options. If I signed, I was out of negotiating power. I had no choice other than to sign and worry about it later. "You better be good," I said, pulling my pen from my inside pocket and leaning the contract on the back of the door.

"I'm better than good. Oh, and just one more thing."

I dotted the "i" in Wilde and glanced up, waiting to hear what she was going to say—she probably wanted input on layouts or a profit share.

"You have to pretend you're my boyfriend—serious-about-to-propose-completely-in love-with-me boyfriend."

I grinned. Was she asking me on a date? "At the wedding?" I asked.

"Yes, at the engagement party and while we're in Scotland and any other event that comes up."

I leaned against the door and took her in. "How many events are there?"

Again, her gaze flitted from my shoulder to the dome of St Paul's cathedral behind me. "I don't know. There's the wedding and engagement party as far as I know."

This must be her way of asking me out. "If you want to make this a real date, you just had to say. You're an attractive woman, and—"

She sighed. "Don't be an arsehole. I don't need a boyfriend. I just need to *look* like I have a boyfriend." She snatched the signed contract from me and stuffed it into her bag. "It's strictly a business deal. Just like this." She waved the paperwork in front of me. "I just need it to be believable. That's all."

It was obviously important to her, but I didn't get it. "So you want us to pretend when we're in public but not when we're alone?"

She tipped her head to the side. "I'm not asking you to be my gigolo, Beck. Everything would be for show." She rolled her eyes as if I was just the stupidest man she'd ever met. Stella London was a new experience for me. I was used to women flirting. Smiling. Playing with their hair when they spoke to me—not being exasperated like I was an annoying little brother.

"But why?" I got the feeling I was an extra in a daytime soap and hadn't received all the script.

"Does it matter? It's part of my terms. Agree or don't go. It's as simple as that."

I wasn't complaining. It was weird but not a deal-breaker. I just was curious about why she'd make it a condition. "Okay. I'll make-believe to be your boyfriend." I wasn't much of a real boyfriend, but who knew, maybe if I faked it, I'd be better at my next relationship.

"Then you've got a deal. Engagement party's this Saturday." She turned toward the door. "Pick me up at seven." Stella headed out of my office.

"Hang on, I need your address. And your number."

"I'm sure you'll figure it out. You tracked me down at my favorite bar, after all." The door slammed shut on me feeling like I might be on the losing end of this deal.

This woman was going to give me a run for my money. But, for ten million quid, my future business and the chance to right the wrongs of my past, I'd put up with it.

EIGHT

Stella

This was what a brave face looked like, I told myself as I looked in the mirror. For once, I'd managed to put on false eyelashes without looking like a hooker. And the tinted moisturizer I'd bought on sale was living up to its promise to even out my skin tone. I hoped it would cover up the hives I was bound to break into any moment at the thought of being within a ten-foot radius of Matt and Karen. Couldn't they have eloped to Tasmania or something?

"Are you sure you don't want me to pick you up? It's on my way," Florence said.

"No, Beck is coming over." I glanced at the time. He was due any minute. He'd emailed me exactly two hours after I'd left his office earlier in the week telling me he'd found my email, mobile phone, and home address. He'd probably had it already but making him work for it—and him figuring it out—felt good. With Matt I'd always been the one to pick the restaurant, make sure his suit was dry cleaned, and the cab was booked. And look where it had gotten me.

Florence sighed. "It was a genius idea of making him your boyfriend for wedding season, even if I do say so myself."

"*Pretend* boyfriend. But yeah. It makes the idea of tonight and the wedding slightly less horrifying."

"It solves a lot of problems for you. I mean you get to go to the wedding, pretend you've moved on—"

"Hey, I have moved on. I'm planning for my future. I didn't even have a glass of wine last night." It wasn't that the fog had lifted, but since I'd been to Beck's offices, I just had slightly better visibility.

A pause at the other end of the line made me think she didn't believe me. But it wasn't like I wanted Matt back. Okay maybe I missed him, or at least missed who I'd thought he was. But no one forgot a betrayal like that.

"Have you heard from Karen since you RSVP'd for you and Beck?" she asked.

"Nope. Just the automatic reply. Have you?"

I could almost hear the grin at the other end of the phone. "Yeah, she called me yesterday. Tell me you're looking white-hot tonight. What are you wearing?"

I stared at myself in the mirror. Hot wasn't how I'd describe myself, but I hadn't had a breakout and my hair hadn't done that thing where it went limp and stuck to my face—the body-building shampoo had done its job—so it could have been worse. "That black, sequined tuxedo jacket and the black trousers with a white cami."

"Ditch the cami. Just wear the jacket."

"You mean just wear my bra? Don't be ridiculous. I'm doing my best *not* to look like a hooker despite my eyelashes' desire to have me change profession."

"No bra. That jacket has buttons. And if you go to the retailer's website, they show it being worn without anything underneath it."

I didn't have much boobage, it was true, but what I had, I didn't want the world to see.

"You have that tit tape, right? Get busy and get rid of the cami."

My buzzer sounded and I jumped before the churning in my stomach returned. This was really happening. If I thought about it too much, I wouldn't answer my door and I'd dive under my bed with a bottle of wine and *Elle Decoration*. "Gotta go. Beck's here. And by the way—call him Beck when you see him, not Hot Suit." Henry wouldn't be at the party tonight and Beck knew that, so he was only coming to the party for me—to fulfill his end of our agreement. Part of me had worried that he'd back out—find another way of getting what he wanted—and I'd be left with egg on my face. Again. Trying to explain why I hadn't turned up to the wedding I'd said yes to.

I ran down the stairs barefoot to collect him. His silhouette filled the stained-glass panels in the door—I'd forgotten how tall he was.

"Hey," I said as I swung open the door and smiled. He might be obligated to come tonight, but that didn't mean I couldn't be nice about it, right?

"Miss London," he said and handed me a small bunch of flowers.

"Sweet peas?" I wouldn't have expected flowers from a real boyfriend, let alone blooms so unusual. "Come up," I said as I started up the stairs.

"My mother's favorite."

"You didn't have to bring flowers." I turned left into the kitchen and pulled a vase down from the cupboard. "The fake boyfriend thing is for other people. I'm really not desperate for male company. But thank you."

He stood in the doorway to the kitchen that Matt used to say was too small for two when I suggested we cook together. "I like to be good at things. And it pains me to say that I'm not a good boyfriend."

I grinned. "It's not a shock. I've yet to meet a man who is." It was strange to see another guy in my flat. There'd been no one since Matt. But it wasn't uncomfortable having Beck in my space. Perhaps because we weren't dating—I wasn't comparing him to Matt. I wasn't worried if the lighting was flattering or whether he was going to see my flesh-colored control underwear. I didn't care what he thought of me.

I took the vase of flowers and shooed him out of the room. "Have a seat, I'll be out in a minute. Don't touch anything."

"I wouldn't dare," he said, raising his palms and backing toward the sofa.

I studied him, trying to figure out if he was serious. "You think I come across as someone who tells everyone what to do?" Matt used to complain about me being bossy, but Florence and Karen used to tell me he was being a dick. Did Karen believe it when she said it, or was she trying to cover up her real feelings? Had she always loved Matt or was it something that had grown between them? A metallic taste burned in my mouth and I swallowed, trying to make it disappear.

Beck's chuckle halted my anxiety's momentum. His laugh was unexpected and warmed the tips of my fingers like a welcoming fire on a cold day. It was confident rather than cocky. He dipped his gaze down to his shoes and then back up to hold my gaze. "I think you come across as a woman who knows what she wants and won't let anything stand in her way of getting it."

If I had any chance at having another successful relationship, I probably needed to learn to be less bossy. Florence would disagree. But it was her job to build me up, so her opinion didn't count.

"It's not a bad thing," he said, frowning. "You look pissed off. Don't be. I like it. It's hot. It's like you're my female equivalent."

"And like the narcissist you are, you find yourself hot?" I laughed and my stomach shifted like the heavy, stone door of an Egyptian tomb that hadn't been opened for a thousand years. How did this complete stranger make me feel so bloody comfortable?

"Nothing wrong with healthy self-confidence," he replied.

There was no doubt that Beck had self-confidence in spades. Maybe if I hung out with him for a bit, some of it would rub off.

"Give me two minutes and we'll get going." As I headed to my bedroom, I called out from down the hall. "I just need to decide on my outfit. I can't figure out if I need a top under my jacket."

"Or what?"

I pulled off my silk cami and slipped on the jacket, buttoning the two buttons. "Or what, what?" I called through to the sitting room.

"A top or what else?"

"Just my bra," I replied and headed back into my sitting room. "What do you think?" I asked, as I peered down at my cleavage. It seemed a little too much from this angle.

"Definitely just your bra," Beck said and when I looked up, I found him staring at my cleavage, too.

"You see? I can't wear this. My boobs are out." I didn't want to look as if I was trying too hard, and I didn't want Matt to think I was slutty. He'd always been really particular about how I dressed, and although at first I'd seen it as controlling, after meeting his family, I understood that he was trying to stop his mother from complaining. I might hate Matt, but I didn't want him to look at me and say, "Thank God it's not her I asked to marry me." I wanted to wear something that made him regret what he'd done.

"They're not *totally* out," Beck said. "They're just giving me a little wave."

I pulled my hands up to my chest. "They're not waving to you or anyone else."

"Winking then."

"Holy crap," I said, turning and heading back to my bedroom. "My breasts don't wink!"

"Well, if you were my girlfriend, I'd be very happy to take you out with winking breasts."

I couldn't stop myself from laughing. "I need to advise you not to say that to a woman. *Ever*." I'd just met this guy and already we were talking about my boobs. I guess we *were* in a serious relationship.

"Good tip," he called out. "But seriously, you look hot—better than with the top, which was a little . . . old."

Old wasn't what I was going for.

"This way, you're sexy," he said. "Your outfit, I mean."

I scooped up my evening bag and called out, "Let's go." He met me at the front door. "I think we're going to crush this fake relationship thing if we can talk about my boobs so casually. Before the end of the night, we'll be peeing with the bathroom door open."

He held the door open and I dipped under his arm to make my way out. "We probably should swap a few details about each other, or at the least get our story straight on how we met, how long we've been dating and stuff."

I paused halfway down the stairs as a rush of ice kissed the base of my spine and shivered up to my neck. "Shit. We're completely unprepared. I mean, I don't even know where you grew up or what your middle name is."

I was planning to go in and lie to everyone about how this Beck guy was the love of my life, and I didn't know what he liked to do on Sunday mornings. Was he a gym guy or a lie-in-and-read-the-papers kind of man?

It was going to be completely obvious that we'd just met.

I was about to be completely humiliated.

I pulled the door shut and locked up. Perhaps I should ask him to leave, call this entire thing off. It was a ridiculous idea. Bloody Florence. Only she could have talked me into this.

"Kent and Robert," he said, holding his arm out for a passing cab.

"I don't think we should do this," I said, my feet fixed firmly to the pavement as Beck held the cab door open for me. "It's insane. People are going to think I'm a lunatic when they find out I'm pretending we're dating."

"Get in the cab, Stella."

"I mean it. I'm a terrible liar at the best of times. But I'm not prepared for this."

"We can talk about it on the way."

Maybe it was the way he was so calm, but I did as he said and got into the cab, telling the driver where to head.

"I suggest we say we met at work. It's easier to stay as close to the truth as possible. You pitched some design work to me, got the job, and I asked you out."

He was either an excellent liar or he'd done this before. "Do you have a lot of experience at this kind of thing?"

"Having a fake girlfriend?" He raised his eyebrows as if I'd just asked him if he'd ever considered keeping a llama as a pet.

"You know, lying."

"Everyone lies," he said. "But I've never had a fake girlfriend, no."

"Oh my God. Do you have a real one?" Of course he had a girlfriend. This guy made the Hemsworth brothers look like they lost out in the gene pool lottery. "She can't like this idea." My heart clattered about in my ribcage, waking my pulse and making my hands sweaty. "What if someone knows her—"

"Seriously, Stella, you need to calm down or you're going to bring on a stroke. I'm not dating anyone."

"You're not? How come?" Beck was handsome, wealthy. He should have had a string of women hanging on his every word.

"If I remember correctly from the voicemail my ex-girlfriend left me last week, it's because I'm a selfish, workaholic arsehole—no, that's not right. I'm a piece of shit. Not an arsehole."

I winced. I had asked. "Were you together long?"

He chuckled again, running his knuckles along his jawline. "A few months. I'm not nursing a broken heart; don't worry about it."

For a second, I forgot about the party, about Karen and Matt, and wanted to ask Beck how long they'd been together, whether he'd been faithful, or if they'd lived together, but somehow I stopped myself.

"Perhaps we should skip tonight," I said. "Do some homework—study each other—then go to the wedding prepared. It's only two weeks away but by then I should at least know if you like tofu or hang gliding."

"It's a mutually exclusive choice?" he asked, grinning.

I couldn't help but smile back. "Please, God, don't tell me you like tofu." I sighed dramatically. "I'm not sure I could have a fake relationship with a bean curd lover."

Pride lapped at the edges of my insides as he chuckled. Creating that laugh felt like it deserved some kind of award or a badge, at least.

"You're safe. We'll be fine tonight. We'll just have to try to not get separated for too long, then you won't get asked questions about me and vice versa."

I admired his optimism. Something was bound to go catastrophically wrong. Even though I didn't want to because I didn't want someone else to feel sorry for me, I had to tell him about Matt. It wasn't as if he was just another guest at the party. He was the groom. This was his party. People would assume Beck knew my history with Matt. I braced myself for that sideways tip of the head followed by either the I'm-so-sorry face or the sharp intake of breath, shocked face. "You should probably know that I used to date the groom," I said.

He turned to me as the cab stopped and the streetlight highlighted the contours of his face, emphasizing his sharp jaw. Men were so lucky—they could just roll out of bed, stick on a suit and look completely fuckable. I'd spent the best part of two and a half hours trying my best to look sexy without straying into slutty territory.

"You did? For how long?" he asked.

I sighed and checked out of the front window to see if the lights had changed. "A long time. We met at university." Things hadn't been great between us for a while, I'd known that, but I'd thought we were in it for the long haul. All couples go through bad patches.

"And you're still friendly enough to be invited to the wedding? How evolved of you."

I shrugged, trying to ignore the weight of his stare pressing into my skin. "We have a lot of mutual friends. It's easier if we're civil."

"Do you like his fiancée?"

I'd expected him to ask me when we split up. My relationship with Karen raised more questions than I answered. "You know, same friendship circle."

"Really?" he asked, as we pulled up in front of the Berkeley hotel.

If he thought it was weird that I was still friends with my ex, what would he think if he knew Karen had been my best friend since primary school right up until the point where she stole the love of my life? "Really," I replied as I opened the car door.

Before my feet hit the ground, somehow, Beck had sped around to my side of the car and offered his hand as I stepped out.

"Do we hate him? Or do we like him? Just so I'm prepared."

Hating Matt would be easier. All I could focus on was why and what if things had been different. What if we hadn't moved to London? What if I'd pushed him to get married years ago?

"We don't care enough to hate him. He's history, and I'm so much happier with you because you're richer and your dick is gigantic."

"Well, that's true on both counts," he said, guiding me toward the entrance, his hand at the small of my back.

Despite the fact that I was walking into one of the most difficult situations in my life, I couldn't help but smile at Beck's arm around my waist. But he was still a complete stranger to me. I didn't see how it was possible for us to get through an evening of pretending to be deeply in love when I knew close to nothing about him. We were bound to be caught out, and if my former best friend marrying my ex-boyfriend wasn't humiliating enough, I'd be exposed as desperate enough to have blackmailed someone into pretending they were in love with me. If ever I needed a miracle, it was now.

NINE

Stella

"Have I got lipstick on my teeth?" I asked, bearing my mouth at him as we made it into the lobby of the Berkeley. Karen was always so perfectly turned out—even first thing in the morning, with a hangover, she was a coat of mascara and a pair of heels away from hosting a charity lunch. Whereas I always had loo paper stuck to my heel or had a button ping off just before the most crucial career moment. Tonight, I wanted to look like I had it together. I wanted people to see me and think Matt was an idiot for letting me go rather than think that the situation was messy but understandable given it was an obvious choice between Karen and me.

This evening I didn't want to feel like the jilted ex.

I wanted to feel pretty. And glamorous. And sexy.

I wanted to feel like a woman that men didn't cheat on. That men married.

Beck slid his hand into mine and my stomach tilted like a giddy ten-year-old in her mother's heels, and for a moment

I forgot that I was about to come face-to-face with Matt and Karen. It had been a while since a man had touched me like a lover. Looking back, I couldn't remember the last time Matt had held my hand. And Beck was ridiculously handsome. The kind of good looking that made me look away because it was just too much.

"You look fucking gorgeous," he whispered. "Now let's go see your friends."

I gazed at him as he led us down the long corridor. Had he meant that, or was he just trying to halt my rising anxiety about this evening in its tracks? Because he wrote the book on gorgeous.

He was walking with intent, but I hadn't seen any signs to the ballroom. "Do you know where you're going?"

"The email you sent me said the ballroom. It's right along here."

"You've been here before?" Were these kinds of parties in five-star hotels what he was used to? Did he enjoy them? What kind of wine did he drink?

So many questions.

"Yeah, a few times. You know, charity dinners. Industry drinks."

"I really don't know anything about you." Tonight had disaster written all over it. We'd just have to show our faces and then make a speedy exit.

Beck squeezed my hand as my friend Jo came toward us, her eyes sliding from me to Beck and then back to me, slightly wider than they were before.

"I'm so pleased you came," she said and pulled me in for a hug. "You're an amazing human being."

"You wouldn't say that if you knew what I was thinking."

"You're here, that's what counts. And you look

completely amazing." She stepped back to examine me. "What a super sexy look."

"It's not really me, is it?"

"It's completely you. It's understated, elegant, and confidently sexy just like you are."

My anxiety stepped down a couple of notches and my shoulders relaxed. Jo turned to Beck. "I'm Jo Frammer."

God, between my panic about not knowing enough about Beck, my apprehension about my outfit, and my anxiety about seeing Karen and Matt, I'd completely forgotten to make introductions. I needed to focus.

"Beck Wilde," he said, dipping to kiss Jo on both cheeks.

"It's wonderful to meet you. I want to hear all about you two," she said, turning and leading us into the party. "Someone's been keeping secrets. Tell me everything immediately. How long has this been going on?"

I'd factored in lying to Karen and Matt, but I hadn't really thought about the fact I'd have to lie to my friends—people I loved—about Beck. Jo didn't deserve me lying to her, even though she'd be completely understanding and sweet if she found out.

I was a horrible person. There was no way I was going to be able to pull this off. I glanced over my shoulder, wondering if it was too late to fake a vomiting bug. But that would be a lie, too—I was surrounded by them.

"Depends on if you mean when we first met or when we started dating. Our first social dinner was a couple months ago?" Beck turned to me for confirmation. I just nodded.

"Wow, you have been playing your cards close to your chest," Jo responded. "I've not seen anything on Facebook or Insta."

Shit. Social media. I hadn't thought about documenting

anything on there, but before I could say anything, Beck interjected. "Yeah, I don't do social media. Unless it's business-related."

"Oh I see," Jo replied. "I've heard about people like you, but I thought you were like the Loch Ness monster or a yeti —just a myth."

"Don't have Instagram, yet I'm still breathing," he said. "Amazing, isn't it?"

"Rather than being amazing, it just means you're old," I replied.

"Or far more interested in being with you than online." He fixed me with those deep, green eyes and those walls that appeared when we first met were back—locking everyone else out, leaving just Beck and me, alone, staring at each other as if we'd known each other a thousand lifetimes and didn't need words to communicate.

Jo cleared her throat, bringing us back to the moment. "The party's in here," she said, nodding toward double doors.

I glanced around the ballroom as we entered. A cacophony of sparkling lights, pastel colors, and the strains of a string quartet surrounded us, and my breath caught in my throat. It was beautiful. A huge arrangement of lilacs and summer flowers hung from the ceiling, drooping down over the central bar designed out of mirrors and glass. More flowers hung around the sides of the room, bringing the outside in and filling the space with a light, floral scent.

This wasn't Matt's choice. His family would have opted for something far more traditional at the family home. No, this was Karen all over—expensive but tasteful. I guessed it was good Matt had learned to compromise. He'd always been so stubborn when we'd been together, but why hadn't he learned to compromise for me?

Chatter, clinking glasses, and laughter swept through the space. I was probably the only person in this room who wasn't happy for Karen and Matt. The only person who, when it was said that they were perfectly suited, agreed, but only because they were both cheating, disloyal, despicable people.

"Are Florence and Gordy here?" I asked. If Beck and I got talking to them, it might save us from having to make conversation with people who asked too many questions.

"I haven't seen them yet," Jo replied.

We settled at a ridiculously thin, tall table that people were supposed to stand around and rest their drinks on. "Stay here, and I'll go and get some drinks," Beck said.

He was going to leave me? I'd thought his suggestion of making sure we were together most of the night was a good one. What happened if he bumped into someone and told them a thousand things about our relationship that I had no idea about? Or if Matt and Karen appeared and Beck wasn't by my side to make me seem less of the bitter ex-girlfriend than I felt.

As I surveyed the room, looking for Florence and Gordy, Karen walked straight into my eyeline as she came toward our table. My vision blurred slightly, and I held onto the edge of the table to steady myself. Jesus, she could have at least let me settle in and find my sea legs.

This was the woman who'd stolen my boyfriend, my lover, my friend.

Or the woman my boyfriend had left me for.

I wasn't sure which was worse.

I tried to look at her like a stranger would—what was it about her that made him throw away seven years?

Was she prettier, funnier, better in bed?

Did he just love her more?

She squealed as she got closer. "I'm so pleased you're here," she said, pulling me into a hug as if nothing had happened.

I'd tried to prepare myself for this moment, but I hadn't come up with a game plan. I could be so nice that I was clearly being sarcastic. I could be cool but distant. I could ignore her, or I could tell her what I thought of her. Except the last option probably would have our invitation revoked so that wasn't really an option. I'd decided to do just what felt right in the moment, but I found myself paralyzed with anger, fear, and a lack of understanding.

"I wasn't sure if you were going to make it," Karen said. "I know you RSVP'd and everything but honestly, I expected you to come down with stomach flu or something."

I put on my best fake smile. She was saying she expected me to lie. I guess she was judging me by her own standards. "My stomach is just fine." Not only did she have a complete lack of remorse, she also couldn't even be nice to me. She'd stolen my boyfriend and now she was acting as if he was hers all along. Maybe he had been.

Perhaps she was embarrassed and hoping that we'd all forget about it. Because that was so easy to do when you'd lost the love of your life to your best friend.

She laughed and glanced at my cleavage. "Well, I'm so pleased it is. And did you bring your . . . date or whatever?"

"Oh, she certainly did," Jo replied for me. "He's over there by the bar. The tall, good-looking one."

I couldn't help but grin at Jo's description as we all looked to the bar. There was no doubt Beck was tall. And good looking. A description that didn't do him justice. He was one of those men that commanded a double take when you passed him on the street. He was pretty enough to look like a male model but the way he carried off that suit—or any of the suits I'd seen him in—gave him power.

The three of us were staring as he started back, carrying an ice bucket and glasses. I locked eyes with him and the tightness in my jaw disappeared. There was something about him that made it feel like I'd known him forever. He grinned and it seemed so genuine that I felt it from deep in my bones to the tips of my fingers.

"Oh wow, that's the look of love," Jo said from beside me.

If only she knew.

"Ladies," he said as he placed the ice bucket on the table.

"This is Karen," I said, remembering my manners this time. "She's the bride-to-be."

I wasn't sure why, but he didn't kiss Karen like he had Jo. Instead he offered her his hand. "Beck Wilde. Nice to meet you."

"Dom Perignon?" Jo asked as she twisted the bottle around to reveal the label.

"Yes, I got them to go and get us a bottle." He began to pour the alcohol into the glasses. "It's kind of our drink."

"Your drink?" Karen asked.

"We had it on our first date," Beck replied. "I was trying to impress this beautiful woman." He handed me a glass and placed a kiss on my cheek. Christ, this guy was good at faking it. "Not an easy thing to do," he continued. "But hopefully I've won her over."

"How did you two meet?" Karen asked.

"Work," I mumbled and took a sip of my drink.

"Oh," she said. "You're a recruitment consultant?"

Beck chuckled. "No. I'd be terrible at that job. You have

to be nice to all your clients and all the candidates. Stella is doing the design on one of my buildings."

"Really?" Karen and Jo both asked in unison.

"I thought you'd given up on the interior designer thing?" Karen asked, her mouth a little pinched.

Thing? It wasn't a thing or a hobby. I'd loved the job. I'd missed it. "Nope. I've just been doing bits on the side."

"Which is insane," Beck said. "You really need to be making the most of your talent." He slipped his hand around my waist and pulled me toward him. The heat of his body coated me like armor, his hand holding me firmly in place as if it were a shield.

"You would say that," I replied, trying to continue our charade. He was so freaking good at this, I needed to step up.

"I say it because it's true," he said and turned to Karen and Jo. "You know how modest Stella is. She never believes how good she is at anything."

I couldn't take my eyes off him as he slid his hand up my back. For a second, I could almost believe he meant it.

My insides began to melt like ice cream in the sun.

But of course, he didn't mean it. It was all just for show.

"I knew I was going to have to ask her out the moment we met, but Stella took some convincing."

I glanced at Karen and Jo to see if they were buying this. Both of them were focused on Beck, as if he were conjuring up white rabbits out of the ice bucket. If how he was being tonight was any indication of how he was with his girl-friends, I didn't understand how he was still single. He was funny, confident, attentive, and generous.

"You wore me down," I replied.

He grinned as if we were sharing an inside joke that no one else knew about. "You drive a hard bargain."

I laughed genuinely. I had to add good company to the list of great things about Beck. "Gotta make you work for it."

"Well, Stella, he seems perfect and completely head over heels with you," Karen said. "Are you sure you didn't pay him to be here?" My stomach flipped as if I'd just been caught trying on my mother's make-up. She grinned as if she were joking, but I knew Karen better than that. It might have taken me twenty years, but I finally had the measure of her. I also knew that if she had a suspicion that Beck and my relationship wasn't genuine, she wasn't going to be easily distracted.

"It's so lovely to finally meet you, Karen," Beck said. "Stella has said so many wonderful things about you. We're both very excited to come to Scotland. I love the place."

I slid my arm around his waist. God, this guy made this faking it thing seem so easy.

Karen's mouth twitched. "Yes, well *Matt* and I are very pleased you could come."

She emphasized the name of my ex-boyfriend like she wanted it to hurt. Like maybe I'd forgotten that she was marrying him. As if I ever could? Had she always been like this? So cold, so heartless? Such a bitch?

"Hey," Florence said as she arrived at our table.

"Florence!" Beck said and kissed her. "Let me go and get you a glass." Beck stalked back to the bar, and I couldn't help but watch him. He had a cute arse. Was I going to discover something I didn't like about him? Hopefully. The last thing I needed was to develop some kind of crush on Beck. We were a business partnership. And I couldn't trust myself to find a good guy. Eventually, when I was ready to start dating again, in twenty years or so, I'd just let Florence handle it. She could pick me a boyfriend. She had far more sense and would never end up with a guy who thought so little of her that he cheated on her or ran off with her best friend.

Florence rolled her eyes as she turned the bottle in the ice bucket, revealing the label. "Dom Perignon again? Doesn't it get old being with such a hot, rich, charming guy?"

I laughed. Perhaps a week in Scotland with Beck wouldn't be so bad. "No one's perfect." Although Beck Wilde might be the perfect fake boyfriend. This guy was sharp. He picked up on things so quickly and ad-libbed like it was his job. No wonder he wasn't worried about tonight. *I was almost convinced we were dating.*

"Exactly," Karen said. "I'm sure there are loads of things about him that drive you nuts, right?"

Beck had said to stay as close to the truth as possible. "Honestly, I've not found anything so far," I replied.

"So, when did you meet him, Florence?" Karen asked.

"When they first met," she replied.

My heart stopped dead and it felt as if Karen's cheating hands were pressing down on my chest, about to break my rib cage. I hadn't briefed Florence on the story of us first meeting—she was bound to give something away that showed us up to be faking our relationship.

I wasn't prepared at all.

I interrupted. "I trust Florence's judgement, so I made sure they met before I agreed to go on a date."

Karen smiled, a small, fake smile. "Really. How nice."

Phew, I'd gotten away with it.

"Well, you two seem perfect for each other," Jo said. "It's good to see you with someone who appreciates how wonderful you are." Jo wouldn't have meant it to be a pointed insult at Matt, not with Karen standing there, but Karen's frown told me she took it as one.

"Yes," Karen said. "It's important to show a man the best side of you."

"I'm not sure that works for me," I replied. "You have to take the good with the bad. You don't have to like every single bit of someone, but hiding stuff doesn't work, either."

Honesty was important to me in a relationship. Even more so now. I never hid anything when I was going out with Matt. Perhaps that's why it had worked between him and Karen and it hadn't with us. Maybe men only liked to see the good, sexy, funny side. Maybe the sides that got irritated at work, liked to wear old, worn t-shirts in bed and no make-up on the weekend were reserved for the terminally single. If that was true, I'd end up alone for the rest of my life. Beck and I were an act—for public consumption—but I couldn't keep it up for long. Not with someone I lived with and loved. It wasn't who I was.

Beck came back to the table with two extra glasses. "Gordy will be here soon, right?" How had he remembered Florence's boyfriend's name? No wonder he'd told me not to worry.

"Yeah, he just went to put our coats in the cloakroom. Thanks, Beck. You gotta stop it with the champagne or I'm going to get used to it."

"You know Gordy?" Karen asked.

"I've only heard about him through these two," he said, lifting his chin toward Florence and me.

"You're going to get on brilliantly," Florence said.

"We have to get that dinner in the diary for next week. And we'll go to that restaurant I was telling you about," he said as he turned to me. "Where they serve the best oysters."

No! Things were going so well.

My mouth went dry and I tried to swallow so I could say something and rescue the situation. Anyone who'd known me for longer than twenty-four hours knew I hated shellfish.

"Why would you take Stella to somewhere they served great oysters?" Karen asked, her smile much more genuine now. She'd caught us out.

Karen's eyes were fixed on me even though she'd asked the question of Beck. She wanted to gloat.

Who was this woman? This girl I'd shared secrets with, dreams, fears—I had a huge history with her. Yet, she'd betrayed me as if I were nothing to her. Like my life, my happiness was meaningless to her.

I took a breath. There was no point in trying to deal with her with honesty and openness. She didn't respond to those things. Perhaps lies were the only thing she understood. "Beck's messing around," I said, pulling back my shoulders, ready for a fight. "He knows I hate shellfish."

Beck chuckled next to me. "I keep hoping I can change her mind. It really is the worst thing about you, Stella."

Karen tilted her head to one side. "It's weird. You didn't seem like you were kidding."

"I guess you don't know me very well." Beck shrugged. He was good. But I doubted he was good enough to throw Karen off the scent.

Karen was like a sniffer dog and there was no way she was that easily placated.

We needed to be more prepared. Karen would now be looking for other things that didn't add up between me and Beck. And the only thing more humiliating than your boyfriend running off with your best friend was being found out to be bringing a fake boyfriend to the wedding.

There was no way we were going to pull this charade off for a week in Scotland unless we were a thousand times more prepared.

TEN

Beck

Most people hate going into the office on Sundays, but I wasn't most people. I wandered through the empty desks of Wilde Developments and headed to my office at the back of the building.

I loved weekend working. The phones were quiet, and I didn't have a constant stream of people trailing into my office asking for opinions or signatures. I could get things done. And now that I was weeks away from getting Henry to sign over the Mayfair property, there was plenty to do. I had to work on the tender document for the architects, go through the blueprints that Joshua had managed to get me of Henry's building, which were much more comprehensive than the plans I'd had previously, and finally, I needed to figure out what I was going to do about the designer. I'd said yes to Stella, given her the benefit of the doubt, but seeing her flat last night brought my concerns back. Nothing about it had screamed luxury, high-end, or cutting-edge design.

I closed my office door as my mobile began to ring.

"Stella," I said. "I was just thinking about you."

Silence and then, "There's no way I can go to that wedding with you. This was a ridiculous idea."

Frustration twisted around my gut. There was no way I was going to let her change her mind. There was too much at stake. "What are you talking about?" I asked, trying to keep my voice even. I wanted to shout at her but knew it would be counterproductive.

"I just got off the phone with Florence. Karen called her, asked loads of questions about you and me, said something didn't seem right between the two of us—"

This woman might be beautiful but she was totally paranoid. "I'm sure Karen will be focused on her wedding and not us when we're up in Scotland."

She sighed as if *I* just wasn't getting it. "You don't know Karen very well. She's focused on trying to make me look bad."

I thought these women were friends? I didn't want to dive down that particular rabbit hole. All I cared about was that Stella was invited to Karen's wedding. That was all that mattered. "You're not going to look bad."

"We were nearly caught out last night. I barely managed to carry off our charade for an evening. I can't keep it up for a week."

I threw my keys down on my desk and perched on the edge, facing the city. "Look, it was your idea to pretend that we were together." It was a stupid idea. Why couldn't we just go as friends?

"I know. And I totally accept that it was a terrible idea and that I'm an idiot. This isn't your fault. I'm just saying I can't do it again. There's no way I'll pull it off. Let's just agree that it's not going to work, and I'll cancel—say that I have a hernia operation or something."

I was going to have to talk her round. She wasn't backing out on me.

"Why do you even care? Worst-case scenario, people figure out we're not dating. It's not the end of the world." I didn't know Stella well enough to know how to change her mind, but I was going to have to try. "You laughed in my face when I offered you work for the recruitment agency but when you stormed into my office demanding that I make you designer on the development, you were laser-focused and determined. It's clearly something you want to do, otherwise you could have just asked me for a check. Are you content to just walk away?" I tried to sound calm and logical, but the realization of a long-time dream hung in the balance. I'd get over losing the money. Probably. But not the opportunity of developing *this* block in Mayfair—I wasn't going to let it go.

"Better to walk away than face complete humiliation in front of everyone I know. I refuse to stay at the center of this scandal. I don't know your birthday or what side of the bed you sleep on. It was insane to think I could carry this off."

So that was the problem. She felt unprepared and out of control. Well, I could fix that. I picked up my keys and stood. "Where are you?"

"In my sitting room, why?"

"I'm coming over and we're going to prep," I said as I pulled open my office door and headed out the way I'd just come a few minutes ago.

"Prep?" she asked.

"I bet you were one of those girls who did nothing but study at university. And you probably mocked up some kind of design for my Mayfair building before you came to see me to offer me the deal. Am I right?"

"Erm, that's why you go to university. To study."

"Wrong." I bounded down the stairs two at a time. "Most people go to university to party. But okay, you're a studier. A planner. I can work with that. We just need to study and plan for this wedding. I'll be over in fifteen minutes."

"No! You can't just come over—I'm in my PJs."

"That's good. I need to learn how long it takes for you to have a shower and get ready. It will all help."

"Help what?"

I pushed open the glass doors to the outside and pressed on my car fob. "I told you that the key to telling lies was to stick as closely to the truth as possible. We're going to get to know each other. That way, when we get to Scotland, you won't need to lie, and neither will I. We'll both have plenty to say that's the truth." I slid into the driver's seat of my sports car that I only used on weekends and started the engine. I'd had it over a year and every time I got behind the wheel, the car still made me grin like a beautiful woman laid out on my bed in nothing but underwear.

"That's a terrible idea. We have two weeks. We can't pack a serious relationship into a day."

"So it might take two," I said, pulling out and heading in the direction of Stella's flat. If I could keep her talking, I'd be there before she could make any rash decisions.

"You can't just assume that I have two days to spend studying with you. I have things to do. Places to go. People to see."

"Right. And we can study at the same time. It will be good for me to tag along with you. I can see what you get up to. Learn your quirks—"

"I don't have quirks."

I grinned and imagined her little frown and pursed lips. "We all have quirks. That's what makes us interesting."

I took her silence as a good sign. "We'll spend some time together and before you know it, we'll know each other well enough to breeze through the week in Scotland."

"There's no way—"

"Hey, I saw how much you wanted this design job. Has that just disappeared? Isn't it worth a little effort? If you do a good job on a Wilde Developments project in Mayfair? Well, you won't be a recruitment consultant anymore."

I put my foot on the accelerator. I'd almost convinced her—I could tell from the way her arguments were waning. "I'm just a few minutes away and then we can start."

"But what about you? I'll need to know what you do at the weekend."

"Well, I was in the office when you called, but let's spend today and tomorrow—and the two weeks before the wedding—like a couple. That way, it will be second nature to us when we get to Scotland. We won't need to pretend. You'll get your career back on track and I'll get Henry to sell me his building. Everyone's happy." I didn't tell her that I spent most weekends working, and that for me, dating didn't involve much more than dinner and sex. But whatever. It was three weeks out of my life in exchange for ten million pounds and victory over my demons.

"I guess we can see how today goes and then reassess," she said.

I kept quiet to avoid inadvertently talking her out of giving this a shot. "You better get here quickly before I change my mind," she said.

"I'm five minutes away."

ELEVEN

Stella

The door buzzer made me jump. That couldn't be Beck, could it? I still had my mobile in my hand—we'd barely hung up more than a few minutes ago. I should have changed.

I glanced down at my pajamas—there was a hole in the knee, and the elastic waistband had grown baggy so they slid to my hips. There were a lot of upsides to being single. One of them was wearing your favorite stuff around the house because no one was there to criticize or make comments about how his mother was perfectly groomed at all times.

Beck always looked like he'd just stepped off a Milan runway, and I was sure his real girlfriends didn't own PJs.

But I wasn't his real girlfriend, so what did I care what I looked like? I buzzed him up and left the door on the latch. Should I have given him a key by two months? No, that was a little much.

"Have you ever lived with a woman?" I called as I heard

him come through the door. Had he seen women other than when they were perfectly made up, hair blow-dried, with their best underwear on?

"Well, hello to you too, Stella. And no. Never lived with a woman." He appeared in the doorway to my kitchen just like he had when he'd come to pick me up last night. Already he looked at home, but Beck was the kind of guy who was probably comfortable wherever he was.

"Have you ever given a woman a key to your flat?" Beck was right—I wanted this design job. I wanted to stop this circle of disappointment I'd been in since I'd found out about Matt and Karen. But we were going to have to up our game. Especially after my phone call with Florence. "You want coffee?" We were going to have to pack in a lot in a very short amount of time. Scotland was only a few weeks away.

"No to the key question. Although I've had it suggested to me a couple of times. And water if you have it. Tap is fine."

"You don't drink coffee?"

He shook his head and I took a deep breath. We had a lot to cover. "You need to tell me these things. Not drinking coffee is a big deal."

"It is?"

"Of course, it is. Do you drink tea?"

"Nope. Can't bear the taste. Coffee either. And anyway, I don't like to be high on caffeine."

"Caffeine gets you high?" It was possible that Beck was one of those oh-so-dull men who didn't know how to enjoy himself. There had to be a catch.

"Not high, but it can amp up your mood. I don't drink much alcohol either."

"Whoa. Really? Not at all? Are you an alcoholic? Do

you take drugs?" I had ten million questions. This was never going to work.

He chuckled. "No, not an alcoholic and I don't take drugs."

"I thought you said you went to university for a good time. Can't have been that great for you if you didn't drink or do drugs—not that I did drugs, but I drank my fair share."

"I didn't go to university."

I stopped, my teabag balanced on my spoon, and turned to look at him to see if he was serious. "You didn't? How come?" In my circle of friends, everyone went to university.

He shrugged. "Wasn't my thing. I wanted to be out making money."

"Well, you've clearly done that."

"Exactly. I had my eye on the prize."

"And your parents didn't mind?"

He rolled his eyes. "No. Neither of my parents went."

I'd made assumptions about Beck that I hadn't even realized. I'd thought he'd come from a privileged upper-middle-class background, just like my friends and I had. But he was changing the picture I had unknowingly built up of him.

"You got into real estate straight away?" I asked. Did he have Russian backers or family money or something? Perhaps his business was a front for mob money laundering. Did London even have the mob?

"Sort of. Worked a lot of different jobs, saved a little money, took out a loan to buy a flat in Hackney, flipped it. Did it again. And again. You know."

But I didn't know. My friends were lawyers and doctors or helped run the family business. Flipping flats in Hackney was not part of my world. "So from a flat in Hackney to a development in Mayfair?"

He shoved his hands in his pockets and looked me in the eye. "Apparently."

"Your parents must be proud," I said, hoping to coax out of him more about his background.

"I guess. Not really thought about it."

"You close to them?"

He laughed. "You're going to need a notepad and pen. Get in the shower and then we can get on with whatever you had planned for the day while we talk."

I'd planned to spend the day cross-legged on my sofa, working on design ideas for his development, but I wasn't going to tell him that. He didn't need to see my haphazard process.

"Okay, you can talk to me through the bathroom door. We don't have time to waste," I said, heading to my bedroom, my tea in hand.

"We're going to be fine, you know." He toed off his shoes and sat on my bed as if we'd known each other for years as I closed the bathroom door. It was weird, having a conversation with a stranger in my flat while I was getting naked. He could be an axe murderer or at the very least a pervert. Although I didn't get a pervert vibe from him. He was too confident, too sure of himself.

"It's not like we're being quizzed by someone *trying* to catch you out," he said.

"I told you, Karen smells a rat. She'll absolutely be trying to catch us out."

"But why? I thought you said you were friends."

"We've drifted apart more recently," I replied. "She's said to Florence that she thinks something doesn't add up between us."

"Why does she care? Because your ex is the groom? Wasn't it over between you years ago?"

I stepped into the shower, grateful Beck couldn't see my expression and I could keep things breezy. "You know how gossipy people are," I said, raising my voice so he could hear my answer and sidestepping the question. "We were together for a long time." I wouldn't tell a new boyfriend all the ins and outs of an old relationship right away, would I? If I had to go to that wedding, then I wanted it to be with the one person who didn't think I was a fool—who didn't know I'd spent years with a man who'd tossed me away and replaced me within weeks with my best friend.

I'd been humiliated enough. I needed a break from the shame, some kind of safe harbor.

"Were you engaged?" he asked, his deep voice carrying through the closed door.

I screwed my eyes shut, letting the water cascade over my face, hoping that dull ache in the pit of my stomach could be washed away. This was why I didn't want to go to the wedding. Ninety-six-point-four percent of the time, I was entirely fine as long as I didn't think about Matt and what he and Karen had done. But if I went to Scotland there'd be no escape from the two of them for an entire week. "Not officially," I said. "But we'd talked about it. I assumed it would happen at some point." I'd thought we were working toward our future together. I'd got that very wrong.

"You lived together?"

"Yeah. In this flat."

Silence from the other side of the door. Good, the Matt conversation was over, and we could move on to more important stuff.

"Did you decorate this place?" he asked.

"Don't worry," I said. "I understand what you need in

your development. I get the styles are different." Most of this flat had been Matt's choices, not mine. "What about you? Why do you think you've never lived with a woman?"

More silence but eventually he said, "I like my own space. Enjoy coming home, putting on the news, opening a beer, and sitting on my sofa in my boxers."

That sounded like the boy equivalent of PJs, ice cream, and a re-watch of *Bridget Jones' Diary*.

"And you can't do that with a woman?" I finished rinsing out my hair and turned off the shower.

"I never have. I just like silence sometimes. I don't want to have to talk all the time. I don't want to have to hear about what happened in her day or remember that she took her cat to the vet or whatever."

"Wow. Harsh," I replied as I dried off and slipped on my favorite robe. It was white with pink flamingos all over it. I'd washed and worn it so often a small hole had appeared under the arm, but it was the most comfortable thing I owned, and I loved it.

Matt hated it.

"Harsh? That I like my own company?" he asked as I opened the door. He was laid back on my bed, one arm tucked behind his head, his long legs crossed at the ankle. My stomach tilted at the sight of him. He might drive a hard bargain, be overconfident, bordering on annoying, but there was no getting away from that sharp jaw and perfect body. The way his shirt fit him just perfectly, the way his trousers hinted at his clearly muscular thighs—it was almost obscene. I glanced away, trying to focus.

"I suppose it makes sense if you've never been in love, which you obviously haven't."

A grin spread over his face like a sunrise. "Obviously?"

I turned away and sat in front of my dressing table, looking at him in the mirror behind me. "Yes, it's clear to me for two reasons. First, you wouldn't think hearing about her day was a chore—you'd want to know about her cat."

"I really don't like cats," he said.

"Maybe not, but if her cat is important to her and she's important to you, then you'd want to know what happened at the vet." Something about the way he looked at me told me he wasn't buying it. But what did I care? "For the record, this is a cat-free zone."

"Thank God. What's the second reason?" he asked, sitting up.

"We all get days where we want to sit around and decompress after work. People in love understand that they can do that together."

He hooked his legs over my bed and began to examine what was on my bedside table. "Is that what it was like with you and Matt?"

I paused as I watched him pick up the silver elephant trinket box that I'd bought on a trip to India with Matt after graduation. Matt's parents hadn't approved of a gap year. But we had a gap six weeks. We'd been so happy then, as if we'd been limbering up for a marathon or in the wings of a theatre before the first show—we were full of excitement and nervousness, hope and expectation. I'd thought we'd be together forever.

A lot had happened since then.

"Maybe. In the beginning, when things were good."

"That's the other thing I don't get about couples. They always seem to stick it out when it's clear to everyone around them that neither of them is happy and they both need to move on. Why the hell is that?"

I uncurled the towel on my head and picked up my hairbrush. "I suppose one or both of them is hoping it will get better. Wishing it could go back to how things used to be. It's hard to walk away when you've invested so much time and effort into someone."

"But it's a sunk cost. That time and effort is gone—spent. No point wasting more resources on a project that's not going anywhere."

"Jeez. Relationships aren't a balance sheet. Feelings are involved. Or are you just a cold-hearted businessman who's all about the cold, hard cash?"

Holding the book I was currently reading—*The Goldfinch*—he turned to stare at me. In actual fact, it was the book I was *trying* to read—what I was actually reading was the latest Nora Roberts. I'd gotten into the habit of having one paperback by my bedside that Matt would approve of and the one I was reading on my Kindle where he couldn't comment on the number of brain cells I was losing by reading it. I suppose I had no one to pretend to anymore.

"Maybe I am. Perhaps I'm just not capable of being in a relationship."

"Who was your last girlfriend?"

"Danielle. She was a pharmacist. Gorgeous girl."

I wasn't about to admit it, but I'd assumed he'd be dating models or ballerinas. Where the hell did men find ballerinas? Every ex-boyfriend Florence ever had left her for a ballerina. "What did you like about her?" I asked.

"She was busy."

I burst into laughter. "You liked that she was busy?"

He shrugged. "I mean, she was pretty. Great body. Her hair was . . . glossy. What do you want me to say?"

I bit down on my bottom lip, willing myself not to laugh again. This guy was totally clueless. "Why was the first thing that popped into your head that she was busy? Because you didn't have to see her much?"

He tossed my copy of *The Goldfinch* on the bed and wandered over to my wardrobe. "No, I don't think so. I just liked that she had her own life, her own friends. She wasn't too needy. Although, I think I might have assumed she needed less attention from me than she actually did."

"So, your ideal woman doesn't need anything from you? You don't have to pay attention to her, hear about her day, concern yourself with what's important to her, just as long as she's around for a shag at your convenience? Is that about the size of it?"

"You're making me sound like a dick," he said, pulling out a pink hoodie that I really should donate or at least fold away in a drawer as if I never wore it.

"I'm just replaying what I heard."

"You're saying I'm a dick."

"I'm not saying that." But I wasn't *not* saying that either. Make-up done, I stood up and pulled out some jeans and a top from the chest under the window. "You need to leave, go poke about in my kitchen or something while I change."

He fixed me with a serious expression. "I really should see you naked if we're doing our research properly."

Heat rose up my body and thundered into my cheeks and I shivered. It had been a long time since I'd felt those first whispers of attraction to someone.

I glanced up at him and he grinned and then slipped out of the room.

Beck was Matt's opposite. Matt had never been afraid of commitment. He'd always envisaged his life with a wife and children. I wasn't sure if it was because we'd met so young, but neither of us had needed to get used to couple-dom. We'd wanted to be together, wanted to hear about each other's day.

Trying to get Beck to act like a man in love—a man more like Matt—was going to require some work.

TWELVE

Beck

Figuring out women had never been a priority for me. But this was business, and although I wasn't good at relationships, I was good at business. I'd done a little digging and found examples of Stella's design work—she clearly had the training she said she did and although her clients were a little different to mine, it was still obvious she'd injected some individuality into each project. But then her flat was stuffed to the brim with a hotchpotch of old stuff that didn't seem to belong together.

"Are we heading over to your place now?" she asked. "So I can root through your stuff and make silent judgements?"

I laughed. She was irreverent and funny but somehow managed to hit the nail on the head. "We're not going back to mine, but I'm happy for your judgement of me to be completely out in the open," I said, clicking down on my key fob, the lights of the Lamborghini flashing as the doors unlocked.

She groaned. "Really? *This* is your car?"

"Is that a problem?" I asked, opening the door for her and then rounding the bonnet before getting in the drivers' side.

"It's just a little . . . obvious," she said as I sat.

"And what you mean by obvious is new money." I didn't exactly snap but at the same time, I wished I hadn't mentioned it. Joshua and Dexter were always ribbing me about this car. But I liked it. What was the point in having money unless you enjoyed yourself a little with it?

"I suppose—not that there's anything wrong with that."

"Fast cars are fun. If that's obvious, I'll take it." I pulled out into almost-stationary traffic. If we weren't in central London, I could show her just how fun cars like this could be. My money might not have been given to me by my father, but it was as good as the inherited stuff.

"I never got the car thing, but each to their own. So where are we going if not back to your place?"

"I don't know. What do you like to do at the weekend?"

She let out a breath, which I'd figured out she did to give herself more time to answer. "I usually end up working, or I'm so knackered from work that I lie in bed, waiting for death." She grinned at me.

She was funny. Like one of the guys. "Level with me about the recruitment consultancy thing. Why are you in a job you clearly don't like when you used to do something you're obviously passionate about?"

She leaned forward and began to fiddle with the air-con. "That's not part of the introductory course. It's the advanced curriculum. And anyway, you've heard a lot about me, and you've been in my flat twice now. I don't know if you live in a tumble-down bedsit in Croydon or a Georgian townhouse in Belgravia."

I laughed, happy to move on from talk of her job, even though I was curious about how she'd ended up where she had. I was confident I'd get her to tell me sooner or later. "I live in Mayfair, of course."

"Of course," she mumbled. "Mr. Mayfair. How could I forget?"

"So, when you're not lying in bed, waiting for death, what do you like to do in London?"

"Eat?" she offered as if it was more of a question than an answer. "Especially at the weekend. Take the papers, settle into lunch. With a strictly no-talking policy."

"Well, we can do food but I'm banning papers. We need to talk or I'm going to have to deal with you having a meltdown because you don't feel prepared enough."

"It's like you've known me a thousand years already. But seriously, maybe we should just accept that this situation is impossible, shake hands, and move on with our lives. If Karen figures out we're not really dating . . . I think I'd have to emigrate to avoid the shame."

"There will be no emigrating. And no giving up. We have a deal." I didn't understand why she needed to have a boyfriend for this wedding in the first place, but if it meant she'd take me then I was up for it. "Do I have to remind you that you really want to be the designer on my new building —when are you going to get an opportunity like that again?" I didn't mention the antique chest in her bedroom that didn't seem to go with anything, or the weird Chesterfield sofa in her living room that looked like it belonged in some stuffy, men-only, private members lunch club. Perhaps they were hand-me-downs and she couldn't afford anything else. I tried to focus on the work she'd previously done and ignore the fear that any talent she had for interior design was purely in her imagination. I'd cross that particular bridge when I came to it.

"And another thing. You lie in bed at the weekends waiting for death." I chuckled at the over-dramatic description of her mood. "This will shake things up a little, make life a little more interesting. Give you a new challenge."

"And if I fail . . ." She trailed off. The hopelessness in her eyes suggested there was more to her story than what she'd told me.

"Do me a favor?" I asked. She had to stop thinking she was being forced to do this. It was her choice.

"Another one?"

"Funny," I said, pulling out of the traffic and turning left off Marylebone Road. "It's not a favor if you're getting something in return. It's a bargain. Give it these next two weeks. We'll hang out. Learn about each other and then if you don't feel prepared, we won't go to the wedding. You can feign illness or something. Stay positive. Keep your goal in mind. We've got this."

I glanced over to find her staring out of the window, drawing a small circle with her fingertip on the glass. "You're right. I've stopped believing that things can go right for me."

The sadness in her voice sent a chill across the surface of my skin, as if I'd been blasted with cold air.

"I've been told before that I change women's lives. So, get ready."

She turned to me and grinned. "You're so cheesy."

Her smile chased away the chill. "So, do we have a deal?"

"Yes." She nodded resolutely. "I'll stop whining, and we'll both do our best over the next few weeks."

I was going to make sure the woman knew more about

me than my mother and my five best friends put together. There was no way I was letting Stella London or Henry Dawnay slip through my fingers.

"NOW WHERE?" Stella asked as we got back to the car after a long, late lunch that had seemed to pass in a flash.

I checked my watch. It was after six. How had all those hours passed without me noticing? What I really wanted to do was drop her off at her flat and head to the pub. That was what I did on Sunday nights. "You don't need to prepare for tomorrow?" I asked over the roof of the car before getting in and starting the engine.

"Prepare for what?" Stella asked. "Another thrilling week in recruitment? No, it's been a bit quieter recently. No doubt I'll walk into the office tomorrow and get hit with a tidal wave of phone calls and emails." We drove in silence for a few minutes. "So, what do you normally do on a Sunday night?"

"Work. Hang out with friends."

"And what about women? Even if Danielle saw the light, surely, for a man like you, sex is on the agenda?"

What did she mean, a man like me? I wasn't a type. I didn't fit in a box. "Not on a Sunday," I replied.

"For religious reasons?" she asked. I turned to see if she was serious and found a wide, warm smile that she didn't wear often enough.

I decided to double back on myself and head toward my flat. She wanted to be prepared? And she could banter like one of the guys? I was going to take her to the pub with me. "Yeah, I'm a regular Benedictine monk."

"I didn't get that vibe from you."

"Weird that. Sunday nights are about chewing the fat and drinking beer with my oldest friends."

"I thought you didn't drink."

"They drink. I nurse a pint of lemonade," I replied.

"Well, you know what I'm going to suggest."

"I'm way ahead of you. We'll drop the car and we'll be there to get the first round in."

"Are jeans okay?" She looked down at what she was wearing. "And this shirt is old."

"I swear, none of these guys will notice what you're wearing."

"Nice. No wonder women aren't part of your Sunday nights if you're full of compliments like that."

"I'm not saying they won't notice *you*. Just that your clothes aren't what they'll pick up on. First will be your smile. Then, no doubt they'll check out your arse, boobs, legs. But they won't focus on your shirt being *so very last season*."

"I don't know whether to laugh or punch you." She giggled and playfully punched me in the arm, and I feigned injury.

"Don't hate the player. Hate the game." I chuckled at myself as Stella rolled her eyes. "What? You told me I was cheesy. I'm just proving you right. You should be happy."

"You think men just break women down into body parts?" she asked as I pulled into my garage.

It was one of those questions that was impossible to answer. I'd either come off looking like a total dick or a *complete* and total dick. I had to reframe the question. "The first thing we notice is a woman's physical appearance. That's just a fact. But that's not the only thing we care about. And you can't tell me it's not the same for a woman." I switched off the engine. "I like attention from women. I don't mind if they see me and like what they're looking at. It's human nature to be attracted to the physical."

We got out of the car and headed to the exit. Yes, we would be early, but there was no point in going up to my flat. I wasn't sure I was ready for Stella to be in my space.

"So you're saying I should prepare myself to be objectified by your friends."

"No more than any other woman walking into the bar. At least they won't be focused on your shirt." I held my hand out as the lift opened at the lobby.

All six of us had women in our lives at various points, some more seriously than others, but only one of us was married. It wasn't that women were banned from our weekly trips to the pub, it was just that none had ever showed up, so I wasn't quite sure how bringing Stella along would go down.

Joshua and Dexter knew that Stella was taking me to the wedding so I could speak to Henry. But I'd have to fill the others in so no one got the wrong end of the stick and thought things were so serious I couldn't be away from her for an evening. It would be so out of character they'd think I'd caught some kind of weird disease. I couldn't imagine ever feeling that close to a woman. The perfect relationship for me was a woman I saw twice a week for dinner and a sleepover. The idea of sharing a bed *every* night was enough to make my skin itch and my palms sweat.

"And I don't have to drink beer, right? Because if fitting in means drinking beer then I'm happy to stick out. I hate it."

"You don't have to but if you want to fit in . . ." I said in mock warning. "I'm drinking lemonade, remember."

I opened the door to the exit of the building, and she stopped in her tracks. "We're not going up to your flat?"

"No reason to. We can go straight there. It's just on the corner."

She eyed me suspiciously but walked through the plate glass doors. "Summer in London is the best," she said.

"When it's sunny," I said, heading right out of my building. The six of us took it in turns to nominate the pub we had our drinks in but over the years we'd settled on three. Tonight, it was my turn, which meant we'd spend the evening around the corner from my flat.

"And not too humid," she said.

"And you don't have to sit in traffic."

"And you don't have to work," she replied. "Let me rephrase. Sunny, not humid, workless, traffic-less, summer evenings in London are the best."

I nodded. I couldn't argue with that. "And kicking back with friends is the best way to spend those evenings."

"Agreed. Oh, the Punchbowl?" she asked, tipping her head back to look at the sign as the softening sunlight caught the strands of her hair. "This is the one Guy Richie owns?"

"He sold it," I said, peeling my eyes from her and opening the door, indicating for her to go before me. "Years ago. Trust me, it's nice." It was my favorite pub in London. It was like an old-fashioned place that had been polished up and made to look nice. And that kind of suited me.

"It's Mayfair. Of course it's going to be nice," she said. We headed inside, and she looked around. "Gosh, it's a lot bigger on the inside."

It had plenty of choice when it came to the beer, which the boys enjoyed, and the dark wood and red leather chairs gave it an authentic feel.

"This okay?" I asked.

She shrugged. "Sure. But I bet you can't get Dom Perignon here," she said.

"I wouldn't bet on it. Grab that table and I'll go and order. You want champagne?"

"I really don't. Wine, please."

"What kind of wine?"

"The house white is fine."

I'd ordered Danielle house wine once. Jesus, she'd been pissed off at me. Apparently, no one drank house wine, and on top of that I was supposed to have remembered the *kind* of wine she preferred. Apparently, I'd found the only person in London who drank house wine.

It was tradition that whoever got to the pub first ordered drinks for everyone, even if it meant beers went flat. It wasn't a complicated order, but I took the barmaid through it three times just to make sure she had it, then returned to our large, round table with a tray of seven drinks. It looked like Stella and I were in for a big night but the boys would be here soon enough.

"So did you guys work together? Grow up together? How do you know each other?"

"Duke of Edinburgh," I replied. "Gangs had just started to build up on our estate when I was a teenager and my mum thought that weekends working toward something positive like the Duke of Edinburgh award—spending time outdoors, climbing mountains, and volunteering—would keep me out of prison. And it did." A number of the kids I'd gone to school with had ended up doing time.

"And you stayed in touch all these years?"

"Yeah. Took three years to get all three awards. And it introduced me to a different future. Did you do it?" I asked as I took a seat on one of the low stools.

She shook her head. "I knew people who did, but I was

indoorsy rather than outdoorsy. Is that what you enjoyed? The hiking? You climb a lot of mountains, right?"

"That's part of it," I replied. "But because kids from all over the area, from all different schools and backgrounds all did the award together, I met people who wanted more out of a life than just staying out of jail or to be a drug dealer," I said as I transferred the last pint glass from the tray to the table. I'd been the only kid from my school to do the Duke of Edinburgh award, and I hadn't told a soul in my class. I learned early not to hand my enemies ammunition. "The kids from other areas had different stories to tell, completely different lives. And I realized my fate wasn't fixed—I didn't have to stay on the estate where I grew up." I took a breath in, still sensing the gratitude I had for stumbling onto the Duke of Edinburgh award. If I hadn't seen that poster tacked up on the notice board by the assembly hall and surreptitiously gone and taken a photograph when I'd been excused to use the loo during a geography lesson, I might have had a very different life. "There was a girl that we did the silver medal with who ended up sailing across the Atlantic—her and her mate. Amazing. They were the youngest all-girl crew to ever do it. Seeing those aspirations in other people sows seeds. The beginning of my ambition was born spending time with the others on the course, understanding what was out there in the world for me, sharing our hopes and dreams for the future. I discovered my grit and determination. By the end of those three years, I'd built the foundations of the man I'd become and made the five best friends it was possible to make."

"Beck, that's amazing."

Stella's eyes were sparkling, and she seemed genuinely enthralled by my story. But it *was* amazing. For all of us. Those hours climbing up and down mountains in the rain, snow, and unbearable heat, volunteering with disadvantaged kids, raising money for the homeless—they had been the time of my life.

"Speaking of—here's Dexter," I said, glancing at the door.

Dexter arrived at the table and his gaze slid from me to Stella and back again, his eyebrows receding farther into his hairline with every second that passed.

"Hey, mate," I said. "You've heard about Stella." I gestured next to me.

"Oh, right. You two are going to the wedding together." He kissed Stella on each cheek before taking a seat next to her.

"That's the plan," I said before Stella could start on how impossible it would be.

"And you're friends now?" he asked.

"We're getting there," I replied. "As I'm going as Stella's plus one, we thought it would be good to spend some time together."

"He's pretending to be my boyfriend, so I need to know everything about him. I'm hoping as his friends, you'll be able to fill me in on all the stuff he doesn't want to tell me."

Dexter shot her a grin that said he'd just won the lottery. "I'm pretty sure we can manage that."

"Manage what?" Joshua asked as he approached the table, setting his wallet down before noticing Stella. I swore one of these days he was going to walk right into the road because he was thinking up some complicated algorithm or something.

"Joshua, Stella. Stella, Joshua." I should have ensured we arrived late, that way we only had to do introductions once.

"We have to rake up every awful thing we know about Beck to tell Stella," Dexter said.

"This isn't a Vegas residency—we're here for one night only," Joshua replied.

I really should have briefed them before bringing Stella. They were joking, but I wasn't sure what would send Stella running in the opposite direction of the wedding. The last thing I needed was for these guys to destroy my last chance to meet Henry.

By the time Andrew arrived, Stella already knew I was shit at football. I didn't bother to add that it was because I hated the game. By the time we'd all sunk our first pints, Stella was almost through her glass of wine and the flush in her cheeks and her near-constant smile suited her. Apparently laughing at my expense relaxed her.

"His legs were so thin, he could have slid down a plug-hole," Dexter said.

"Fuck off," I said. "I was just lean, that's all."

"Spindly more like," Tristan said. "My mum used to pack chocolate bars into my rucksack to give you. She thought you were malnourished."

"That's a lie. You never gave me any chocolate."

"Of course not. I kept it for myself." Tristan shrugged as if I were stupid.

"You all did all the levels together?" Stella asked.

"Yeah. We all did bronze, silver, and gold, so it took a while," Tristan said. "Years. I couldn't shake these guys even if I wanted to."

"One of the best things I've ever done in my life, even if it did mean I hung out with this lot of losers," Dexter said. "Getting all three medals is one of the achievements in my life I'm most proud of."

I nodded and looked up to see the other four guys

nodding too. Tristan was a billionaire who'd built up his online pharmaceutical distribution business from scratch. Dexter was a diamond dealer and as sharp a man as I'd ever met. All six of us were the best in our field. We all had a lot to be proud of. But Duke of Edinburgh would make top three on our list of accomplishments any day of the week. We all owed a good portion of our success to the skills we developed during those times.

"And you get to go to Buckingham Palace, right?" Stella asked.

"If you complete gold, you sure do. We met the Duke of Edinburgh." Dexter pulled out his phone and brought up a picture of him and his mum and dad in front of the palace gates. We all had a similar picture. And of course, we had plenty of the six of us.

"You all seem very passionate about it," Stella said.

"Well, Beck here is," Dexter said. "If he hadn't done Duke of Edinburgh, he would have fallen down a plughole."

"Fuck off. I was *lean.*"

Stella laughed and part of me wanted to strip down naked and challenge anyone to take the piss out of me. I was still lean, but unlike when I was fourteen, I now had the muscles that defined my shape. I didn't get out into the country to hike as much as I'd like, but I was committed to running and the gym.

"So, what else do I need to know about this guy?" Stella asked.

"He's disgustingly competitive," Tristan said.

"Coming from you?" He had to be kidding. Tristan was one of the most competitive people on the planet and the worst loser who ever lived.

"We're not talking about me," he replied. "We're talking about you."

"We're all competitive," I said. None of us could argue with that. What went unspoken was that we'd all step in front of a train for each other.

When Gabriel's father died when I was seventeen, I caught three trains and walked seven miles to get to the funeral.

Two years ago, when Tristan's sister's boyfriend punched her, Joshua tracked him down online, drained his bank accounts of money, destroyed his credit rating, and gave him a criminal record for aggravated assault.

When I bought my first flat in Hackney, all of them showed up and helped me gut the place.

We were brothers. I'd learned some time ago that family wasn't about blood that you shared but experiences that bound you.

"Okay, what about current bad habits?" Stella asked.

"Honestly, he's not got the greatest track record with women," Joshua said. "But other than that, he's a pretty decent guy."

"What does his track record with women look like?" Stella asked.

"Women just aren't my focus," I replied before anyone else could add something I couldn't row back from. "So I can be a bit thoughtless."

"Have you ever had a serious relationship?" she asked.

"Serious?" Dexter asked with a chortle.

"I work too much," I mumbled.

"Like I keep telling you, mate, you won't have to consciously try to make an effort when you find the right woman. But until then, a fake relationship sounds like a good idea. Make sure you keep him on his toes," Dexter said.

"So this is some kind of immersion weekend before you

go to the wedding?" Joshua asked. "I guess you had to squeeze it in before you go to New York next week."

Fuck, I'd completely forgotten I was headed stateside next week. Stella wasn't going to be happy.

"You're going to New York?" she asked. "For how long?"

"The trip is ten days in all. I'm spending a few days in Chicago, but I don't go until Thursday."

"Can you cancel? We have prep to do. I won't make a total fool out of myself in front of all my friends."

I'd been winning with Stella before my trip had been mentioned. She'd relaxed and I'd begun to enjoy her company. I already recognized the beginning of a spiral into meltdown territory.

"I can't cancel. These meetings have been arranged for months. But it will be fine. I feel like you know me better than my own mother at this point." The meeting in Chicago was about the possibility of converting an old hotel into luxury flats. It could turn out to be very lucrative. And I was looking forward to diversifying and spreading my wings a little.

Stella set her drink on the table and sat back, looking as though dark clouds had gathered above her. Her mouth was downturned, and her eyebrows pulled together. "I'm serious, Beck, Karen will stop at nothing to embarrass me. And I don't think I could handle it. I've had enough humiliation to last me a lifetime. Being at the wedding is bad enough."

"Humiliation? What do you mean?"

Her eyes filled with tears, which was the last thing I was expecting. Despite her claim that she and Karen were friends, it didn't seem that way at all. But why would going to the wedding be so awful? I didn't want to ask and risk upsetting her even more. "You could come with me to America?" I suggested.

"Don't be crazy. I can't follow you to New York. Apart from anything else, I don't have enough holiday left. Especially since I have to take a week for the wedding."

"So, hand your notice in. You're not going to be able to do that job and do all the design on my building anyway." What was I doing? I shouldn't be encouraging her to give up her job. It would be better for me if she realized herself that she couldn't do the two things and ended up pulling out of my project.

"I'll figure it out." She tapped her finger on the bottom of her wine glass. She didn't sound too convincing. "In the meantime, you need to cancel your trip."

"That's not going to happen. I'll be at the end of the phone. We can even FaceTime. But I'm not cancelling. End of story."

"Oh, did I mention how stubborn Beck is?" Joshua asked.

"Piss off," I replied. "You wouldn't cancel in my position either. And there's no need to. If we were having a relationship, we would talk a lot by phone, so that's what we'll do. I'll call you five times a day if necessary." Truthfully, going to the US when Stella was so jittery wasn't ideal, but I'd have to make good on my word and call her a lot—ask her questions, answer hers. It would be fine.

"I guess, like you said, I can wait and see how confident I'm feeling and tell them I'm sick if I don't think we're ready."

"We're going to be ready. I promise you." One thing Stella would learn about me was that I didn't make promises I didn't keep.

THIRTEEN

Stella

With Beck in New York, I was going to have to make the best of things. It wasn't as if he were on a desert island somewhere without his mobile. After elbowing my way through the lunchtime crowds of Seven Dials, I threw my salad onto my desk and pulled out my phone. It was nine in the morning in New York. Beck should be ready for a few questions.

Me: *Are u there?*
Beck: *Where?*
Me: *On the other end of the phone?*
Beck: *No.*

He was *almost* funny.

I had to use the time he was away as efficiently as possible. I needed to think of the kind of digging Karen was going to do. No internet research was going to tell her anything that would be a problem. It wasn't like Beck was secretly gay or married or a priest or something.

He liked women. His friends had assured me of that in the pub. I grinned to myself. He was always so cool and confident, it was nice to see he wasn't perfect—the way his friends ribbed him about stuff in front of me had clearly irritated him.

It was cute.

Almost as if he wanted to present the best version of himself to me. As if he wanted me to like him.

And I did like him. So far. Not that it mattered. Although, obviously he was attractive. An eighty-five-year-old lesbian nun would be a little giddy around Beck.

But it didn't matter. Because we weren't dating. We were getting to know each other. That was different.

Somehow.

Me: *What's your favorite restaurant in London?*

Nothing.

Two minutes later—nothing.

Ten minutes later—still nothing.

Five hours later just as I was logging out to go home—Beck was still radio silent. What could be more important to him than this? I thought he desperately wanted to go to the wedding.

Three dots popped up, indicating he was online, not that I had the phone jammed in my hand or anything.

But then nothing.

I typed out "hello" and then deleted it. Then typed out another less polite message and deleted that one as well.

I knew if any sane person could see me now, they'd wonder what the hell was going on. Time to call in the only person I was completely sure was sane: Florence.

I shot past the lifts and took the stairs where I could get mobile coverage.

"Hey," she answered.

"I need you to talk me off a cliff. Oh, and hello."

I heard her take a deep breath and it made me copy her and fill my lungs.

"What's going on."

Florence understood how difficult this wedding was going to be for me. She'd understand a little freaking out. "Beck isn't answering my messages."

As I exited the building, by some miracle my bus was waiting for me at the stop. I climbed on and pressed the phone harder against my head, hoping I'd hear Florence over the traffic and announcements on the bus.

"At all? Or has he just not answered one text. Yet?"

"The one I sent him five hours ago hasn't been answered. And before you ask, he's seen it and it's after lunch in New York." I wasn't being entirely unreasonable and expecting him to answer in the middle of the night or anything.

"You know what I'm going to say," Florence replied.

I stared out of the window, watching the push and pull of the office workers trying to escape the area and the tourists pouring in. "That I should never have agreed to go to this wedding in the first place?" Well, that was completely certain. "It was a deal I couldn't say—"

"You know that's not what I was going to say. He's in New York for a reason, not just to message you the entire time. He'll reply. He knows he has to keep you happy and stop you from completely melting down."

She was right. He was probably in a meeting. Or multiple meetings.

But didn't he get a loo break?

"Karen is going to do her best to figure out if we're an act. I can't give her any chinks in our armor."

"Yeah, she's on a mission now. If I didn't know better, I would say she's more interested in you and Beck than she is about the wedding itself. She called me again last night and asked a ton of questions about when you two met and then when I'd met him."

My heart pounded, sucking up blood from my toes and making them turn marble-cold. I'd half hoped Florence would tell me Karen had forgotten by now and that in Scotland she'd be far more focused on her wedding and her guests, but she'd done the opposite. "Maybe I should have gone to New York," I replied. I could have phoned in sick, although knowing my luck, I would have bumped into someone from the office on the Heathrow Express.

"Who cares what Karen thinks, anyway," Florence said. "She's a witch. You don't need someone like that to believe you."

I thought Florence got it. "Karen can't know that Beck and I aren't a real couple. Gordy hasn't said something, has he?" Was she trying to warm me up before she told me that Gordy had spilled the beans?

"Gordy doesn't speak to Karen. And actually he hasn't spoken to Matt much either. Between you and me, they've had a bit of a falling out. Gordy really doesn't approve of what he's done."

Gordy was a sweet, kind man who might just deserve Florence.

My thoughts tumbled down into the I-can't-believe-this-has-happened valley. I'd spent a lot of time in that place, ruminating and wondering what had gone on, when things had gone wrong, how long Matt and Karen had been together—I couldn't go back there.

"Well, he's done what he's done. I'm trying to look to the future—otherwise I wouldn't be going to this wedding."

The bus pulled up at my stop just three doors down from the flat I'd thought would become the place where Matt and I lived as newlyweds.

"Exactly, so who cares if Karen figures out you and Beck. You still get the job. You still move forward."

I might still get the job of a lifetime but somehow, I needed more than that. I had to believe that I could be more than the girl whose best friend and boyfriend got married. "I need evidence," I said. "Yes, the job's important. I need the chance to get my design business up and running, but I need something else too. I'm in a rut—or I'm on a losing streak or something. At the moment, if I got that job, I'm worried something would happen to stuff it up. I need this pretend boyfriend thing to go right to break the pattern."

"To end your losing streak?"

I put the key in the lock and pushed the door open into the hallway. Absolutely nothing about coming home had changed since Matt had left. Except Matt wasn't here. The coat hooks still had too many coats on them, even though they were just *my* coats and jackets now. The succulent his mother had brought on her last visit still sat on the console table. The deep red carpet still made the hallway look dark. "Exactly. Maybe." It wasn't exactly a run of bad luck I was having. But I'd gotten into a pattern of bad stuff happening and it was starting to feel normal. "Something good needs to happen. And you know what? I want to convince everyone at that wedding, including Karen, that Beck is my boyfriend because I want to know that people think it's possible."

"I'm not following you. Think *what's* possible? That you could date a guy like Beck?"

"Sort of. I mean, he's good looking, hardworking, he has a great body, his own business. He's funny—sometimes.

He's got nice friends. I don't know, I just want people to believe that I'm worth someone like that. That I'm worth something more than a cheating boyfriend. I swear people think that I must have done something to deserve it." The fact was, I was always trying to figure out what I could have done differently. What I could have done to have stopped Matt cheating.

"Stella, I believe you're worth more than a man like Matt."

I didn't like the tinge of pity I heard when she said my name.

"You don't count. You're biased." I pulled open the bedside drawer that had been Matt's. When I'd packed up his stuff, I'd forgotten this drawer, and when I realized, I didn't bother to tell him. And I hadn't emptied it. It was almost as if I didn't want to get rid of the last pieces of him for some reason. Now a packet of mints, a pen that he'd gotten from his dad when he got his first job, and a dog-eared copy of *Into the Wild* were the only things of Matt left in this flat. In my life. I slammed the drawer shut. "It's not just the Beck thing—I want people to think I'm strong and capable. And that my whole life hasn't been busted into a million pieces."

"You want everyone else to believe that?"

I did. I wanted the entire world to believe that I was okay. That I was not only capable of surviving Matt and Karen's betrayal, but I had thrived despite them.

If everyone else believed it, maybe I could too.

The sound of a message arriving bleeped on my phone.

"I'm putting you on speaker," I said. If Beck was online, I wanted to make the most of it.

Beck: *J Sheekey. You?*

So he hadn't died. And I liked his choice in restaurant.

Matt always liked Rules for the venison, so we used to go there a lot. I preferred something a little more modern and less stuffy. Like J Sheekey or Scotts. But Matt didn't like fish.

Me: *Scotts*

Beck: *Nice. I like it there too. Do you have brothers and sisters?*

I grinned and flopped back on my bed. Beck was taking this seriously.

"You think this will be one of those things that I look back on and say, thank God that happened? Thank goodness Matt cheated on me and ran off with Karen and married her within weeks?"

"Absolutely," Florence said as if she were in no doubt. "Wouldn't surprise me if they were divorced by the end of the year."

"And I won't even notice they're divorcing because I'll be so busy at work."

"And you'll be having amazing sex with an intelligent, handsome, funny guy who treats you like gold."

"Actual sex? Or the make-believe sex like I'm having with Beck?"

"You never know—by the end of a week in Scotland you might be having *actual* sex with Beck," Florence replied.

I ignored the fizzle under my ribs at the thought.

"I just want the design job. I can live without his penis."

"I bet it's super handsome. Just like him," Florence said.

"I'm going," I said through my giggle. "You're ridiculous and Beck just replied. I need to pepper him with questions."

"I hate to say I told you so, but I knew he'd reply," Florence said. "I'll be saying the same thing when you two end up hooking up in Scotland."

"I'm hanging up," I said.

Beck and I weren't going to hook up. We were going to nail this fake boyfriend and girlfriend thing. Beck was going to get his Mayfair building, and I was going to get my life back.

FOURTEEN

Stella

"You think we're ready?" I asked, unzipping my case in our hotel room. Between Beck's meetings, the time difference, and my dragon of a boss, Beck and I had texted every day, spoken a handful of times, and even squeezed in a video call over the past ten days, but I was still nervous. I'd been trying to dampen down the rising panic all morning, but now that we were here, an hour away from beginning the celebration of a marriage of the two people who'd betrayed me, being here seemed ridiculous. Being here with *Beck* made it worse as if he emphasized that I was alone. I had no one. "I'd not considered the logistics of sharing a room. I need a drink."

"The logistics?"

"You know. Two people. One bed."

"I think it would raise suspicions if we had separate rooms," he said.

He obviously thought I was too stupid to live. Of course

I understood we had to share a room in the hotel, but I'd not mentally prepared myself. All my energy had gone to focusing on getting through the weekend. The day of the ceremony, my plan was to take a seat on one of the pews at the back, on the side away from the aisle so I could see and hear as little as possible. Then, rather than wait around for photographs, I'd disappear back to the hotel. But we had days to get through before that final obstacle.

And here we were at the first obstacle—I'd not given sharing a bedroom with a perfect stranger much thought, and as if my suitcase wanted to provide me with proof, I pulled out my pajamas. If Beck and I were really dating, my pink nightwear with daisies speckled all over them would not be the way to go. No doubt he was used to seeing women in something sheer, sexy, and impossible to sleep in. Well, tonight he'd get to see what women wore to bed when they weren't sharing it with an attractive man. "I know," I replied. "But, it's weird. We hardly know each other."

"That's not even remotely true. I know more about you than anyone, barring my immediate family and my five closest friends."

The more time I spent with Beck, the more questions kept popping into my head. "What about your mum's middle name?" I asked.

"Bridget."

"I should have probably met her."

He chuckled, like he did most times when I began to sidestep into meltdown territory. He'd had to talk me down from a cliff at least three times since we'd made our pact. He was good at it. Knew what to say and which buttons to press. It was weird—I knew he was doing it to make sure he got what he wanted, but it always came across as if he had my best interests at heart. He was dangerous like that because he was just protecting what he wanted. I needed to remember that. He wasn't just being nice. He had an agenda, however convincing he might be. Everything he did was pretend.

"You know we're not really dating, right?" he asked. "And we're only *pretending* that we've been dating for just less than three months." He'd unpacked at lightning speed, zipped up his suitcase, and stowed it behind the door.

I sighed dramatically. "Beck, when you know, you know. Three months is a long time. It's time we thought about taking things to the next level. We're in love. It's serious. What are we waiting for?"

He paused for a second. "Three months is a long time? Would you be expecting to talk to someone you're dating about the future, about *marriage*, after three months?"

I thought about it for a second. I couldn't remember when Matt and I had started talking about marriage and the future, even names for our kids, but we'd been so young when we'd met it hadn't seemed imminent. Just something we'd do in the future. Except the future had never arrived. "I think it would depend on the relationship, but if it was the good kind, then sure. Why not?"

"Three months in I'm not even making dinner reservations a week in advance—I'm certainly not thinking about honeymoon destinations."

"So, are you just waiting for the right girl to come in and bowl you over or are you refusing to settle down before a certain birthday or . . . What's your deal?"

He scooted back on the bed and watched as I continued to unpack, unzip, and tidy. "You think I've scheduled in *getting serious with someone* on the day after my thirty-fifth birthday?"

"Some men do." Matt had been a planner. Whenever I'd mentioned marriage, he'd always tell me how he wanted to get to a certain point in his career or be living in a different house. There had always been some practical reason why it wasn't the right time. Although seeing how quickly he'd married Karen had changed all those reasons into excuses. "You're saying you're not one of them. Have you had your heart broken—is that the issue?"

"There's no issue and no history of a broken heart. I'm just happy doing what I'm doing. What about you? You're looking to find a man who's going to march you down the aisle within three months?"

"God, no, but if I was going to marry someone, I think I'd know within three months."

I couldn't imagine marrying anyone now. Matt and I had grown up together. There was nothing we didn't know about each other. I'd never have that kind of intimacy with someone again, but that was what I was looking for—someone who knew me inside out and back to front and vice versa. I wasn't into hiding, pretending—presenting my best side as Karen would say.

"I'm not sure I'll ever be ready to commit to anything but a particular cocktail from now on. It's difficult to find someone you want to spend time with and want to share every thought in your head with and hear exactly what they're thinking. Imagine if the last few weeks with us had been real—squeezing in phone calls, texts. It's hard and it has to be worth it." It hadn't been difficult with Beck because I was hell-bent on not being humiliated. And he was easy to talk to and valiantly put up with my crazy questions.

"Just so we're clear, if anyone asks, we're not engaged, right?" he asked.

"You look terrified at the prospect of even pretending." I shook my head. Thank God I wasn't dating Beck. We wouldn't last an evening. He screamed *scared of commitment* from every pore. "We're desperately in love but there's no engagement. But of course, if someone nudges you and says, 'You next,' you have to try not to look as if they've just asked you to carve your leg off with a rusty knife. Smile and say something positive like—"

"'If she'll have me' or 'I hope so.' I get it, Stella. You don't need to worry that I'm going to mess up."

I wasn't really worried about Beck. He could more than handle himself. I was worried about me. How would I react to seeing Karen and Matt celebrating the official start of their lives together? Would I be able to swallow down the pain at the sight of everyone gathered to wish them well? Would I be wishing it was me and then hating myself for being so pathetic? "Is there a mini-bar? I need a drink."

Beck glanced at his watch before heading over to the cabinet under the window. It was barely lunchtime, but I needed something to give me the courage to get down those stairs. "What do you want?" he asked, peering into the small fridge.

"Do they have wine?"

He pulled out a bottle and set about getting a glass and pouring it for me. "It's going to be fine, Stella. We've totally got this. We just need to stick together like we did at the engagement party."

What did he know? It wasn't his ex and ex-best friend getting married. I just needed to remind myself that it was just a week out of my life and in return, I'd hopefully get my career back.

I could do this.

I could make people believe I hadn't been broken by Matt and Karen's cheating.

I could convince everyone I had a new, better life.

Probably.

FIFTEEN

Beck

I didn't like weddings even if I'd been invited. There was always someplace better to be—work, hiking with the boys, an abattoir. But this wedding was different. This wedding *was* work. And Henry Dawnay was the only meeting I had planned. I scanned the bright, sunny room where they were having welcome drinks, trying to look as if I wasn't looking for anyone. Which I totally was. It might be day one, but I didn't want to miss an opportunity to run into Henry.

"God, this is pretty," Stella said. I wasn't sure if she realized she'd tightened her hand in mine as if I were her life jacket in choppy, open waters. I looked around the room again, trying to see what she did. I supposed it was pretty. There were blue and white fresh flowers everywhere I looked—framing the doors, in swags around the picture rails, and small arrangements on every table. The French doors opened up to a brick patio where people were spilling out onto a lawn. Perhaps Henry was out there. It sounded like they had a string quartet playing—maybe he liked the music?

As we walked through the room, a waiter approached us with a tray of champagne. I took two glasses and handed one to Stella, who promptly downed hers, so I handed her mine. She smiled, slightly embarrassed, but took the glass nonetheless. She needed to take it easy on the alcohol, or I was going to have to carry her back up to our room. She was beyond stressed out. And I wasn't sure if it was just because it was her ex's wedding or if she was worried that we'd be caught faking it. Getting to know her had been eye-opening. I'd gotten an insight into how women thought. With me, what you saw was what you got. I'd realized over the last couple of weeks that the women I normally spent time with didn't tell me half what they were thinking. In contrast, Stella didn't hold back. I had a near-constant running commentary on what was going on inside her head. She'd assured me that all women thought similarly about various issues—men who only called late at night, men who wouldn't go down on a woman but wanted a blow job, and men with back hair, among many other things. I also knew her opinion on men who ghosted women—which had happened to Florence before Gordy came along, apparently —on the joys of working from bed, and the importance of hedgehogs. It was as if I'd suddenly inherited a sister.

Except Stella was hot.

"You look beautiful," I said, trying to calm her nerves. If I didn't know better, I'd think she had a drinking problem, but I'd never seen her like this before.

She was looking particularly stunning today. She'd picked out a floaty, floral dress with long, billowing sleeves and a deeply cut neckline. When she walked, I got a glimpse of her toned, tanned legs. It was a dress that looked demurer than it turned out to be.

And that suited Stella—one thing on the face of it, hinting at something more interesting underneath.

That dress could have been made for her. But my favorite thing about her today was the way she'd scraped up one side of her hair with a clip that had fresh flowers on it. It was innocent and sexy at the same time. It showed off her long neck and emphasized her cheekbones. She was gorgeous, even if she didn't realize how gorgeous.

She had nothing to worry about. I'd only laid eyes on the bride once, but the first time I'd seen Karen, I wondered why on earth Stella's ex had dumped her. Not that Karen wasn't attractive, but she wasn't as beautiful as Stella, either. Not even close.

"I don't see Henry," she said, emptying her second glass of champagne and catching a passing waiter, swapping her empty glass for two full ones.

She handed one to me.

"Are you sure you're not going to take both of them?" I asked with a smile.

She grimaced. "Sorry. I need to be medicated to get through tonight. Hopefully it won't be so difficult after I see them for the first time."

But she was friends with them, wasn't she? I wasn't getting the full story from Stella, but given she'd been so open about so much with me, she must have her reasons to keep secrets. I wasn't going to make her feel uncomfortable.

"Here's Florence and Gordy. They might have seen Henry."

"How are you holding up?" Florence asked once we'd all greeted each other.

"I'm fine," Stella replied. "Well, you know, as fine as can be expected."

"You need a drink," Florence said. "Or maybe you don't," she added as Stella stumbled on a completely flat surface. It wasn't even eight yet. At this rate she'd be throwing up within the hour.

"That was my shoes, but I have to admit, this isn't my first glass. At this rate, Beck will have to carry me upstairs."

"And that's not part of the package," I replied, and Stella blushed and put her finger to her lips.

I hadn't meant part of our deal—it was an offhand comment that was just meant to be a joke, but I could feel the heat in her cheeks in the tips of my fingers even though I hadn't touched them. She needed to stop being so fixated on what was fake between us and focus on what was real.

I really knew her—more than any woman.

I really liked her.

And I really wanted to get to know her more.

RIGHT ON CUE at just before ten, Stella clutched her stomach and said, "I'm not feeling great. I might head back up to the room."

I hadn't spotted Henry and felt sure he wasn't about to arrive just as everyone was leaving. I'd have to be patient. It was just that all of my patience had been used up getting to this point. I needed his signature on the contract. I had exactly a week after the ceremony to get his signature. Then I could call the bank to tell them to call off the dogs and I could start on redevelopment. I was done waiting.

"I'll come up with you," I said, taking Stella's glass from her before she could down the last half a glass of champagne that we'd likely both see on the way back up. Luckily, Stella was a harmless, funny drunk. Cute really. I'd had a couple of girlfriends who turned into two-headed, fire-breathing monsters after a couple of glasses of wine. I'd not dated one of those for a while. The last one had been Joan. She'd been cool and sexy, and it was all going so well until one Friday night we went for dinner after she'd been drinking—it was as if she'd been possessed by an evil spirit. She'd started telling me how no one was going to fall in love with me because I was such a cold-hearted bastard who used women for sex. Her cool-girl act had been exactly that —an act.

Stella just got more relaxed. Her shoulders fell by several inches each drink and then her head had tilted to one side as she kept telling Florence and Gordy how much she loved them.

Stella grabbed Florence and they hugged each other as if they were expecting to never see each other again.

"It'll be about nine hours until you see her at breakfast," I said.

"Yes, and Bea and Jo will arrive soon. It will be so great to see them." Stella launched her hand in the air and cocked out one hip. She was going to take somebody's eye out. "To see all the girls from St. Catherine's."

Hopefully, Henry would arrive tomorrow. Joshua better have been right when he'd said Henry would be here all week, or we were going to fall out.

"Right. Bed," she said.

I placed my hand at the small of her back, gently encouraging her forward.

"Beck, you're a very nice guy," she said, pointing her finger at my cheekbone as we started up the old, oak stair-case, her toned thigh slipping out from under the fabric with every step she took. The dress was perfect for her—sweet and sexy. If the dress had downed at least a bottle of wine, I'd say they were related. "You've been the perfect gentleman tonight."

"Were you expecting something else?" I asked as we reached the landing, and I pulled out the key to our room.

I turned when I realized she wasn't by my side—she was frozen in the middle of the hallway.

"Am I attractive?" she asked.

The ground beneath my legs suddenly felt less stable—was she about to turn into a Joan? Was this a trick question where any answer I gave provoked rage? If I said yes, I would be objectifying her, and if I said no, I'd be some kind of mean bastard. "Of course. Let's go inside." I gestured to our room, holding the door open.

"Do you mean that?" she asked as she slid past me. "Or are you just saying that?"

I took a deep breath as I got a great view of her bottom as she bent from the waist to unclasp her shoes. There was no doubt she was attractive. From the moment I'd laid eyes on her, I'd been struck by her openness. And her high cheekbones and her eyes that watched me so intently. "I rarely say things just for the sake of it," I replied, shrugging off my jacket and placing it on a hanger.

"But am I *marriage* material?"

Oh God, were we really going to do this? I wasn't her therapist. I wasn't her sister or best friend. I didn't do girl talk. "I have no idea what marriage material is."

"Karen's marriage material." She struggled with the zip on the back of her dress, and I stepped forward to help her. "Well, clearly. We're at her wedding. But I obviously wasn't. Not for Matt anyway. And not for anyone, according to my left ring finger." Before I could turn away, she let her unzipped dress fall to the floor. For a half-second, I expected her to proposition me, but she seemed to have moved on from worrying about sharing a bed and a bathroom and now seemed perfectly happy to walk around in her underwear. I wasn't about to discourage her. Not with a body like that. Her skin was flawless, and her curves were in all the right places. Some men liked big boobs, but I liked a woman whose breasts were in proportion with everything else. Like Stella's.

She bent over and reached under her pillow and began to put on her PJs. "I bet the women you normally go to bed with wear super-sexy negligees, right?" She stumbled on the word negligee, and I had to bite back a grin. She was verging dangerously close to adorable.

"Usually they're naked." There was little need for clothes if a woman was staying the night with me. I didn't do sleepovers to watch Game of Thrones and drink tea.

She scrunched up her nose. "Urgh. That's gross. And cold. And what happens if there's a fire alarm?"

"So you're saying I should leave some clothes on?" I asked.

Her eyes widened and she started to giggle. "Yes! Cover your penis."

It wasn't the usual thing I was used to hearing in the bedroom.

"Do you think someone will marry me someday?" she asked, looking down at her bedclothes before collapsing on the small, blue sofa next to the mini-bar.

I pulled on a t-shirt and padded toward her. She needed a glass of water. "Do you just want to marry anyone, or does it matter who?" I asked. I'd never understood women who had a *goal* of getting married. Didn't that just happen if it happened?

I crouched at the drinks' cabinet, pulling out glasses and water.

"I'm just saying that I think some girls are the type men marry and some aren't."

I handed her a glass.

"Thank you," she said. Her eyes were dull and the corners of her mouth downturned. She was usually so upbeat—determined and focused on our preparation. I took a seat beside her.

"I'm not sure that's true. But then again, I'm probably not the guy to ask."

"I bet you're the type that just goes out with models and bloody ballerinas."

"I'm not sure I've ever dated a ballerina. Is that a thing?" I stretched my arm across the back of the sofa cushion, angling myself toward her. Why did she have a thing about ballerinas? And marriage? Maybe it was just because we were at a wedding of her ex.

"But I'm not your type, right? I can tell."

There was no doubt about that, but not because I wouldn't give her a second glance if I passed her on the street. I would. I'd notice across the room. I might even buy her a drink—or dinner. But getting to know her these past few weeks—she was different. Worth more somehow. "Stella, you're an attractive woman—"

Before I could finish my sentence, she lunged at me, pressing her lips to mine.

I froze.

Ordinarily, I had no problem with women kissing me. Especially a woman as attractive as Stella. But I knew Stella well enough by now to know her kissing me wasn't about me. It was all about being at this wedding, the nerves and the alcohol. Tomorrow she'd be shrouded with regret and that wasn't the way it should be. If I was going to kiss Stella London, she wouldn't regret it. She wasn't going to be thinking about her ex or getting caught and she wasn't going to be under the influence of a bottle of champagne.

She pulled away and covered her face with her hands. "Oh my God. I'm sorry. I don't know what I'm doing. Of course, you don't want me."

I didn't know what to say. "It's not that, Stella. It's just—"

She covered her ears and screwed her eyes shut. "No, please don't give me a rundown. I'm tired, drunk, and emotional. I'm really sorry." She bounced up from the sofa and headed to the wardrobe, pulling down blankets. "I'm going to sleep on the sofa. Please, can we pretend this never happened?"

Bloody hell, as if I was going to let her sleep on the sofa. The last thing I wanted to do was embarrass her. If she hadn't had so much wine, I may well have been the one kissing her rather than the other way around. What a shit-storm. "Don't be silly. I'll take the sofa if sharing a bed makes you feel uncomfortable."

"The other way around, more likely. I'm an idiot. I was just lonely and feeling sorry for myself. I'm really, really sorry."

"Please don't apologize. I'm very flattered—"

She groaned and dragged the blankets to the sofa, shooing me off as she set about creating herself a makeshift bed.

"I'm serious. You're gorgeous." It wasn't like I could tell her I'd be completely up for getting naked if she were sober and not so obviously sad about her ex-boyfriend or not being married. Or something.

She got under the blanket and turned toward the back

of the sofa, her legs curled up so she could fit. "I'd be really grateful if we could just forget all about this."

I scraped my hand through my hair, desperate to make her feel better. It really was no big deal. "Of course. Consider it forgotten, on one condition: you sleep in the bed. I'll take the sofa if it makes you feel better."

"You can't sleep on here. You're about six foot fifteen."

I'd much prefer not to spend the night with my legs wrapped around my head. I'd probably take the floor instead. "Six foot two. So, let's both sleep in the bed. I'll build a pillow wall down the middle if it helps?" I set about pulling the pillows down to the middle of the bed but by the time I finished, Stella hadn't moved a muscle. There was only one thing for it. I scooped her off the sofa, and before she could ask me what the hell I was doing, I put her down on the bed.

"There. Now sleep. You'll feel better in the morning."

"Thanks," she said in a small voice, and I grinned to myself. She was cute when she was embarrassed. I had no idea why she didn't think she was marriage material, she outshone everyone in the room tonight. She might not believe it, but she was entirely kissable and almost irresistible. But tonight, between us? The time just wasn't right. When it was, I would kiss her, and she wouldn't be thinking of any ex-boyfriends when I did.

She wouldn't be drunk.

She wouldn't be sad.

And she wouldn't ever be sorry.

SIXTEEN

Stella

Oh. My. *God.*

Every time I thought back to last night, my stomach dived into my feet and I had to pause whatever I was doing to make sure I wasn't about to throw up. Why could I have not passed out rather than decide I'd try to kiss Beck? It was as if I wasn't content with the humiliation of being at my ex-boyfriend's wedding with a stranger who was *pretending* to be my boyfriend. I had to bear the additional shame of trying to kiss the most handsome man alive.

I was an idiot.

I wasn't sure anything was worth spending the rest of the week here. If I'd been sober enough to charge my phone, I was pretty sure I'd have booked a flight out of this cave of mortification by now. It didn't help that we were all being bused to Matt's uncle's castle from the hotel for a day of *activities*. It might only be a fifteen-minute journey, but the narrow, winding roads mixed with the memories of the evening before were threatening to bring up last night's dinner. At least I was at the front of the coach—last on, first off. I'd nearly missed it, and I was almost certain that by the end of the day I would wish I had.

The bus pulled up in front of Glundis Castle. Last time I'd been here, Matt and I stayed in the west wing in the Churchill bedroom, named after its most famous occupant. I tried to push away the memories. Things were different now. I couldn't change it. Every time we'd been away together in the last few years, I'd wondered if Matt would propose. Last summer when we were here, it hadn't been any different. I pressed my head against the window to take in the turrets on top of the four stories of weathered red brick. The wide, stone steps narrowed toward the entrance and a red carpet had been laid to give everyone the VIP treatment as they entered. Last time I'd been here, I'd been treated as a member of the family. This time, I was one of many guests.

When I got off, I stood in the rare Scottish sunshine, trying to focus on something other than the sloshing in my stomach. "Hey," Florence said, bounding over to me. "I didn't see you get on the bus. I wondered if your head was hurting a little too much this morning."

"Don't remind me. I was a mess."

Jo and Bea came up behind us and I opened my arms and pulled them into a four-way hug. My girls. At least today I wouldn't see much of Beck—hopefully by tonight, by magic, his memory would have been erased and he wouldn't recall my sad, pathetic humiliation. Today the men and women had been separated and different things planned for each group. Apparently, the boys were shooting. We were probably flower arranging or something. The invitation assured us it would be an enjoyable day. I knew better.

"It's so good to see you," Bea said. "I love that I get to hang out with you for an entire week!"

Thank God there was finally an upside of being here. I was beginning to wonder if I should just spend the rest of the week with fake tonsillitis. Or something more contagious that would give me an excuse to check into my own room, where I'd be as far away as possible from Beck Wilde. If only I could just rewind and make myself go right to bed without speaking a word to him.

I was never drinking again. Ever.

"Can you believe this pottery shit?" Jo said as we followed the rest of the party around the back where five long trestle tables were set out with chairs on either side. Free-standing shelving full of plain pots and glazes flanked the tables. "Why can't we go shooting with the boys?"

If I hadn't made a complete fool of myself with Beck last night, I would have agreed, but today I was grateful we'd been divided by gender—even if it was sexist bullshit.

"Matt would never agree to pottery painting and Karen wouldn't go shooting, so I guess it makes sense," Florence said. "It's kinda like the hen and stag parties they didn't have."

"I know, but I'm desperate to meet Stella's new man!" Bea said as we took our seats at one end of the table. If I thought I'd have a reprieve from my nausea, I was wrong. Florence was the only one who knew Beck was actually a fake boyfriend. She'd convinced me that the fewer people who knew the truth the better. I hated lying to Bea—she was always so open about her dating life.

"Well, we've got another four days so I'm sure you'll get to see him at some point," I said, trying my best to give a genuine, newly-in-love smile.

"Speak of the devil," Florence said as we followed her gaze to see Beck heading toward us.

Oh God. What did he want? I'd faked being asleep when he got up for a run, then dashed into the shower and made it out before he returned. I'd given myself a metaphorical pat on the back—it wasn't as if we had anything in particular to say to each other. And I needed a few hours for my humiliation to be brought down to a simmer.

Now I was going to have to act like the dutiful girlfriend. "Hey," he said. "Hi, Florence. Jo."

"I'm Bea, Stella's friend from St. Catherine's." Bea stood and beamed at Beck.

"I'm delighted to meet you, Bea," Beck replied as he bent down to kiss her cheek. "I've heard so much about you. And I've just met James."

Impressive that he'd remembered Bea's boyfriend's name and put them together. He was so bloody convincing he should take acting up for a living.

"Stella," he said and my heart ping-ponged in my chest as humiliation, confusion, and a little lust fought to be first in line. "Can I have a word?" He beckoned me toward him and started walking away from everyone.

I followed him over the grass. What the hell was he doing here? I'd been such a complete lunatic last night. I'd never tried to kiss a man before. Why had I started with Beck Wilde? He was probably going to make us have some awkward conversation about how he thought of me as a friend, and I'd have to explain that last night hadn't been about him—it had been about wine. And trying to make myself feel better. Maybe it had been a little about him, because he was so bloody nice to me on top of that six foot two of good looking. It was hard to resist *without* wine.

He stopped about twenty meters from where everyone

was choosing their pottery, so no one would be able to hear what we were saying.

"Look, I'm really sorry about last night, Beck," I said, trying to head off the talk he was about to initiate.

Beck pushed his hands through his hair as if he were gearing up to deliver bad news.

"You don't need to worry," I said. "I promise it won't happen aga—"

He cupped my face in his hands, his warmth heating my skin.

"What?" What was happening? Why was he touching me? Was this part of the show? I searched his face, looking for answers.

"I'm going to kiss you now. Are you ready?" he asked.

I took a step back and he stepped forward, keeping his hands on my face.

"Did you hear me?" he asked.

"I don't understand—"

Before I could finish my sentence, his lips were on mine, and sparks of energy raced from his lips across my skin.

What was happening? His mouth was soft but insistent, and he smelled of coconut shower gel, freshly mown grass, and something indescribable but undeniably male.

He broke our kiss but didn't move away, instead resting his forehead against mine. This *had* to be for someone else's benefit—he'd done this to prove we were a couple.

"I've been waiting to do that." He straightened and took a half step back, as if he wanted to check not just my face, but my entire body's reaction to his kiss. Which was entirely understandable because his kiss still reverberated from the bottom of my toes to the breath escaping from my lungs to the buzz of my jaw under his fingers.

I felt it *everywhere*.

"Did I miss something?" I stuttered, trying to figure out why he'd kissed me. Who was watching?

He snaked his arm around my waist, and he pulled me toward him, kissing me again, this time his tongue parting my lips. He groaned as he moved deeper and my insides tightened, my heart sped, and my skin pricked like popping candy under my tongue. My knees weakened and I had to lean into him to stop myself from falling. But it didn't stop the dizziness, the way the world seemed to sway as he touched me.

"Christ," he said, pulling away but keeping me in his arms. "I'm not quite sure how I'm going to be able to leave you alone for the rest of the day, but I'm going to have to. I'm thirty seconds away from pulling you down onto the grass and dry humping you like my fourteen-year-old self."

I smiled up at him, confused and a little disorientated. "What . . . I mean, did something happen? Did someone say something?"

He paused, and there was a softness in his eyes I'd not seen before. "Last night . . . Well, I wasn't expecting it. You were . . ."

"Hammered," I finished for him.

He shrugged. "I didn't want to take advantage last night. On my run this morning, I decided I didn't want to wait a moment longer to kiss you." His expression changed as he caught me—presumably looking as dazed and confused as I felt. "This is okay, right?" His thumb stroked my jaw. "Last night you seemed to be on for the kissing."

This entire situation was so weird. Last night I'd been a mess—a lunatic. And this morning, when I'd thought about trying to kiss him, all I'd felt was complete mortification. I hadn't been picking out pottery to paint wondering if I still liked him or if he'd kiss me today, so I wasn't prepared for his question. "It's fine," I replied. "Unexpected. It's not because anyone has said something?" I asked.

"Stella, listen to me. I don't kiss women because I have to. I kissed you because I wanted to. I want to."

I wanted to turn away from him so he couldn't see how much his kiss had affected me, no matter the shame from the previous evening. "Last night, I shouldn't have—"

"Last night was last night." He paused. "You'd had a lot to drink."

I'd completely thrown myself at him, and though I'd been drunk, I could unfortunately remember every moment of it. I pressed my palm against his chest to get some space. "We're here to introduce you to Henry, not to be . . . you know."

He pulled me closer and kissed me again. "Business comes first. But I really like kissing you."

I pressed my fingertips over my mouth to hide my smile. He really was an excellent kisser. And in the sixty seconds since it had happened, I'd not thought about Matt or Karen or their betrayal once. Apparently, kissing Beck was like pressing a temporary delete key in my brain. I nodded. "Me too."

The sound of breaking pottery brought me back to where we were, and I glanced over my shoulder to find Florence staring at us. I was going to have some explaining to do. Not that I had much to say. It was just a kiss. "I should get back to . . ." I grimaced. "Painting pottery."

"Sounds fascinating. Once you're done, do they fling them into the air for us to shoot?" he asked. "These people do the weirdest things for fun."

"These people?"

"You know. People with money."

"Do I need to remind you that we flew up here on a private jet you use all the time?" I asked.

"Yeah, but my money isn't old money. I'm not one of *these* people," he said. "I don't shoot at inanimate objects for fun. I like good food, sport, and sex. I'm a simple man."

I laughed—I wouldn't have made the distinction between Beck and *these* people. But I suppose there was a difference. Most of the boys I'd grown up with had been wealthy, but he was right. There was a difference now that he'd pointed it out. It wasn't obvious, but beneath the surface, there was a hunger, a drive Beck had that I didn't see often. "Simple pleasures are the best," I replied.

"Absolutely." His mouth twitched at the corners, and his eyes sparkled with a hint of wickedness. "I have to get back to clay pigeon shooting. I wonder if how they have sex is as unsatisfying as what they call sport."

Like a fourteen-year-old girl hearing the word *sex*, I shivered as he spoke. I couldn't imagine sex with Beck could possibly be unsatisfying. I glanced at the ground, hoping to hide the heat I felt in my cheeks. "Yup. We both have to go and enjoy ourselves." At least I'd managed to sit on a table with people I loved and away from Karen, but now being away from the boys for the day didn't seem so much of a relief as it had on the coach ride over here.

"So, I'll see you back at the hotel?" He dipped to catch my eye, as if his question carried more meaning than it first appeared.

I nodded and folded my arms, turning away but feeling a pull toward Beck that hadn't been there before.

It had been so long since I'd been kissed the way Beck had kissed me. In fact, I wasn't sure, I'd ever felt a kiss so deeply before. With Matt, we'd been too young to realize what a kiss could mean—how it could be the promise of something, good or bad. Beck's kiss had been so powerful that if it was the promise of something, it would either be catastrophic or the best thing that had ever happened in my life.

I wasn't sure I could withstand either.

I wandered back to the tables, carefully avoiding looking at Karen's table.

"How's Beck?" Florence asked, grinning at me as I approached as if she was just dying to tell me she'd told me so.

Bea and Jo were both looking at me like baby birds waiting to be fed scraps of gossip. "Oh, you know—tall, dark, and handsome."

"He most certainly is," Bea said. "And a phenomenal kisser by the looks of things."

There was no doubt about that.

"Let me help you choose what you're going to paint," Florence said, springing up from her chair and shooing me over to the shelves stacked with the different types of pre-prepared pottery.

She handed me a vase. "Oh my God, what's going on?" she asked in a loud whisper.

I glanced back at our table to see if anyone was watching or close enough to hear, but they were all engrossed in what they were doing.

"Nothing, I mean—"

"Stop that right now. Don't tell me that was nothing. That wasn't a kiss for show. Are you sleeping with him? I can't believe you didn't tell me this even though I completely knew it was going to happen."

"No, I'm not sleeping with him. This is as far as it's gone —what you've seen is the entire extent of what's happened between us."

"Wait—that was the first time you've kissed? What's going on?"

"He said he'd been running this morning and had realized he wanted to kiss me."

Florence narrowed her eyes, silently accusing me of not telling her the entire story.

"You know how drunk I got last night? And being here —it was all a little overwhelming. And at some point, I might have lunged at Beck."

"Lunged?"

Lunging wasn't really my style. Not that I had a style with men. There had only ever been Matt. "Yeah. It was horribly embarrassing and if you tell anyone, I'll kill you—"

"But he was down for it?"

"No, he politely declined." My insides began to curl up in shame as I remembered last night. Despite him kissing me today, I still wished it hadn't happened.

"But then today?"

"You know as much as I do. He said that he wanted to kiss me."

Florence took a deep breath. "Well, he's obviously crazy for you," she said matter-of-factly. "It's so nice that he didn't kiss you when you lunged but did just now in front of everyone. He clearly couldn't wait."

Florence was a hopeless romantic, even when things weren't going well with her and Gordy. "He's not *obviously* crazy for me. It was just a kiss." One that I'd felt in my bones and gave me goosebumps just remembering it.

"You're together for the next week. Sleeping in the same bed. Something more is bound to happen."

I rolled my lips together. It was just a kiss. But what if Florence was right and he kissed me again? Wanted more?

Obviously, someone had to come after Matt. Unless I

was going to check in to my local nunnery for the next fifty years, there would be another man. I knew that somewhere deep down, I just hadn't gotten to the point that I wondered who that someone was or wanted a particular someone to be next.

Not that I could have ignored Beck and his handsomeness. It hit you in the face like a freight train.

And he'd been so nice to me—confident, reassuring, and concerned.

There was a reason I'd lunged at him and not the bellboy.

"You're clearly both attracted to each other, and if he still likes you post-lunge, then that says a lot," Florence said.

"Post-lunge? Really? Can we not focus on the lunging? It's humiliating enough." But Florence was right—if he could see me drunk and emotional and not be running for the hills, perhaps Beck was the next someone. The problem was I didn't know which way was up and I didn't trust anyone enough to tell me.

"He has a vested interest in being nice to me," I said, my mind whirring with doubt and distrust. "He was probably worried about me abandoning him after his rejection last night and kissing me was his way of trying to keep me happy." Was that what his kiss had been about? Had he just been protecting his own best interests? He seemed genuine enough but if he'd wanted to kiss me, was he really such a gentleman that he'd held back last night?

"Stella, I witnessed that kiss. There was nothing fake or forced about it."

But she didn't know Beck.

I didn't really know Beck. And even though what I did know of him I liked, the fact that I was at the wedding of the man I thought I was going to marry told me my judgement wasn't to be trusted.

No, I was here for business—fighting for my future. I wasn't about to get thrown off course by a man's showstopping kisses.

No way.

SEVENTEEN

Beck

I was sticking out like the sorest of sore thumbs. I was wearing a navy-blue Tom Ford shell jacket in a sea of green and brown Barbours and tweed. It said everything you needed to know about me and the people here—I was new money versus their old.

But fuck it, I was a better shot than most of them. Shooting clays was so fucking boring. I didn't understand the appeal. It was no better than shooting cans at the back of the abandoned garages with an air rifle. And I'd mastered that around thirteen.

In any other scenario I would have just gone back to the hotel. My emails were piling up, and I had a thousand missed calls, but nothing, not even clay pigeon shooting, was going to drive me away. Henry Dawnay was ten meters away from me, and I wasn't going anywhere until I'd introduced myself.

Obviously, I didn't want to stare, but out of the corner of my eye I could see he was standing with three or four other men, one of whom was Stella's ex-boyfriend. We hadn't been officially introduced but I'd caught Matt's eye a few times, first at the engagement party and then last night. It was strange. He'd obviously moved on because he was getting married, but I got the distinct impression there was some unfinished business with Stella from his perspective.

But perhaps I was imagining things.

My imagination had been working overdrive recently. Last night when Stella had tried to kiss me, I'd been a second away from pushing her against the wall and kissing her until she didn't know what day of the week it was. Ever since, I'd been imagining what she tasted like, how her skin felt under my hands. I'd been wondering if the floral scent that I couldn't quite place was a perfume or just how she woke up. And now I'd kissed her, I'd been thinking about when I'd get to do it again.

But that would come later. Right now, I needed to focus on why we were both here.

A table with drinks and snacks on it had been set up, and when I saw Henry break off from the small group he was talking to and head toward the table, I decided to seize the opportunity. I took a settling breath. I couldn't blow this by going in too hard and fast, which was my usual MO. In my experience, men like Henry didn't like to feel ambushed. They were used to having the control in most situations, so I needed to take my time and stick to my plan.

When I got to the table, I set about making myself a cup of tea. "It's a lovely day to be outside," I said, trying to sound as casual as I could—as if I didn't want to pin him down and sign away his property in Mayfair.

I was used to doing business with all different types of people. When I'd been flipping bedsits in East London, the people I'd worked with had been the opposite to the ones I now dealt with when developing luxury residential property in the W1 postcode. I prided myself on finding common ground with some people, flattering the egos of others. I did what was required to get what I wanted. The difference was whoever I normally worked with, wanted or needed something from me. Henry was different. The Dawnay building wasn't on the market.

Henry didn't need me.

And that together with the fact he was old money meant I was so far out of my comfort zone I needed oxygen and a parachute.

"A perfect day," he replied and held out his hand. "I'm Henry Dawnay. How do you do?"

I shook his hand. "Beck Wilde." I couldn't bring myself to say "How do you do" back. I liked to find common ground with people, but I wasn't a faker. I couldn't pretend to be someone I wasn't, and I'd never said "How do you do" to anyone.

Henry smiled and the muscles across my upper back began to unlock. I was finally here. In front of the man who could give me what I most wanted: a closed door on my past. I just had to bond with a man I had nothing in common with. A man who would no doubt look down on me because I hadn't been to a school he'd heard of. I had to get him to like me, trust me. I had a lot of work to do.

First thing was first, I needed to point out the coincidence of us being at the same wedding. "Henry Dawnay, that name's familiar to me," I said, poised to put two and two together in front of him.

Before I'd gotten much past giving Henry my name, we were interrupted. By Stella's ex. I held back a groan. I just needed a few more minutes to tell him we had a connection and that I'd been trying to get in contact with him.

"We haven't met," he said, holding out his hand. "I'm Matt, the groom. You're Stella's plus one, right?"

Plus one? That was an interesting way of referring to me and it gave away a lot more than he intended. He was clearly trying to dismiss me, and if I *had* been Stella's boyfriend, perhaps I would be offended. But he served it up with such transparency it didn't earn my offense. I nearly laughed at his petty point-scoring, but there was no need for him to know that I saw through his bullshit. "Beck Wilde. Stella's boyfriend. Great to meet you and congratulations."

He held my gaze as if he were trying to stare me down. Christ, he'd be getting his dick out in a second and suggesting a pissing contest.

I cast my mind back—I didn't think Stella had ever mentioned why she and Matt had split up. But if they were still friends, and they had been together a long time, I guessed it was something innocuous like they just fell into a brother and sister relationship. I would have to ask her. It was the kind of information you would tell a new boyfriend you were serious about. And anyway, I was interested.

"Looks like it's going to be a beautiful week," I said. "Perfect wedding weather. You're a lucky man, given it's Scotland."

"Indeed. And of course, I'm marrying the perfect woman," he said. "How are you enjoying the day so far?"

Perhaps it was my imagination again, but it seemed like his reference to Karen being perfect was rather pointed.

"Great company, wonderful weather, and a cup of tea. What more could a man wish for?" I replied, glancing across at Henry.

"Here, here," Henry said, raising his teacup.

Matt smiled tightly. "Absolutely," he said. "I've spent almost every summer of my life up here, enjoying the spectacular countryside. And to get to enjoy it with the wonderful weather is the icing on the cake."

"You're very lucky," I said. Matt and these people weren't like the rest of us. They could take entire summers off to shoot and ride horses while I pulled out rotting floorboards from a flat in New Cross. Now I had people to do the physical work, but my summers were still spent in the office, negotiating the price of my next property or managing builders and designers.

My money had to be earned.

Theirs just had to be babysat.

"I don't think we run in the same circles," Matt said. "What is it that you do?"

I might not want to answer Matt's questions because he was no doubt wanting to know so he could judge me. But at least it was information I wanted Henry to know. "I'm a property developer," I said. "Residential mainly. It's how I met Stella. She's a designer on one of my buildings."

Matt's mouth twisted as if he'd taken a bite of something sour. "Really? What kind of building?"

"Luxury residences. My latest is in Mayfair."

This was the perfect moment for Henry to tell me he had property in Mayfair. That he owned some rundown building that needed to be redeveloped, but he was staring out across the countryside, as if I'd been talking about the weather.

Patience. This was our first conversation. And I had a plan, even if it had been thrown off track a little.

"How interesting," Matt said, clearing his throat and seemingly flustered.

"Excuse me, I need to make a call," Henry said, and I tried not to inwardly groan. Losing an opportunity to chat with Henry was bad enough. There was no way I was going to get left with Stella's tool of an ex-boyfriend.

"That reminds me," I said. "I have to return an email. Good to meet you both."

I pulled my phone from my pocket and wandered toward the knoll that led down from the house. I wasn't sure how I was going to get through the next week surrounded by these people, who were all sweetness and conversations about the weather on the surface. Perhaps it wasn't just the surface. Maybe an indulgent life and summers shooting clays and playing croquet provided unlimited charm.

I'd never know. I'd never fit in with these people. My father had made sure of that.

EIGHTEEN

Stella

I cleared the smudge of mascara from below my right eye and set about trying to avoid the same mistake on my left eye. I couldn't remember the last time I'd felt this way before seeing a man. I couldn't even quite figure out what it was I did feel. Was it nerves? Even when I was first dating Matt, I didn't remember a *physical* reaction just at the thought of a man. The way my breath got higher in my throat when I thought about Beck, the way my skin seemed to tighten when I remembered our kiss—it was all new. I kept replaying our kiss in my head, wondering what had brought it on—whether he'd kissed me out of necessity or desperation or if it had been, as he'd described, just about desire. And when I saw him again, would he have had a change of heart and not want to kiss me? And if he did want more kissing, should I resist him, reminding myself that everything between us was a lie?

Too many questions.

I popped the mascara wand back in the tube. Beck

wasn't back from whatever it was the boys were doing today, and I didn't want to look as if I'd been waiting for him. Thankfully my pedicure had made it to four days without a chip, so I grabbed a pair of black sandals. Tonight, women and men had separate dinners, again in some kind of effort to recreate hen and stag nights. It seemed a little forced and ridiculous and although I didn't want to admit it to myself, part of me wanted to spend the evening with Beck despite knowing this growing warmth I felt for him might be entirely in my head.

I jumped at the rattle of the door handle but managed to do up my second sandal and stand as Beck entered the room.

"Hi," I said as if I'd just been caught doing something I shouldn't and nerves tumbled about through my stomach like autumnal leaves in a breeze.

His gaze swept down my body. "You look . . ." His eyes grew bigger and then finally met mine. "Nice." The way he said it reverberated in the base of my spine as if he'd pressed his tongue against my skin. How did he make the word "nice" sound so sexy?

"Thanks," I said, hoping he couldn't read my thoughts.

"You look as if you're leaving," he said as I picked up my evening bag.

"We have this separate dinner thing," I replied, opening up my bag and checking that I had everything I needed, despite having checked it just before he came in. I just couldn't look at him in case he saw how much I enjoyed our kiss earlier. I wanted to be cooler than that. Like it was no big deal that this hot, sexy guy sought me out to kiss me in front of everyone. Like it was real. "Drinks started at six-thirty."

He checked his watch. "I was hoping we could talk."

The leaves landed with a thud. In my experience, whenever men wanted to "talk" it was never about anything good.

He pulled his jacket off, tossed it on the bed, and stalked toward me as if he were on a mission. I took a step back when it looked like he was going to mow me down, but as he reached me he circled an arm around my back and slid his hand behind my neck, kissing me again. This time it started more urgently, as if he'd been storing up his kisses all day. My body sagged—soft against his hard, marble-like chest. He was warm and smelled so good, like a forest floor after a rainstorm.

His moan sent vibrations through my body, weakening my bones and making me gasp.

"Talk, huh?" I said as we pulled away.

He swept his thumb over my cheekbone. "Yeah. I didn't want anything to be . . . I wanted to check I wasn't out of line earlier."

"When you kissed me? So you did it again?" Nothing about him *seemed* fake. But then again, I'd believed everything Matt had told me as well.

He shrugged. "Apparently."

"Don't sweat it."

"Don't sweat it?" he asked as he toed off his shoes and sat on the bed while he removed his watch.

"You felt the need to kiss me, so you did. No big deal."

He chuckled as he stood and unbuttoned his shirt. I needed to get the hell out of there. The way he was going, he'd soon be naked, and I couldn't guarantee I would be able to keep my hands to myself. "No need to have a discussion? I thought women liked to talk about these things."

"It may have escaped your notice, but women aren't one

large homogenous group of people who all think and act the same way."

"Ahhh," he said as he peeled off his shirt, and I came face-to-face with his hard, bronzed chest. At least he didn't wax. A man as good looking as Beck had every right to be vain, but there was something distinctly un-masculine about bare chests in my book. "That's where I've been going wrong." He began to unbuckle his belt, and I turned and headed to the door. Someone had turned the heating up and I was trying to keep my cool. "I'll see you later," he called after me as I headed out into the corridor.

I suppose I had half an answer to my wondering what was going to happen next between us—no change of heart from Beck and a follow-up kiss.

Beck and I were supposed to be pretend. But the constant flip of my stomach and the way my heart sped as if I were running the hundred-meter final in the Olympics whenever he was around was undeniably real.

NINETEEN

Beck

I was prepared. I'd tweaked my strategy of how to approach Henry about the Mayfair property. I'd just tell him how I hadn't made the connection earlier, but that he must be the Henry Dawnay who owned the Dawnay building and go from there.

I was ready to see him again.

Primed to make my move.

But he wasn't bloody here.

I checked my watch for the seventieth time that evening. It was almost ten and this thing was supposed to be over by ten-thirty. He was a no show. I'd kept my ears open all night, but I'd not heard anyone mention him. I swirled the tonic water in my glass, keeping the door to the reception room in my eyeline as it had been all evening, hoping he would make a last-minute appearance.

It was useless. I might as well go back to the room. I drained my glass and headed out. Maybe I'd check the car park to see if Henry's car was still there. Although, that wouldn't tell me much—he might have simply done something else for the evening. I kept telling myself to be patient, but I didn't have an infinite amount of time. There was just over a week left.

As I turned the corner, laughter from the conservatory caught my attention. Through the small-paned glass, I saw Stella chatting to Florence amongst the other women of the wedding party.

I paused and just as I did, she turned and saw me watching her almost as if she knew I was there. She looked stunning, her hair scraped up into a ponytail, her face slightly flushed. Without thinking, I grinned at her, and she smiled back before dipping to say something to Florence and then heading in my direction.

"Hey," she said as she got closer. "You okay?"

I shrugged. "I thought I'd head back to the room and catch up on emails."

She blinked a couple of times as if she were waiting for me to say something else, to tell the truth.

"I'll come too," she said after a couple of seconds.

"You don't need to." I needed to catch up with work but at the same time it would be good to have some company. Someone to ruminate with on where Henry was. Someone I could run my newly tweaked strategy by.

She looked up at me as if she were peering into my brain, wanting to know if what I said and what I meant were matching. "I know. But I want to. Let me just get my bag."

As Stella went to leave, the bride caught up with her and Stella visibly stiffened when she pressed her hand on her arm. "You're leaving?" Karen asked, all smiles.

Stella smiled back, but I knew her well enough now to distinguish a real smile from a fake one, and there was nothing genuine about the smile Stella wore. "We want to save some energy for all these different events," Stella replied.

"Yes, it's spectacular, isn't it? It was Matt's idea to make a week of it—a real celebration. And I love Scotland, as you know, although I'd not been to the castle until Matt brought me up here to convince me that this was where we needed to get married."

Karen continued to chatter on, but Stella didn't say a word—she just nodded and gave intermittent tight smiles. It was a side of Stella I hadn't seen much of, like a deer caught in the headlights. She seemed vulnerable and . . . stuck.

I stepped forward, taking Stella's rigid hand. "I'm dragging her away. I hope you don't mind," I said as Stella's palm melded against mine.

"Of course not," Karen said. "I'm so delighted you're here to celebrate with us. I'll see you tomorrow."

Stella's fake smile faded, and she turned to me. "Thank you. I always get tongue-tied around . . . her."

I'd seen a very different Stella to the one holding my hand. One who was determined and unafraid to ask for what she wanted. Someone confident. Sure of herself. What was it about Karen that made Stella lose her ability to speak?

We made our way toward the stairs, still hand in hand. "You went out with Matt for ages, right?" I asked.

"Since university."

"But you know Henry, who is Karen's godfather—you said you went to stay with him. So you knew her before she was going out with Matt?"

"We've been best friends since the age of five," she said as she tried to pull her hand from mine, but I tightened my grip.

"And now she's marrying your ex-boyfriend. Is that weird?" It seemed weird to me but horses for courses.

We reached the top of the staircase and turned down the corridor toward our room in silence.

Eventually, Stella said, "It's a little weird."

I didn't spend enough time talking to women about personal stuff to know much, but I knew from the silence, the way she'd gone stiff and looked at the ground when Karen came along, that *a little weird* was an understatement.

"How long after you and Matt splitting did he and Karen get together?"

She gave a half laugh, half sigh and then shook her head. "I have no idea. Matt and I broke up about three months ago. I didn't know there was anything between him and Karen until I got the wedding invitation."

"Jesus, Stella. I had no idea." It made sense why it had taken so much to get her to come to this wedding. "Why the hell were you invited?"

She twisted her hand out of mine then dug about in her evening bag. "Oh, you know, I think they wanted to pretend it was all fine or something. Act as if it shouldn't be a big deal because Matt and I had split. And they wouldn't have expected me to come." She held up the key card and I took it from her, unlocking the door and holding it open before she stepped inside.

"You must want to design the Mayfair building pretty badly."

"More now than when you first asked me. It's like I didn't realize that's what I needed—as if it's given me a future, something to aim for," she replied.

I stayed silent as the words stuck in my throat, weighed

down by sorrow for her. If she hadn't been able to see a future for herself, she'd clearly been devastated.

"I'm just going to go and get changed," she said, scooping her nightclothes from the bed and heading for the bathroom before I thought of something to say.

I stripped down to my boxers, turned on the TV, and lay against the headboard as I scrolled through my phone as if that had the answers.

"Hey, where's our pillow wall?" she asked as she emerged from the bathroom, her hair piled on top of her head and her pajamas on. She looked fantastic when she was dressed up, all magazine-glossy, but Stella was one of those women who looked even better without all that stuff.

"Housekeeping must have demolished it."

"Well, I guess you're safe tonight. I'm sober," she said as she peeled back the covers on her side of the bed.

"I sort of like drunk you," I replied, putting down my phone and sliding under the covers.

She laughed as she lay down on her side facing me. "It's not a look I wear well."

"From what I've seen, you wear most things well," I replied. "Want to talk about Matt? Or Karen?"

She shook her head and placed her hands under her cheek. "There's nothing to say. I thought he would be the man I'd spend the rest of my life with and later this week he's going to marry the person I thought was my best friend. Safe to say my judgement's a bit wonky. I've just got to get through this week, focus on my future and not my past."

Silence stretched between us.

"That's what I keep telling myself, anyway," she added.

I curled her hair around her ear, not knowing how to make it better for her. I'd done nothing but make it worse. "I'm sorry I brought you here." I'd made her come face-to-face with these people who'd hurt her. She'd said she didn't know when Karen and Matt started seeing each other, but to be getting married only a few months after Matt and Stella split, there must have been something going on while they were still together.

I hated cheaters.

"Don't be. You're helping me with my future, remember?"

It didn't seem enough. "Did you not want to marry him? Is that why you split up?"

She stared across me at the dresser under the window. "I'd have married him years ago and he knew that. I thought we were just waiting for the right time. Apparently, it wasn't the time that was wrong, but the girlfriend."

Listening to her, it was like my stomach was filling with curdled milk. "You expected him to marry you, and he led you on and then found a better option?" It sounded familiar. At least Matt hadn't left Stella pregnant and then made her homeless.

"I'm not sure he led me on." She turned and lay flat on her back facing the ceiling. "I thought we were heading toward marriage and spending the rest of our lives together. Even when he ended things, I thought he was just having a bit of a freak out before making such a big commitment. I'd never really considered us split up and then . . . the invitation."

"Jesus, that's closure."

"It was a shock."

"What did you say to him. To Karen? How did they excuse what they'd done?"

More silence.

"Nothing," she said. "I mean, I never asked him. Or her."

I sat up. "You've never spoken to him about it? Not even when you got the invitation?"

"What was there to say? It wasn't like I was going to talk him out of it or negotiate a wedding for myself instead. What would have been the point?"

"You could have done a lot of shouting, gotten it off your chest, let them know how you feel." I wanted to do it for her.

She shrugged. "I'm already the kind of woman they think they can lie to and cheat on. I'm already the girl they invite to the wedding because they think I'll be happy for them or something. Or they don't care. I suppose I didn't want to give them reason to respect me even less."

"Who cares what they think? Either of them. They're clearly people you don't want anywhere near you. You should have confronted them for you, to make yourself feel better. Stand up to them. Don't be the woman who takes everything they dish out with a smile."

Tears welled in her eyes. I'd gone too far. I didn't mean to call her weak. She was here—at her former best friend's and ex-boyfriend's wedding. With a smile. That took courage and strength. But it was okay to feel wronged. To be angry. I was angry for her.

"I'm sorry," I said. "It's just . . . people like them . . . they act as if it's their world and we just live in it. Like we don't matter. They're so entitled or so they think. They don't care who they mow down on the way to getting what they want."

My mother was a victim of that entitled attitude—it still made me so angry. "You deserve more, Stella."

"I've rehearsed it," she said in a small voice almost as if she didn't want me to hear it. "What I'd say. To him and her. I didn't sleep much in that first week after I got the invitation. I had plenty of time to prepare a speech. Probably spent more time on it than the father of the bride has on his."

"So, say it to them."

She took a deep breath. "I'd end up getting tongue-tied and Matt would try to talk over me . . . and would I feel better?"

"You won't know if you don't try."

"I think I'd prefer to just avoid him. He hasn't come near me at this wedding. And as long as he doesn't, I'll be fine. I don't want to be made to feel like the entire situation is my fault. And that's what would happen."

"You've not spoken to him at all while you've been here?"

She shook her head. "If I know him at all, he's angry that I've come—despite the invitation."

"Karen can't keep away from you. I've seen her come up to you a few times."

"Yeah, I've come close to saying something to her, but then I think I only have myself to blame. Our entire lives, Karen has taken what she's wanted, and I've never spoken out, never criticized her or told her what I really thought. At school she made us swap beds because she didn't want to be near the loo. When we ate out in restaurants, she'd make me order a pudding and then she'd eat it herself. She would borrow my clothes and not return them. I've let that happen. For years. And I've done the same thing with Matt —I've wanted him to be happy more than I wanted me to be happy."

"You don't know how to put yourself first," I added.

"It sounds like a cliché."

"It sounds true."

"I think they just have such forceful personalities, and I genuinely want people I love to be happy."

"But they've got to want you to be happy too, otherwise people will ride roughshod over you." It had happened to my mother—used when there wasn't anything better to do and then dropped when life moved on. It made me sick. "Promise me you'll start pleasing yourself before you start pleasing other people."

"I can't make promises that I don't know I'm capable of keeping."

"Promise you'll at least try. And if Matt says anything about you coming to this wedding after what he's done and then sent you an invitation . . . he'll have me to contend with."

"You're going to be my knight in shining armor?" she asked.

"No swords. I'm going to tell him what a useless human being he is."

She turned back toward me and placed her warm, soft hand over my arm. "Please don't say a word. I've managed to avoid him so far—that's all I've got to do until we leave on Sunday."

"He better keep away from you."

I couldn't stand up to the man who'd discarded my mother like she was nothing because he was dead, but if Matt even breathed in Stella's direction, I couldn't hold myself responsible for what I'd do.

"Promise me you won't say anything," she pleaded.

"Stella, I can't make promises that I don't know I'm capable of keeping," I said, replaying her words back to her.

"Don't think I haven't seen that steel in you. I know you are perfectly able to control yourself if that's what you want to do." She slid her hand over mine. "Don't think I'm not grateful. Just you *wanting* to protect me is . . ." She sighed. "More than Matt ever did."

"But why should I control myself? That guy needs some home truths—"

"For me. That's why."

With those two words she'd stolen the wind from my sails.

For *her*.

It was a simple reason, but the best. And one that couldn't be argued with.

"I promise I won't say anything," I said. *For her*—she was worth the promise.

For her, I'd keep decades of frustrations locked up and wouldn't unleash them on Matt, however tempting it was.

For her, I wasn't sure if there was anything I wouldn't do.

TWENTY

Stella

Beck held my hand as we left the hotel room to join the others downstairs for a lunchtime picnic. I'd woken up feeling sore—not on the outside but somehow the inside of me was bruised. Maybe it had been that way for some time and I just hadn't noticed. I couldn't believe I'd confessed to Beck last night about Matt and Karen. He must have thought I was a total doormat.

Just as we were stepping onto the brick veranda, Karen appeared. There was no heading off in the opposite direction or avoiding eye contact—we were face-to-face, and shame rose from my feet and seeped into my belly. Shame for not saying anything to her and for allowing myself to be treated the way she treated me.

"Hi," she said, glancing down at my hand linked with Beck's. "It looks like the sun is going to hold."

"Looks beautiful," I said, trying my best to smile. Even if I did have the courage to say something, I couldn't risk upsetting things for Beck. Henry was Karen's godfather after all. If I ruined her wedding, we'd be asked to leave, and Beck would lose his chance of getting Henry to sell him his building. But if I *was* to say something, I might tell her how her first boyfriend had turned up at my house the week before he ended things between them and told me he loved me. I might say how her little sister, Elsie, had told me once that she didn't like the way Karen spoke to me. I might even show her the message I got from her mother the day after the invitation arrived, telling me how sorry she was for what her daughter had done.

But of course, I stayed silent.

"Well, head over to the weeping willows where everything is set up," she said. "I'll catch you later."

"She's very upbeat," Beck said as we made our way down the steps. "It's annoying."

I laughed. "Yeah. She's always been that way—nothing much gets to her." It had always seemed like Karen had some kind of internal suit of armor.

"I think it's genetic," he said. "Life's always wonderful."

Different colors of tartan picnic blankets were laid out on the grass by the river. On each blanket there was a wicker hamper and a square card with names printed on them. Beck would think this was normal and put it down to the idiosyncrasies of the upper classes, but set seating at a picnic was anything but normal—it didn't matter who you were.

Beck and I wandered from one empty blanket to another looking for our names.

"People are different. You can't know someone just by virtue of the fact their family has money." Beck was looking at name cards intently, and I wasn't sure if he was ignoring me or hadn't heard me. "There we are," I said, spotting my name two blankets farther up, at the very edge of the party. I kicked off my ballet flats and took a seat.

"Have you thought anymore about confronting Matt or Karen—or even better, both of them?" he asked, handing me the card while he unbuckled the hamper.

"You might enjoy making enemies, but I don't."

"It's not about making enemies. It's about standing up for yourself."

There was no point in having this conversation again. It wasn't as if I'd helped Karen pick out her wedding gown or was a bridesmaid or something. "Well, if I had confronted her, I wouldn't have been invited this week and you wouldn't be here. So, count yourself lucky and zip it."

He chuckled, handing me two wine glasses. "Yeah. Okay. Point taken. I just don't get it, that's all."

I spotted Florence and Bea on the other side of the sea of blankets, down by the river. Karen must have given them a blanket for four.

"Look, Florence is waving," Beck said.

I nodded. "Yeah. She's over there with Bea and there's Jo, too," I said, spotting the rest of our gang.

"No doubt your good friend Karen was in charge of the seating plan."

"Come on," Beck said, standing up. "We're going to take our blanket over there." He tugged at the green wool I was sitting on. "Get up."

"Beck, no. We can't. There's a seating plan for a reason. Anyway, it doesn't matter if we're back here."

"We bloody well can." He scooped up the hamper. "This week is difficult enough for you without her seating you nowhere near your friends."

"It won't be malicious from her perspective," I said, not entirely believing it. She probably hadn't wanted me in her eyeline as a reminder of what she'd done, although in that case she shouldn't have invited me.

"I suppose it depends on your definition of malicious. If not giving a shit about you or your feelings is malicious, then that's the least she's being. Get up," he said again, "or I'll put you over my shoulder and carry you. If you won't stick up for yourself, I'll do it for you."

I shivered. I couldn't remember any man coming to my rescue before. I wasn't used to a man who worried about my feelings or the enjoyment of my day.

Something ignited inside me, giving me energy, and I got to my feet.

Matt should have been that guy.

He should have been the man who wanted better for me than I wanted for myself, who stood up for me and did things to make my day better.

Because we'd been together for so long, what I had and what I should expect for myself had melded together and I'd lost sight of what I was worth. Beck might be a fake boyfriend, but on every measure, he was better than Matt had ever been.

He was nicer to me. More respectful. He was in my corner—batting for me, cheering me on. Not to mention more handsome, funnier, and a better kisser.

Matt had done me a favor by dumping me. The constant, subtle putdowns, the lack of affection and kindness, not to mention the way he always pushed his needs to the top of the list, even if I'd let him. Beck had provided me with a new normal, and I could never go back now.

It really said something when having a fake boyfriend was better than having a real one.

Instead of sadness, the realization about Matt freeing me provided relief. And uncertainty—if I'd been wrong about Matt for so long, what else was I wrong about? Who else?

Before I got a chance to overthink, Beck tucked the blanket under his arm and made his way between the other guests. I had no choice but to follow him as I hastily put my shoes back on and gathered the wine glasses. Although it felt a bit naughty, it also felt liberating. For once, I was doing something to make myself happy.

"Hi," Beck said, as we arrived at the spot where all my friends were. "Do you mind if we join you?"

"Of course not," Florence said. "I don't know why you weren't over here with us in the first place. And who the hell has assigned seating at a picnic anyway?"

Beck shot me an I-told-you-so look and, despite him being a tiny bit irritating, I couldn't help but admire how he just didn't give a shit. It felt like a small victory over Karen and Matt, and Beck was the man who'd made it happen.

"Who's having wine?" Beck asked, offering up the bottle in our basket. When everyone passed, he filled my glass and put a few mouthfuls in his. "Day drinking and staring out at that river," he said as we all looked through the screen of willow branches down to the jetty that led into the river. "It's like something out of an E.M. Forster novel."

"You read much E.M. Forster?" I asked, laughing.

"I read *A Room with a View*," he said, which stopped my smile in its tracks.

"You did?" I asked. "For school?"

"No. I saw the film and liked it, so I decided to read the book."

He was obviously serious, and I had to stifle a giggle. He seemed such an unlikely audience for anything Merchant Ivory.

He looked at me. "Are you laughing at me?" he asked, smirking.

"Never," I replied and took a sip of my wine. I was such a horrible liar.

"What can I say? It's a good film and a better book."

"It doesn't seem like your kind of thing. Isn't it wistful and romantic?" Beck was dogged and determined. You didn't get to be as successful as he was from a standing start without having an edge. A love of costume drama didn't seem to fit. But what did I know? I couldn't tell good people from bad. Friends from foes.

I wanted to ask more about his taste in films—prod to see if it was a character trait or a fluke—but I didn't want to give away how little we knew about each other. "I've never seen it," I said. "So I couldn't possibly comment."

"When we're back in London, we'll watch it one night."

I glanced over at Bea, to see if she was taking any notice, but she was talking to Florence about something. Was this conversation real or fake? Either way, I was enjoying it.

"You'll have to point out all your favorite bits," I said.

He chuckled. "I can tell you don't believe me, but my sister went through a phase of reading everything by him, and I was a dutiful younger brother and sat through the film a couple of times. Looking back, she must have been recovering from heartbreak. I guess she was around fifteen."

Shit, I'd forgotten her name. I lowered my voice. I couldn't not ask but didn't want anyone to overhear. "Are you still close with . . . your sister?"

"She's older and married with two kids. I don't see her much but when I do, I enjoy it."

"Tell me that's not Karen and Matt arriving on a boat," Florence said, pointing at the water, interrupting me imagining a sun-kissed, younger Beck reading E.M. Forster.

People began to murmur and, sure enough, Karen, dressed in white, and Matt in his usual summer outfit of chinos and a blue shirt, climbed out of a small rowing boat and up onto the jetty. I might have been hoping that one of them would go head-first into the water, but I wasn't about to admit to it.

"She's such an attention seeker," Jo said. "Who has an entire week of wedding celebrations in the first place. And then this?" She cocked her head at the river.

If Karen had told me she was going to sail into her wedding picnic on a rowing boat in a white floaty dress when we'd still been friends, I would have thought she was fun and carefree. "It's not a bit of fun?" I asked.

"Everything's fun for Karen if everyone's looking at her," Bea said. "Haven't you noticed?"

"If she's so selfish and self-involved, why have we all been friends with her for all these years?" I asked. Had Bea and Jo seen this side of Karen since she got engaged to Matt or had they always felt this way?

"Because you always wanted the four of us to do stuff together," Bea said.

"You're always the one who includes Karen on the email chain or suggests she gets the invitation to dinner."

It hadn't been conscious. I just liked to include everyone. "I never noticed . . ."

"Because you see the best in everyone. Want the best for everyone. It's lovely, but people like Karen eat up your goodness like summer pudding," Florence said.

Karen always liked to be at the center of things, the rest of us just looking on like we were members of the audience rather than on stage, but it had never really bothered me—I hadn't seen her as taking advantage of me. Maybe Matt was the same. When we were together, I'd thought we were costars, but perhaps I was just backstage sweeping up after him.

"Or Eton Mess," Bea said. "Matt was no different—they both took advantage of your kindness."

Beck nudged me and nodded toward Florence and Bea as if to tell me I should pay attention to what they were saying.

The thing was, I vaguely remembered Florence and Bea saying these things to me before and me dismissing them. But now, with what had happened, what Beck had said and kept saying . . . I couldn't ignore who Karen and Matt really were anymore. But who else was going to reveal themselves as my enemy rather than my friend? If two of the people I was closest to in the world could betray me, then anyone could.

As the happy couple walked up the riverbank to join us, people began to clap. Beside me, Beck chuckled. "I was hoping one of them would go in."

I bit down on my bottom lip to stop myself from laughing. Today had kind of summed Beck up—moving the blanket and calling out this spectacle, forcing me to acknowledge what was really happening.

He dared to do what I didn't, say what I couldn't, made me see things the way they were rather than how I wanted them to be. Whether our kisses had been real or fake, Beck was changing the way I saw the world and the way I saw myself.

I just hoped I wasn't as wrong about him as I had been about Matt and Karen.

TWENTY-ONE

Beck

Stella's eyes dipped to my bowtie, then up to my jawline and finally up to meet my gaze. "You look cute."

The sun cast a golden, hazy light across the hotel room, making her look even more beautiful than usual, lighting up her face, highlighting the beauty spot on her cheek, emphasizing the deep v of her cupid's bow. The short skirt didn't hurt—she had killer legs.

"Cute?" I asked. "I'm not sure cute is a compliment."

"Maybe I wasn't giving you one," she replied.

This girl never let me get away with anything, and I couldn't remember when I'd ever had quite so much fun. No woman had ever given me a hard time like Stella did—certainly none of my girlfriends had. I ended up dating women who were easy. Not in the sexual sense, but in the sense that they fit into my life and didn't require me to work at anything, which left me to put all my energy into my business.

It suited me. Perhaps Stella would be easy as a real girlfriend but as a fake girlfriend she was challenging and funny and had told me I was irritating on more than one occasion.

"You look a lot better than cute," I replied.

She spun around, black and white sequins clinging to every curve. "You think it's thirties enough? Everyone is bound to have gone to costume shops and had stuff made. I bought this for one of Matt's work dos when we were up in Manchester."

"It's a sexy take on the thirties. And why would you want to be like all these people anyway?"

She smiled. "They're not so bad, you know. Anyway, I don't have anything else, so it will have to do."

"It will more than do. I'll struggle to keep my hands to myself all evening." We hadn't repeated our kisses from the day before, but looking at her now, kissing her was all I could think about.

"I have a feather boa," she said, ignoring me. "But I think it looks tacky. What do you think?"

She hung the black feathers around her shoulders. Normally, when a girlfriend asked me my opinion on her outfit, I'd say whatever was going to get us out the door fastest, but with Stella, I studied her. I wanted her to look as good as she could, feel the most confident she ever had. I wanted her to feel like she had all the power when she was with these people. Because she was better than all of them. "I think without. The dress is enough on its own."

"You're right," she said, discarding the boa on the bed. "It's kind of distracting. And I look like a stripper."

"If it's going to get you in character, then maybe I'll change my mind."

She picked up her evening bag and whacked me with it. "Let's go." She led the way out of the hotel room.

"So, it's just cocktails tonight?" I asked as we made our way down the corridor. "No food?"

"I have no idea. I can't imagine Karen hasn't thought of that. So perhaps substantial canapes?"

"I might be ordering room service when we get back," I mumbled. "There's Henry," I said, nodding toward the party making their way toward us from the other end of the corridor. "He's rarely alone. It's part of the reason it's so difficult to speak to him."

"This is perfect. I've not seen him yet. Come on," she said, picking up speed so we could run into him.

"Henry," Stella said. "How wonderful to see you." Her grin lit up her face and a pang of jealousy bloomed in my gut. Had she ever smiled so widely at me?

"Stella, darling. How are you? You're looking wonderful." Henry was all charm and warm smiles.

"I'm wonderful, thank you. Can I introduce you to Beck Wilde?"

She placed her hand lovingly on my arm, tucking her body into mine as if she belonged to me. My breath caught in my throat, not because it was uncomfortable but because the idea of her belonging to me felt . . . right.

"Mr. Wilde, very nice to see you again. You did very well with the clays the other day. I hope you leave some grouse for us tomorrow."

"You have my word on that, sir," I said. Maybe I was a hypocrite—I couldn't even spell the word vegetarian—but I didn't want the souls of tiny birds haunting me. I'd leave that to old money. "After we met," I said, "I realized our paths have almost crossed a couple of times in London." I wasn't about to mention the time at the Dorchester when I tried to introduce myself. "There was a property of yours I was interested in."

Henry frowned. "Really? I don't recall."

"Yes, the Dawnay building in Mayfair."

He took in a deep breath and then shook his head. "Yes, place still isn't let. But I don't remember any offers."

"Well, perhaps we could find some time to discuss it," I said.

"Yes, of course," he said. "Right now, I must go and see Graham." He shook his head and turned back to Stella. "You look wonderful, darling." He turned to me. "Look after her . . . Mr. Wilde."

Great, I thought as Henry headed toward the bar and left Stella and me at the entrance to the party. He hadn't even remembered my first name.

"Who's Graham?" I asked.

"No idea," she replied. "Tell me what happened?"

"What? When?"

"Henry mentioned that you shot well," Stella said as we found ourselves a table and took a seat.

"Oh yes. It's surprising how often these men miss considering they do this kind of thing all the time."

Stella groaned. "Give it to me straight. Did you beat everyone else?"

Why was she groaning? I thought she'd be impressed.

"Easily," I replied. "That's what too much time with an air rifle and three empty tomato soup cans looks like."

She leaned toward me. "I'm going to ask you a straightforward question and I want you to give me an honest answer—how badly do you want this building in Mayfair?"

Had she missed something? I thought I'd been more than clear. "Badly."

"Put your ego to one side, hand over your credit card, and follow my instructions 'badly'?"

"You want me to buy everyone a round of drinks?" I asked.

"That's the very last thing I want you to do." She pulled out her phone and began scrolling. "We're free tomorrow morning—no wedding events. We'll try in the village but if not, we're going to have to make a trip into Inverness," she said like I knew what she was talking about.

"For what?" I asked.

"You're clearly not winning over Henry. That introduction was a car crash."

Car crash seemed a harsh way of putting it. It hadn't been that bad, had it? He might not have remembered my name, or asked me anything about the Dawnay building and my interest in it. He might have cut the conversation short, but it was progress, wasn't it? I suppose it hadn't been great, but I'd at least spoken to him.

"So, we need to get you back on track," Stella said. "We're going to go shopping and buy you some things, and I'm going to help you build a relationship with Henry."

"What sort of things are we going to buy that will help me negotiate with Henry? A rope, duct tape, and some chloroform?"

"Funny," she replied. "Clothes. We're going to give you a makeover."

"You're going to give me a *Pretty Woman* moment?" I asked.

"Think of me as Richard Gere. And you're Julia Roberts, just not as hot."

"Well, for the record, you're a lot better looking than either Richard or Julia."

"See? You can be charming." She smoothed down the lapel of my jacket, and I had to fight back the urge to pull her on to my lap.

"So Tom Ford's not good enough?"

"It's far *too* good. You know these people aren't cash rich. Their wealth is in property and art and trusts . . . They are caretakers of a fortune—they spend their time trying not to spend money. You know this; you're not stupid."

"That's the point. I can make Henry cash rich if he'd give me the time of day."

"Your way hasn't worked so far, and he didn't show much interest in speaking about your offer on his building. If you want him to sell you that property, you need to play by his rules. No one likes a show-off."

I liked Stella's feistiness, had since I'd met her that first day when she'd turned me down flat. But a step farther and I'd officially be pissed off. "I'm not showing off."

"Then why did you win yesterday?"

"You're not suggesting I should pretend to be less than I am so I puff up these people's egos, are you?" I asked.

"If all it took was ego-puffing, then that would be easy. And I can't imagine that you are so pig-headed that you wouldn't be prepared to puff, puff, puff if that's what it took. You can be so completely charming, so utterly convincing, I don't get why you're being so stubborn about using your powers of persuasion with these people. If I didn't know better, I'd say part of you doesn't want the Dawnay building at all."

"You know that I want the building more than anything."

"Why? You have plenty of money. It can't just be a financial thing."

She waited as if I was going to answer her, as if I was going to tell her all my secrets.

I stayed silent.

"It's like you're trying to antagonize people. You need to

get them on your side, but you know this, and so I don't get it—the Tom Ford when everyone else is in tweed. The winning at clays even though what you should be concentrating on is talking to Henry and letting the host win. None of this makes sense."

"Oil and water," I said. "We don't mix. They don't like me."

"I like you," she said.

Didn't she get it? She wasn't like the rest of them. She wasn't like any woman I'd ever met. "You're different."

"Then trust me and let me take you shopping tomorrow."

"If you let me kiss you," I countered. It had been too long since our last kiss.

A small smile curled around her lips. "You always want to make a deal. But you're asking for something I'm more than willing to give without anything in return. Maybe you need to sharpen your negotiation skills."

This woman was as sharp as a pin.

"Well, then maybe I'll make you wait."

She sighed. "More waiting."

I pushed down a grin and tried to ignore the ache in my balls at the thought of denying her.

Yes, I wanted the Dawnay building. But right at that moment, I wanted Stella London more. Tonight was going to be a long night, and I was going to have to use every ounce of my self-control to stop myself from pulling her out of this cocktail party, back to our room, and stripping her naked immediately.

TWENTY-TWO

Beck

If I told Stella what I had planned to do to her tonight, she'd no doubt rip off one of her ultra-high heels and thwack me with it. Stella was sexy as hell, gave as good as she got, made me shift my focus about a lot of things, but best of all being with her felt easy, comfortable—like being at home. It was like being with a friend, but better because she was gorgeous, and I wanted to get her naked.

Patience. I'd had to exercise a lot of it this evening and I was fast running out.

I unlocked the door to our hotel room and held it open as she walked through.

"You promised me kissing," she said. "But it's later and still I'm kissless."

"Kissless?" I asked. "Well we wouldn't want that." I spun her around to face me, cupped her face, and pressed my lips to hers.

Her hands slid up the sides of my shirt and I held back a

shiver. When had a simple touch over my clothes ever had such a visceral effect on me?

I wanted this woman. *This* woman. Not just sex with a pretty girl. I wanted to undress Stella, to lick and bite every square centimeter of her until I knew her better than I knew myself.

I wanted to *devour* her.

She sighed under my touch and her hands caught my wrists. I pulled back. "You okay?"

She grinned, her lips reddened with heat. "Absolutely."

"You know that this is more than kissing tonight?"

"Oh yeah?" she asked. "What did you have planned?"

I circled my arms around her waist and pulled her tight against me. "Naked stuff."

She laughed. "Such a Casanova."

The smooth guy I used to be, the one who knew how to seduce a woman, had disappeared. I'd never really understood the concept of being disarmed until Stella London. I bent and kissed her neck. "Not trying to be anyone but me," I replied, tugging at the buttons at the back of her dress.

I stripped her down to her underwear and walked her backward to the bed. I needed to get a grip, to take back control of this situation. I leaned over, pressed a kiss to her soft stomach and let myself breathe her in. Tonight, she'd be mine. Finally.

I hooked my thumbs into her knickers, dragging them off as I pushed her back onto the bed and kneeled at her feet. My dick started to throb at just the thought of what she tasted like. Of how she smelled.

Jesus, what was the matter with me? I was like a teenager leafing through the underwear section of my mother's catalog.

I pressed a kiss at the juncture of her thigh, and she

groaned. Good. It wasn't just me. She was worked up too—she wanted this. Wanted me.

I made my way up to her perfect hip bone, across to the other side and down, enjoying her warm, smooth expanse of skin, needing to take my time but greedy for all of her all at once.

"Beck," she groaned, sliding her hands into my hair, the sound vibrating through my body in a way I was sure would register on the Richter scale and gathering in my balls, building my need for her by the second.

I pressed a kiss over her clit. "You're going to have to be patient." I said the words as much to myself as to her.

She sighed and I began to lick—slow, dirty strokes, going deeper and deeper. I wanted to bury myself in her. I took a breath, trying to dampen down the starting growl of my orgasm and focus on making the strokes longer and longer. Her hips lifted off the bed, and I pressed one hand on the hot skin of her stomach and the other on her thigh to keep her in place.

"Tell me before you come," I said.

A gush of wetness spilled out onto my tongue and Stella began to grind against my mouth. "Beck," she cried.

I moved away. "You close?" I asked.

"Yes. No . . . but . . . Oh God," she groaned again as I pressed my fingertips into her milky skin—warm like sun-kissed seawater.

For a split second I wondered if Matt had ever gone down on her. I doubt he had any idea of what to do with a woman. I would show Stella that she wasn't missing anything by not being with him.

I resumed my exploration of Stella, kissing, licking, and sucking, reveling in her sighs and moans, savoring the way she squeezed her eyes tight shut as if trying to block out the pleasure she was feeling. Her body was perfect from this angle, all smooth curves and goose-bumped plains. Her pulse tripped under my tongue, sending sparks of lust right to my cock. She definitely wasn't far off, and I pulled away to assess her expression.

She was lost. Floating. Her cheeks flushed, her hair spread out on the bed.

I'd never seen her look so beautiful.

"No coming," I barked.

"I'm close," she said, her voice breathless and weak.

We'd just have to do something about that. I gave her one final lick and then sat back. "Take a breath."

She gave me a confused look.

"I said no coming and I meant it."

I liked that her orgasms didn't come too easily. By the time I'd finished with her, she'd be coming on command.

She lifted up onto her elbows. "Beck, what . . ."

"You're getting nothing else until you promise you won't come without telling me."

"I p-promise," she stuttered.

I resumed my position, blowing on her clit and circling her entrance with my finger. She moaned. "I mean it, Stella. Relax and take a deep breath or I'm going to stop."

"What are you doing to me?" Her gaze flitted around my face.

"Trust me and you'll find out."

Her ribcage rose as her lungs filled and then she exhaled—a long, slow breath pushed from her lips.

"Better?" I asked.

"Define better."

"You're not going to come straight away?"

"Yeah, you and I have a different definition of better."

I pressed a kiss to her hip bone to stop myself from smiling. "You'll see." I twisted my fingers, working around her entrance, and lay my tongue flat against her clit. Her body tightened, her breaths shortened, and her hands fisted in my hair.

She was close. Again. "Stella," I growled. She needed to get better at communicating.

Without further prompting, she took another deep breath and relaxed her body into the mattress.

"Better." Her compliance made my mouth wet and my dick hard. Stella was fucking fun and fun to fuck.

As fingers and tongue worked, I luxuriated in the way Stella tried to keep her breaths deep and her body relaxed, but when I slid a third finger inside her, her back arched and she spluttered, "I'm going to come."

I withdrew my fingers and sat back. I wasn't ready yet.

"So, this is what you do?" she asked, her skin flushed and her words tripping into each other as if she were exhausted. "You torture women?"

I could do this for hours with Stella.

I couldn't hide the grin she provoked. "I'm playing with you, not torturing you. And believe me. It will be so much better when I finally let you come." I stood up, my erection raging against my stomach, desperate for release. It wasn't just Stella I liked to deny.

"The things for which you have to work hardest taste the sweetest." I dropped a kiss on her mouth and headed to the bathroom. I undressed and poured two glasses of water.

Her eyes went to my cock as I returned. "You're going to fuck me now?"

"We're going to fuck all night. But you're not having my dick yet. You're going to have to work a little harder until you've proved you're ready."

She groaned and this time it wasn't in pleasure.

"Drink this. I don't want you getting dehydrated."

I expected her to argue, but she lifted herself up on her elbows, still eyeing my hard-on as she took the glass from me.

My cock jerked under her inspection, and she sighed and gulped down the water as if she couldn't wait for her reward.

She'd get it. Eventually.

She gave me back the glass and lay down.

"Legs open," I said as I retook my position and began working my fingers and tongue. Her hands gripped the sheets, but without my prompting she released them and blew out a breath.

Good girl.

I took her to the edge three more times, but she didn't complain. In fact, she seemed to see it as a challenge.

She sank into the mattress, her limbs heavy, and the glazed look in her eye suggesting she'd fully embraced my *torture.*

I worked harder and she tried to muffle her cries, but the rippling of her stomach and the curl of her toes gave away her pleasure. She finally gave up and exhaled on a loud moan. "Beck," she cried. "I'm going to come."

"Keep breathing deeply and come for me."

She shot me a panicked look as if she were afraid of what her orgasm might do to her.

"You're going to be okay," I said as the convulsions in her body began to spread. I could almost *see* her orgasm crawl up her body. Her nipples peaked, her back arched, and silently, she reached for me—in reassurance or need?

I had no idea but something in my gut stirred.

I crawled up her body, and she circled her arms around my waist as her orgasm enveloped her.

"You okay?" I asked as she recovered. I rolled to my side and she came with me, hooking her leg over mine.

"Um, yeah. That was . . . I don't know. Intense. I've never . . . I mean . . . *intense.*"

I chuckled. "You enjoyed my torture."

"I'm not sure about the torture bit. It was a challenge but the orgasm . . . It was like the mother of all climaxes. I've never felt anything like it."

It was no less than she deserved.

"We're just warming up."

"I'm plenty warm," she said as she pushed herself up on her elbows then straddled me.

She was deliciously wet, immediately coating my cock in her juices. "Where did you learn that shit?" she asked as she moved her hips forward and back. "I mean, I expected you to be a little more . . ."

I tucked my hand under my head as I waited to hear her explain her misconceptions of me.

"I don't know. Selfish. Impatient."

"You've clearly been fucking the wrong guy."

"Apparently," she said, pressing her palms against my chest. "I mean, there's only ever been Matt. I guess I don't have a lot of experience."

Jesus, on top of it all, she was at the wedding of the only guy she'd ever slept with. Every time I thought I understood how difficult this week was for her, I found out something else.

"Well, now there's me." She deserved the best sex that life had to offer. And I couldn't help but enjoy the fact that I'd been the man who showed her how good it could be.

I flipped her to her back and grabbed a condom from my wallet on the bedside table where I'd left it. I didn't want to wait a moment longer.

The more I got to know Stella, the more I wanted to know. When she'd first had her freak out and I'd spent the day with her, listening to her reel off information, all I'd wanted was to make her feel better so she didn't bail on this wedding. But now, I wanted to *know* her. I wanted to know things about her that were completely unnecessary to fake a relationship in front of strangers. I wanted to get inside her head. Inside her body. I wanted to *feel* this woman.

"Are you ready?" I asked as I positioned my cock at her entrance.

"It depends. Are you going to torture me again?"

"I'm going to fuck you. No more torture."

"Then I'm more than ready." She ran her hands down her body then pulled her legs wide apart. Fuck, I wasn't even inside her, but just knowing that in seconds I would be was enough to have my jaw tense and my cock jerking in my hand.

I moved inside her, just enough so she'd feel me.

"Oh God," she said on a sigh as if she'd been lost in a desert for days and I was giving her a cold glass of water.

Slowly I inched into her, and she took deep breaths as if she was trying to control her orgasm, as if a single stroke of my cock was going to tip her over and have her coming. That didn't hurt my ego.

I shoved in the last centimeter, wanting to get as deep as I could, and she arched her back, lifting off the bed.

"So deep, Beck."

It was deep, tight, and fucking perfect.

I had to take a breath. I wasn't ready to give in, and I wanted her to come again.

I withdrew just as slowly, trying to get used to the feel of her around me. Trying to get used to how she looked—the way her breasts shifted as I moved over her, the way she bit down on her bottom lip in concentration, the way she looked at me as if I'd wrapped up the moon and given it to her.

I wasn't sure I'd ever been *aware* of anyone in bed before. Not that I wasn't focused on a woman's pleasure—that was always part of the package. But compared to how I was taking Stella in—how I wanted to savor it all, remember it—it made me see that before her, it had always been anatomical, biological. With her it was . . . different, burrowed deeper somehow.

She grasped my arm. "You okay?" she asked, pulling me out of my own head.

I was more than okay.

I nodded, pushing into her faster this time. She closed her eyes and pushed out a heavy, slow breath. Christ, even her breathing was sexy.

I shut my eyes in an effort to block everything out—blanking my mind, seeing only white. I needed to focus. I began a rhythm, trying not to be so fucking aware of how soft and tight and perfect Stella London was.

"Beck," she whispered, bringing me back to the moment. "It's so good. How is it so good?" She trailed her fingers down my back, and I couldn't stop the guttural roar that rippled up from my gut and out of my throat.

Sweat gathered at my hairline—not from the physical but from the mental effort of holding myself back from pouring into her. My cock was swollen with need, my muscles heavy with desire, and I kept thrusting, kept pushing into her. I needed to make it good for her, but more than anything, I wanted to keep these feelings, these new sensations that floated around me, whispering and wondering and new.

"Beck, Beck, Beck," she began to chant in panic.

"Hey," I said, folding myself over her so my chest was flat against hers.

"I'm so close and it feels so good. I don't think I can stop it."

I exhaled, almost relieved it would soon be over. I couldn't stand this any longer—I couldn't bear how fucking good it was.

I knew I wouldn't be able to stop my orgasm as hers arrived. "Shhh," I said, pressing a kiss to her neck. "You can come, baby."

She blinked lazily and her hands dropped over her head. I felt it begin. The pulse under her skin, the tiny shiver that morphed into a shudder. She arched her body, and it flicked a switch in me.

There was no more holding back. I pulled back and thrust in one more time, my orgasm creeping up my spine, circling and spinning, higher and higher until it exploded into every cell in my body.

It pulled every ounce, every molecule of energy from me, draining me of everything but the sensation of coming. All I felt was the buzz of her skin against mine and how fucking perfect that was.

I slumped against her, burying my face in her neck, and she tightened her grip around me, as if she thought I might go somewhere.

As if I could.

I didn't have the energy to lift my head.

And even if I did, there was nowhere I'd rather be.

TWENTY-THREE

Stella

The windscreen wipers were working overtime to clear some sort of path in front of us. The roads were ridiculously narrow around here, but it didn't seem to faze Beck, who was at the wheel of the Land Rover he'd rented.

"You think we should turn around?" I asked as I gripped the papers I was carrying.

Beck shot me a look, then patted my leg, his hand staying a little too long on my thigh for it to be a friendly reassurance. Up until last night I'd doubted things between us—unable to understand what was real and fake. But last night was real and I had the bruises, the bitemarks, and the near-constant buzz under my skin from being with Beck that proved it.

"It's fine. Just rain. I can slow down if you're nervous." I didn't know if it was the words or the tone, but I believed him when he said it was fine. Still, he lifted his foot off the accelerator a little and we slowed without me having to ask. At every opportunity, he showed me that he thought about my feelings, my desires, my needs. Being with him was a revelation. "It's meant to clear in a couple of hours, so the journey back should be easier. At least we're not going to Inverness. A helicopter would be more difficult in this visibility."

There was no way I would have gotten into a helicopter in this weather, but thankfully there was a shop in a village about twelve miles away that would have most of the stuff we needed.

Not that buying things was going to help. What I really wanted was to get to the bottom of what was driving Beck. He was smart. He'd had money long enough to know how these things worked—it didn't matter what world you came from, people did deals with people they liked and trusted, yet Beck was doing his best to not fit in.

"We have a trip to Fort William next," I said, looking at the detailed itinerary we'd been given when we arrived. "That should be relatively easy to dress for. We have that hike—we need to deal with that. And then the shooting. It's too late to get you a dinner jacket—"

"I've brought a perfectly nice dinner jacket."

This guy had a thing for Tom Ford, and who could blame him? He looked spectacular in everything he wore, but old money went to Saville Row. And they could tell the difference.

"Just because I don't have a tailor that my family has been using for four generations doesn't mean my dinner jacket isn't a perfect fit."

"You need to stop focusing on how things should be and just figure out how they are so you can get what you want."

His knuckles whitened on the steering wheel.

"Why are you so determined to stand out from everyone around you?" I said, sliding my hand onto his leg. Beck's comments about people with money still weren't making sense to me, and I was determined to get to the bottom of it. I wanted to know him better. I wanted to understand exactly what made him tick. I'd thought I'd known Matt and it turned out I'd been living with a stranger all these years. I wasn't going to settle for what Beck told me. I wanted to dig deeper. Not least because we were sharing a bed.

Last night had been . . . unexpected. It was impossible to deny that Beck was attractive. But he wasn't my type—well, physically, he was everyone's type, but Beck was so . . . brash wasn't the word. But he had a confidence about him that Matt had been missing. Matt was confident on the outside and comfortable in the world of public school and old money, but he didn't have the core of steel Beck did.

He also didn't have the penis Beck did.

But it wasn't just Beck's dick that had made last night so memorable. It was the way he'd made me feel. Like it was me, rather than sex, that he wanted. I couldn't ever remember feeling like that with Matt. Being with Beck was . . . liberating. It allowed me to stop focusing on where I was and what had happened, and I'd been forced into the present. But it wasn't as if Beck was going to be part of my future. As much as Beck and I were enjoying each other's company, as much as I'd been convinced that things between us were real, we were both in Scotland—together—for a reason. And it wasn't to start a serious relationship.

The corners of Beck's mouth twitched as he fought a grin as he faced the blurred road in front of us. I wasn't sure if it was what I'd said, my hand, or whether he was thinking about last night, too.

Beck cleared his throat, caught my wrist and placed my hand on his thigh. "The hike won't be difficult," he said.

"We're not going up Beck Nevis. We don't need poles and shit. I've brought some gray hiking trousers."

I'd bet they were brand new. And I'd bet his arse looked fantastic in them. "Yeah we can probably solve that with a nail brush and some scissors."

"I have no idea what that means, but I know you're not cutting up those trousers. I went up Scarfell Pike in them last year. There's nothing wrong with them."

That sounded promising. At least they wouldn't still have their label on and crease marks on the legs from the packaging. That was the thing with old money—nothing was new. Nothing looked as if you'd just spent money on it. But Beck knew this. He wanted to stand out. But why?

"You went up Scarfell?" I liked the idea of Beck out in the wilds, his hair a little tousled, a smear of mud across his perfect jaw. I'd witnessed Beck a little sweaty and it looked good on him.

"Yeah, some charity thing that Dexter was doing."

"So you sacrificed your pristine, expensive gym for the outdoors? I thought you left that behind when you got your Duke of Edinburgh?"

The road veered to the right and some signs of life came into view. "Looks like where we're headed," he said, nodding at the buildings up ahead. "And I have no problem getting outdoors. Never have, never will. I might live in the city—"

"In a penthouse in one of the most expensive postcodes in the country, in Europe even."

"Doesn't mean I don't like getting out. I grew up in the country. And you're the one getting wiggy because it's raining." He took my hand from his lap and pressed a kiss to my wrist as if it was totally normal. His lips were like a shot of lust injected right into my veins.

I pulled away, unsure of how long I could withstand the intensity of his touch.

"Oh, this must be the village," he said. "Can you spot the shop you want to go to?"

I glanced to either side of the street as Beck slowed down. "There on the left," I said.

"You sure we're going to find what we need?" he asked as he pulled in front of a shop with dark-green window frames and a cream sign on the front that said *Cameron James-Gentleman's Outfitters*. "It looks like a ghost town."

"It's not Saville Row, that's for sure. What I do know is that I didn't bring an umbrella." It was only about three meters between the car and the door to the shop, but it was enough distance to drown in this weather.

Beck pulled his jacket from the backseat. "Use this."

Before I could say no, he'd stepped out of the car and instead of making his way to the store he rounded the bonnet and opened my door.

I could get used to a man doing that for me, although I couldn't tell him that. "I can open my own door. You'll get soaked."

I slid from my seat, holding his coat over my head, enjoying the scent of him as it surrounded me. "Here," I said, trying to share the shelter of his jacket.

He ignored me and took my hand, pulling me forward.

The bell was still tinkling as we closed the door behind us and let the rain drip onto the mat in the entrance.

I looked up at him and my stomach did a deep dive from a mile-high cliff. I wondered if I'd ever come up for air. The rain had emphasized his beauty. His face was splattered with raindrops and his hair was slick with water, as if he'd just stepped out of the shower. "You're . . . ." I traced his brows with my fingertips and he lazily shut his eyes.

A man behind us cleared his throat. "Can I help you?"

Beside me, Beck scrubbed his face with his hands and slicked back his hair.

"Yes, we need something for Beck to wear when he goes shooting."

"Very well. My name's Angus. Please follow me."

The shop looked tiny from the outside but seemed to go back for miles. We were the only customers, but the place was stocked as if they were expecting a sudden surge of people to descend on them at any moment. From the floor to the admittedly low ceiling were built-in, aged-oak cabinets and shelving stuffed full of shoes, shirts, jackets, walking sticks, boots, coats, trousers, kilts, wellingtons and binoculars. Every so often there was an island cabinet showcasing socks or cravats or ties. It was as if it had been airlifted from Saville Row right to the highlands of Scotland. We were bound to find everything we were looking for right here.

"Miss, if you'd like to take a seat." Angus indicated a small, buttoned, red velvet chair to the side of a cabinet full of blue ties of differing patterns. "Sir, if you want to make your way into the changing room, just there." Angus nodded toward an oak door right beside me. "I'll bring you some things," he said, then scurried away.

"What? He doesn't want to know my size or what I like?"

"This guy is what? Sixty? My guess is he's been doing this job about forty-five years. He'll know your size from looking at you and will know what you want better than you do."

"What I want is Henry's signature on those papers."

"Exactly."

Beck sighed, then his face cracked into a grin. "Wanna come in and make out with me before Angus comes back?"

I laughed. That was exactly what I wanted to do. But before I could respond, Angus returned, his arms weighed down with tweed, and he shooed Beck back into the changing rooms.

"I was expecting the fit to be less fashionable," Beck said as he came out in a three-piece, dark-green tweed suit.

"Yes," Angus said, apparently able to read minds. "It's a traditional label that likes to throw in a modern twist in some of their designs. May I say, it fits you as if it's been tailored."

Angus was right; the jacket clung to Beck's shoulders perfectly and the dark green seemed to bring out the green in his eyes.

"And you think a tie?" Beck asked, unbuttoning the jacket, showing off the waistcoat.

"Not everyone will be dressed formally, but Henry will be," I said, trying not to focus on how freaking good this guy looked in tweed. How was that even possible?

"And the color is right for grouse," Angus said.

"Then let's take it," Beck said. "What else?"

"I have a list," I said, pulling out the pad of paper and pen I'd brought from the hotel. "We need some shooting boots, a waterproof jacket. I think some moleskin jeans for the Fort William trip. Maybe a casual tweed jacket and a hat?" I wasn't sure I'd manage to get Beck into a hat, but it was worth a try.

"You can forget about the hat," Beck told Angus. "But the rest is fine."

Angus scurried away, and Beck turned to me. "I'm not a hat kind of man."

"You didn't think you were a tweed kind of man until

five minutes ago." He rolled his eyes. "If I ask you a question, will you tell me the truth?" I asked.

He frowned. "I've never lied to you."

Beck was right. He'd never given me any reason to doubt what he told me, but I was doubtful of everything at the moment.

"Why's the Dawnay building so important?" I asked. "You're a rich man. You own the rest of that block. You could make a lot of money without that property." He stepped forward to see if Angus was approaching and I got the feeling he'd welcome the interruption. But lucky for me, Angus was still gathering Beck's new wardrobe. "You're going to a lot of effort," I continued. "It feels personal."

Beck took a breath and exhaled as if he were surrendering. "Maybe it is."

I stayed silent, willing the words to flow. I wanted to know more. I wanted to know everything about this man.

"My mother used to live in the building. When she was first pregnant with me."

I knew there was something more to that building than the real estate, but such sentimentality was a shock. "You want to buy it for old time's sake?" I asked.

"Hardly. She was asked to leave just before she gave birth and she had nowhere to go. She told me the story when I was sixteen. I've been fixated on the building ever since."

The way he said it made everything completely obvious.

"Because she was asked to leave?"

He nodded, fiddling with the display of blue ties next to me. "Henry inherited the building from his cousin, Patrick Dawnay." He paused. "My biological father."

A chill snaked up my spine.

He'd talked about his dad—a man he clearly loved from

the way he described him. And a man who was very much alive. "I thought your dad was—"

"I never knew Patrick Dawnay. My dad raised me and is the only man I consider a father. Patrick Dawnay got my mother pregnant and then threw her away like she was nothing. She was his mistress and was provided with a flat in that building. But when she got pregnant, she got an eviction letter from his lawyer. Along with money for an abortion."

The edges of me curled up and I tried not to shudder.

Everything made sense now.

His obsession with the Dawnay building.

The determination to be different from people with old money. He didn't want to fit in. He didn't want to be a man who would do that to his mother.

I stood, stepped toward him and slid my arms around his waist. He stepped back, out of my reach.

"Don't feel sorry for me."

I looked up at him. "Not for you. For your mother. No one deserves that."

He nodded and this time he relented when I put my arms around him and placed my head on his chest.

"The Dawnay building won't exist when I'm finished with it."

"When *we're* finished with it," I corrected him.

"Do you always have to have the last word?" he asked.

"Pretty much. And I'm not done. The clothes aren't enough—they'll just make sure you don't stand out. You need to switch up how you are approaching this. You're self-sabotaging."

He sighed. "I know. I'm letting these people get under my skin. Every time I speak to someone, I want to ask them when they last did a full day's work."

"You'd be surprised," I said. "Have you met Matt's uncle Richard?"

"Nope."

"He doesn't have to work—his family trust is gigantic—but he's a pediatric neurosurgeon. Works full time in the NHS, doesn't even see private patients." He'd think I was making it up if I told him he liked to take on complicated cases from abroad on his off days.

Beck just nodded, and I could tell he was just thinking that there was always an exception, but people were people —rich or poor. Some were nice and some were arseholes.

"And Nancy Meadows, who I will introduce you to if I get a chance, works seven days a week, raising money for one charitable cause after another. The woman never takes a holiday. Last year she raised thirteen million pounds for a homeless charity. Not everyone born with money is worthless. And not everyone who made it on their own is a decent human being."

"I know, it's just . . ."

"You'll like Henry. He really is one of the good guys. Just give him a chance to show you."

"I *need* this building," he replied.

"Then you know what you need to do. You need to be charming, and friendly, and get Henry eating out of the palm of your hand. Once you connect, you'll like him—respect his opinion. I swear to you."

He nodded. "I need to focus on the goal and not get bogged down in the injustices . . ."

"Yes, keep the endgame in mind, but it might not be such a chore if you give these people a chance."

He pressed his lips to my forehead. "I don't know what I'd have done without you."

I closed my eyes, grateful that he'd needed me because

I'd needed him right back. Without him, I'd still be mourning a man who wasn't worth my tears, but now I was focused on my future. On the Dawnay building and the Mayfair development. We were going to get Henry to sign that building over, and we were going to rip that building to bits and rebuild it.

TWENTY-FOUR

Beck

I was hoping that Stella remembered I was supposed to be Julia Roberts in *Pretty Woman* and not Steve McQueen in *The Great Escape*. We'd stopped by Boots to pick up a nail brush and a pumice stone, which was on Stella's list, then at the entrance of the hotel, she'd scooped up some soil from the flowerbed, putting it in a small plastic bag she pulled out of her purse.

"I still don't understand what's happening," I said as I took a seat back in our hotel room. Stella was laying everything we'd purchased out on the bed.

"I'm going to show you. Can you get the scissors from the vanity pack in the bathroom, please?"

I'd just have to humor her. As I flicked on the bathroom light, images from the night before flashed into my head. Stella's skin was so smooth it was like gliding my tongue over gin-soaked ice. My hands had fit perfectly over her hips. And she'd smelled so good.

But sex was sex. It was rare not to enjoy it—even though

it had been exceptional with Stella. What was more surprising was how completely alluring it was that she'd been entirely focused on our mission today. And the way she'd held me when I'd confessed my connection to the Dawnay building had been . . . comforting—no, more than that, it had bound us together somehow. No one else knew why I wanted that building so badly. It had just sort of tumbled out earlier. I couldn't help it.

I'd always professed to like the shallows when it came to women, but I couldn't help but wade deeper with Stella. Every step forward, things got better between us, felt more right, as if I'd been waiting for this woman and now that she was here everything in my life made more sense.

She was kneeling by the bed when I handed her the scissors, completely focused on the lining of the jacket of the five-thousand-pound suit I'd just bought and would wear once. She snipped the thread of the lining and made a hole in the seam about three centimeters long.

"Is this some kind of passive-aggressive shit where you make me buy things and then destroy them because you're annoyed about me not going down on you for long enough or something?" I asked.

She paused what she was doing and looked up at me. "What kind of girls have you been dating?" Her expression was part horror, part pity. "And you went down on me plenty. Couldn't you tell by my nineteen orgasms?"

Stella had made me work for her climax, which meant I appreciated it all the more when I'd finally coaxed it from her. And it had made mine all the stronger. "I'm happy to try it again if you think it wasn't quite long enough. Wouldn't want to disappoint."

She grinned but shook her head as if I was some incorrigible fifteen-year-old boy obsessed with his older sister's best friend.

"Let's focus. You need this signature from Henry. Then after . . ." She shrugged. "Let's . . . let's just grab the trousers and sit on them," she said. "We don't want them looking too new." She reached for the pumice stone and started to rub it over the seam on the shoulders.

"You know, I'm starting to think you're a little bit crazy."

"Everything needs to look worn and not like we bought it ninety minutes ago."

"You mean you want it to look as if my grandfather bought the trousers and I'm so fucking stingy I've raided his wardrobe." I toed off my shoes.

"Open mind, remember." She looked at me with a grin so warm I felt the heat in my bones.

I took a seat next to her on the floor and picked up the pumice stone. "So, you know why I want the Dawnay building so badly. Why do you want the design job bad enough to watch your ex marry your best friend?"

She blew out a breath. "Shouldn't you be encouraging me, not questioning why I'm such a lunatic?"

I shrugged. "You're here now. For which I'm very thankful. But if I were in your shoes, I'm not sure anything could have dragged me here."

She blinked, closing her eyes for a second longer than normal, as if she were trying to wipe her mind clean of a memory. "Ironically, designing your Mayfair development is an opportunity to move forward after all that's happened. I hate my job, but I can't leave it until I have something else. I had a successful design business in Manchester but Matt had a job opportunity in London, so we moved down. I had started to build a new business, but when he . . . left, I'd only managed to get two small jobs. I wasn't properly established and I had a mortgage to pay—London's expensive."

"He left you with the mortgage?"

"I told him to leave. I didn't think through the cost of the place."

"He should have done the right thing and kept paying his share." My jaw tightened at the thought that Matt believed he could just drop Stella and leave her to pick up the pieces.

"It was my fault. I should have thought it through." She always took on every problem like it was her own.

"You should have asked him to contribute."

"I couldn't do that. He wasn't living there."

"But you gave up your business, moved cities for him." Stella didn't seem to see the injustice that was obvious to me.

"For me too. I wanted a life together and anyway, I love London. I always wanted to be there."

She didn't look at me the entire time she spoke. I wanted to tell her how sorry I was, but I knew she wouldn't want my pity. "You're good at giving. Not so good at taking," I said.

Ideas spun through my mind of what I could do for her. Maybe I could buy her something, pay her mortgage or something. It wasn't that Stella was a woman who couldn't look after herself—more that she was a girl who deserved to be spoiled.

This Matt guy needed someone to show him that girls like Stella didn't come along all the time. She'd made sacrifices to make him happy. She'd given things up for the good of their relationship, for a future together. She'd been part of a team, whereas he'd only been thinking of himself.

"As long as Henry signs on the dotted line, this Mayfair

development will turn things around for me. I've started sourcing suppliers already."

As nervous as I was about her taking on the project, I wanted her to do well and create a better future for herself. "Maybe I can put you in touch with a few people as well."

She looked up at me from beneath her lashes. "You'd do that?"

Didn't she get it? There wasn't a lot I wouldn't do for her.

"It's no problem. And I don't think I've ever said thank you for coming here and doing all this."

"It's not like I'm not getting something in exchange."

Was that what it was? A simple exchange? Perhaps I was making too much of what she was doing, but it felt like we were a team. That she was sitting on the hotel room floor, her arms deep in a sea of tweed because she *wanted* to help me.

"The Dawnay building's going to be a game changer for both of us," she said.

"Agreed. But can we stop calling it the Dawnay building?" I asked.

"What will you name it? The Wilde building?

"The entire development will be called One Park Street."

I didn't need to name the building after myself. I just wanted to erase its legacy. And at the same time, create a new one for myself. And Stella.

TWENTY-FIVE

Stella

I had a hot, semi-naked man in my bedroom, but the itinerary specified that *I* had to be semi-naked with a bunch of *women*.

There was nothing better than a day at the spa.

Usually.

And as well as not being with Beck, I risked having to speak to Karen.

"Stella," Karen called as soon as I stepped into the relaxation room—a darkened space, lit only by candles that reflected off the gold walls. Whale music played in the background and loungers were organized around a central display of stones and crystals. "There's a free seat here."

Typical that she'd be the first person I'd run into.

Before she'd run off with my boyfriend, I would have assumed she was being nice by offering me a seat, but now, I couldn't imagine it was possible for her to do anything nice for anyone. Perhaps she wanted to put on a show for the other people, or maybe she just needed to feel better about herself. Either way, I wasn't going to give her the satisfaction of making a scene by refusing her offer.

At least Florence was on the other side of me.

"I was just telling Florence that I hadn't seen much of you," she said, patting the chaise lounge next to her. "I want to hear all about your new man."

I had to dampen down a smile instead of the panic that usually came when I had to talk about my fake boyfriend. If nothing else, Beck was now my very *real* lover. "What is it that you want to know?" I asked.

"Is it serious? What's he like?" she asked.

"It is from what I've seen," Florence interrupted. "He's charming, generous, funny, and crazy about Stella."

Florence was quite possibly the best human being. She knew I was a useless liar. But for the first time in a long time, I didn't feel the need for protection. "You've not seen anything until you've seen him naked," I added.

Florence's eyes widened, and I nodded.

"Good for fucking you," she said, and I grinned. "You know what? With a man like that, I'm not sure I'd make it out of the bedroom."

"I needed some recovery time," I said and that was the truth. After our first night together, I needed some mental space to process the things he'd made me feel. But after last night, it was physical recovery I needed. Every muscle and bone ached. And I wasn't sure if it was from the things we'd done or my desire to do each one again.

"So, it's just casual sex?" Karen asked.

Nothing I'd said had suggested that. "I didn't say it was casual." I grabbed a magazine from the pile on the table between Florence and me.

"But it can't be all that serious," Karen said. "You've only been together a few months."

There were lots of things that were unbelievable about me being at this wedding, but Beck was right, one of them was that I'd never confronted Karen and Matt. Maybe the reason they thought they could betray me so fundamentally and then expect everything to be hunky-dory was because I wasn't the kind to confront people—that I was too focused on not making people uncomfortable, that I wanted everyone to be happy and get along.

I'd been trampled on for far too long.

"Who cares if it's casual?" Florence interjected. "Beck's so hot, I'd take whatever he was offering."

"Yeah," Karen said. "He doesn't look the marrying kind."

"Well, someone looking for marriage isn't necessarily the best kind," I replied, flicking through the pages of my magazine but not taking them in. I wanted Karen to stop commenting on my love life like she hadn't stolen my boyfriend. Clearly Matt was available to be stolen but still— she should have some shame. "Just a few months ago, I was dating someone who I thought was the marrying kind and look how that ended up." I put my magazine down and turned to Karen, my pulse thudding in my ears as I tried to gather my courage. "I spent seven years with Matt and he's marrying you. Perhaps I don't want someone who pretends to want to marry me and then ends up marrying my best friend."

I could almost hear Florence's jaw hit the floor behind me as I blew out a breath and my shoulders slid down from where they were up by my ears.

I'd been keeping all that in, squashed up like a ball, and now it was out, I had more room.

Karen blinked, furiously. "Well, if you felt like that, I don't understand why you came."

"Felt like what? Hurt? Betrayed? Devastated?" Did she really think I'd be fine with it? "Given what you did, I don't understand why you invited me," I replied.

"I thought you'd be happy for us. It wasn't like the two of you were still living together."

I snorted, blown away by her lack of empathy. I'd been trying to find a reason for what happened—if only I hadn't insisted on the blue lounge chair or agreed to move down to London, but it was obvious now.

None of this was my fault.

The elephant that had been sitting on my chest since I received the invitation had moved on to rest his arse somewhere else. "If that were true then you would have had the decency to tell me to my face that you were marrying my boyfriend. I wouldn't have found out when I opened the invitation." She didn't think I'd be happy for her; she just didn't care.

"People can't help falling in love, Stella. I thought you'd understand."

She thought I'd understand because I always had. I'd always excused her selfish behavior, constantly put her happiness ahead of my own—I did it with everyone. And I'd had enough.

"I was in love with him for seven years, or did you forget?" I asked. After all these years, Karen's motives for most things still flummoxed me. Was it possible that they were truly in love?

Either way, I didn't have to pretend I was happy for them.

She looked at me, her eyes wide and her mouth parted as if she didn't know if she should run or scream at me.

"Was it worth it? Are you happy?" I asked, genuinely wanting to know. Would marrying my ex-boyfriend fulfil her? Had losing a friend she'd had since she was five years old made her feel good?

"Of course," she said, and I could almost see her feathers bristle. She checked her watch. "I think they might have forgotten about me. I'm going to see what the delay is."

"Absolutely," I agreed. "They shouldn't be keeping the bride-to-be waiting."

My limbs were floating, like I'd already had my massage. I always assumed confrontation brought anger and frustration but for me, telling Karen how I felt seemed to have instilled some kind of peace.

"Well, good for you," Florence whispered as we watched Karen leave. "I've been waiting for years for you to stand up to her. I can't believe she thought you'd be happy for her."

"That's how much of a doormat I've been," I said.

"It says far more about her than you, but I do like this new Stella. Has spending time with Beck made you brave?"

"I'm not sure brave's the word." Time with Beck hadn't given me courage, but it had given me a little bit of distance and perspective, away from the drama and debacle. Beck was an outsider, who had no skin in the game. Florence had been telling me for years I should stand up to Karen, but somehow seeing myself through Beck's eyes changed things.

"If Beck doesn't make you brave, how does he make you feel?" Florence grinned so wide I couldn't help but smile back—because of Beck but also because I had a friend like Florence who wanted me to be happy. Friends like her were rarer than I used to believe.

"Like I have more room to breathe," I replied. "He's . . . I mean, it's nothing—we're stuck up here together and it's . . .

convenient. But I'm twenty-six and I've never had a fling, so I guess this is the holiday romance I never had."

"It's way overdue. And you never know, it's not like he's Marco Russo and heading back to Italy in a couple of months."

I laughed. Marco Russo—how did Florence remember things like our Italian student teacher when we were fourteen? Every girl in the school had been utterly distracted by his swarthy looks and had completely underperformed in the end-of-school exams. "Back then you were all about going to Italy when we finished the exams."

"Like he would have even remembered our names at the end of the year," she said.

"Right? He never knew our names in the first place."

"I'd never seen a man so attractive," Florence said. "I was sure that if I could find him in Italy, he'd fall in love with me, we'd get married, live in Tuscany, and paint and be happy forever."

We'd all had childhood fantasies that seemed ludicrous now. Just like the thought that I was going to marry Matt seemed now like something that had always been utterly impossible.

"You seem happy," Florence said. "When you're with Beck."

I guess I was. But I wasn't going to let myself think that it was something more than it was. "You're ridiculous." I tossed my magazine back on the table between us. "Beck is a stopgap. He's a something that happens before real things happen. Like the anesthetic before an operation or the canape before the main meal." The words tasted bitter on my tongue. I wasn't sure that was true for me. Beck felt like the start of something, but I didn't want to be that naïve girl who tumbled into something and got taken advantage of, again.

If Beck wasn't my future, he was a whisper of a future— a hint that there could be something after all that had happened. For the first time in a long time, I was starting to wonder what would make me happy.

TWENTY-SIX

Beck

I'd woken up resolved. Stella was right. I knew what I needed to do. I just had to focus on the goal and not get hung up on what these people—Henry's cousin—had done to my mother.

Stella had helped me focus. She brought out the best in me.

My new clothes, pumiced and muddy in places, made me look like everyone else, and I nodded at a few people as I made my way toward the group of men gathered at the edge of the sweeping drive.

"Morning," I said. "Beautiful day for it." I'd come across these people in my life—hell I was good friends with a couple of trust funders. Stella told me that Henry was a good man and although it was difficult for me to believe that someone related to Patrick Dawnay could be decent, I trusted her.

Henry was over by the keeper, so I headed in that direction.

"We're shooting wild birds today, not grouse reared on the estate." Matt stepped up beside me, dressed in a light-green tweed suit, brown socks up to his knees and a flat cap to match.

At a distance, he could have been fifty years older than he was. I'd drawn the line at headgear, and although Stella had wanted me to wear breeks and wellies, I'd insisted on trousers and walking boots. "Are you ready?" he asked.

"As I'll ever be," I replied.

Stella had insisted that I do my homework on what a grouse shoot involved. I was usually well prepared, but I'd been resisting it, rejecting every part of this way of life—perhaps because I'd been rejected by it in the first place. Patrick Dawnay hadn't wanted me, had pushed me and my mother aside, and I didn't want to want any part of it. But, as Stella said, if I wanted the Dawnay building, I had to do whatever it took.

"Do you like shooting?" Matt asked.

"Golf is more my thing," I said.

"Excellent," he said. "Perhaps we should play a few holes when I'm back from my honeymoon. The girls can get together for lunch and leave us boys to it."

Why on earth would he think I'd want to spend time with him? He was Stella's ex-boyfriend. And even if he wasn't, I had enough friends. Five super-competitive arse-holes were enough to contend with. There weren't any vacancies in my friendship circle.

"How are you enjoying Scotland?" he asked. "That rain yesterday was dreadful, but at least we're seeing the sun today. I didn't want to have to cancel."

"You don't call off a shoot because of a spot of rain, man," Henry barked at Matt as he came up beside us. "We wear waterproofs and get on with it."

"I enjoy the rain," I said, because it was the truth. "I never miss a run because of weather."

"Quite right," Henry said. "You'd never go outside in Scotland if you were afraid of a bit of water." He sniffed, then turned to me. "So, you're Stella's new chap, are you?" he asked.

"Yes, sir."

"Well, she's a lovely girl. I'm very fond of her. Known her since she was a small child. She was always clever but never shouted about it. I liked that about her."

Henry and I agreed on one thing at least. "She underestimates herself," I said. "Very modest despite being quite . . . wonderful." It was easy to be honest when I was talking about how great Stella was.

He nodded. "Puts other people first. Other people who frankly don't deserve it." He shot a glance at Matt, who had the good sense to be pretending not to hear what we were talking about.

"I've just seen Phillip. Please excuse me," Matt said. "I must go and ask him about his speech."

"Yes, he should scuttle off," Henry said. "The way he and my god-daughter have treated Stella has been absolutely terrible. Selfish and entitled—both of them. Stella's better off without him."

A grin filled my face. "I couldn't have put it better myself. But his loss is my gain."

"Just make sure you realize what you've got in that girl."

I'd liked Stella from the moment I'd met her, found her attractive, enjoyed her feistiness. But getting to know her had brought an entirely new level of captivation with her. I respected her as well as enjoyed her company and couldn't keep my hands off her. "Every day I realize it a little more," I replied.

"I've never understood womanizers. When I found my wife, I was determined to marry her. I saw how kind she was. She brought out the best in me and I could make her laugh. What more could I possibly want? And all these years later? It's still the same—together we make each other better."

I looked out onto the countryside, all mossy greens and muted browns. That was Stella—she made me better. She saw things in me that others didn't, and she coaxed the best out of me.

"All Matt knows how to do is take," Henry said. "Perhaps Karen is what he needs. If he'd married Stella, she would never have known what being adored and respected felt like. And she deserves that. She's a special soul."

"Very special," I agreed. Gut instinct had guided me well during the course of my career, and at that moment it was telling me that there was more to what Henry was saying than him just giving me a warning to look after Stella. It was almost as if he knew that we weren't really together, and he was warning me not to pass up the opportunity to keep her in my life when this week was up.

But perhaps that was my mind playing tricks on me.

"You've shot grouse before?" Henry asked.

"Never," I admitted. "Not really my scene. I've shot clays a few times. And a lot of soup cans."

"Ahhh, sounds like me as a boy. With my air rifle at the back of the stables." I chuckled. Perhaps Henry and I had more in common than I imagined. "That's clearly why you were such a good shot the other day."

"Soup cans come in handy," I said.

"I take it you haven't brought your own gun?"

I shook my head.

"I didn't bring mine either. I'll help you pick one out. Follow me."

As we walked toward the keeper, Matt's chortle echoed out across the party. Henry cleared his throat. "I told Karen that a man who's prepared to cheat on a woman, will cheat on *any* woman."

"I think those are wise words," I replied.

"You look after Stella. Maybe the next time I see you, after this week, it will be at your wedding."

I didn't have to make an effort to agree with Henry. The last few weeks with Stella had been fun. She'd found the whole idea of pretending we were dating more stressful than I had. Relationships for me had never required any effort but with Stella . . . I was much better at being a fake boyfriend than a real one. Being a fake boyfriend was far more demanding—we were more like teammates with a shared goal. But I preferred it like that, which had me thinking that maybe that's what relationships were meant to be about. I laughed. "Well, we're not quite at that point yet."

Henry stopped and looked me dead in the eye. "You seem like a man who knows what he wants. If you want Stella, then don't mess her around."

I admired how protective he was over her.

Stella had a way of making me see things differently, even if she didn't do it on purpose. She shook things up like a snow globe, and when everything settled down still again, things were back to normal but were forever changed.

"Yes, this will do for you," Henry said, handing me a shotgun, and pulling me away from my thoughts of Stella and wondering what things would be like when the snow settled and I went back to life before her. Whether that was even possible.

"Perhaps we can carve out some time this week to talk more about the Dawnay building," I said.

"Oh that's right," Henry said. "You said you'd tried to set up a meeting about it. Did you want to lease it?" he asked. "It would need overhauling, I'm afraid. It's in a dreadful state."

"Actually, I'd like to buy it from you."

His eyebrows disappeared under his hat. "I don't think it's for sale." He didn't sound very convinced. "At least, I've never considered selling it."

"I can offer you a good price. But I need to move things along quickly, I'm afraid. It's a short window of opportunity, but like you say, the place needs work, even to let. If you sold it to me, you could invest in something else that's easier to generate revenue from."

Henry nodded but stayed silent. I didn't want to push. I needed to be patient. Let the idea settle.

"Let me know the price you're thinking. I'll give it some thought. In the meantime, if you've got any paperwork I can look at or I can send to my lawyers, then let me have it."

I was holding my breath as he spoke, not quite believing that we were having this conversation and that he hadn't dismissed the idea out of hand.

I wasn't sure if it was the tweed I was wearing or the warning I'd gotten from Stella to give Henry the benefit of the doubt, but something had shifted. If I kept listening to Stella, the Dawnay building might finally be mine.

TWENTY-SEVEN

Beck

The lock on the hotel room door whirred and Stella appeared in the doorway, grinning as if she'd been waiting to see me. Her expression hit me like a physical force, almost knocking me off my chair. It was like seeing me made her happy.

It felt fucking fantastic.

"How many defenseless little grouse did you murder today?" she asked as she kicked off her shoes. I put down my phone on the table to give her my full attention. Her hair was piled high on her head, and her face was free of make-up.

She looked beautiful.

"Funny. And you'd be proud." I gestured her over with a nod of my head.

"I would?" When she was close enough, I grabbed her hand and pulled her between my thighs.

"I bonded with Henry. You have quite the fan there."

She forked her fingers through my hair. "I do?"

"Yeah. He likes you a lot. Not Matt's biggest fan from what I can tell."

"Really? Well, that makes two of us." She leaned against me as I rested my hands at the tops of her thighs.

"You sure about that?" I asked her. "If he dumped Karen and told you he'd made the biggest mistake of his life, what would you do?"

"Agree with him."

"Would you take him back?" I asked. Stella had so much to offer—she didn't need to waste that on an idiot who didn't appreciate her.

"It's never going to happen, so I don't need to spend time and energy thinking about *what-ifs*."

It was such an evasion—did she really not understand that she was worth more?

"You'd just go along with it?" I asked. Because that's what Stella did. She went along with things to make other people happy, without really thinking about what she wanted.

"I've not given it much thought." She paused. "But no." She exhaled, her eyebrows pulling together as if she were deep in thought. "No, I don't think I would. I'd always be waiting for it to happen again. And anyway, Matt's not the man I thought he was. He's . . . different. I mean, I was wrong about him. What he's done is unforgivable, but . . ."

"There's a 'but'?" I asked. She couldn't think that what he had done was justified.

"Yeah. There's part of me—a very small part of me— that thinks it's not the worst thing that could have happened. What if we had got married and *then* I'd found out he and Karen were sleeping together or that he didn't love me the way I loved him. I don't know if it's being here at their wedding but, although it's still painful, I believe things will get better for me. I'll get to London and I'll figure stuff out."

I couldn't stop smiling. I hoped I'd had a part to play in her believing the future held promise. I pulled her down onto my knee. Perhaps I'd show her how good things could be.

I slid my hand up her skirt. I was done talking about Matt. "How was the spa? What did they do to you?"

She squirmed as my hand dove between her thighs.

"Erm, I had a massage?"

"Who touched you? A girl or a guy?"

"A girl, why? Are you jealous?"

I nestled my finger underneath the lace of her knickers. "It depends," I replied. "Did you have a happy ending?"

She threw her head back and laughed and I grinned—not at my question but at the glorious sound of Stella happy. It was indisputable that Matt was an idiot for cheating on her with her best friend. But what if I gave her up when we got back to London? What did that make me?

She gasped and grabbed my shoulder as my fingers delved into her. "No, you're the only instigator of my orgasms this week."

Which was how it should be.

"You haven't told me how it went with Henry," she said, shifting so my thumb grazed her clit, enjoying her shiver.

"You want me to talk to you about my day while I'm getting you off?" Did couples do that?

She smiled then pressed a kiss on my cheek. "No, but I do want to hear about it."

"Orgasms first," I said, and pulled my hand away and lifted her onto her feet. She looked confused and then I began to undress her, lifting her t-shirt over her head. "And then we'll talk shop."

"If you insist. I'm not going to complain."

"No, I'll make sure you have nothing to complain about." I released the clasp on her bra, and she shrugged off the straps as I knelt to unbutton her skirt. These clothes were for the people outside of this room. They were part of the act—a mask, armor—but this space, the private time between her and me, that was real.

Once naked, she lay back on the bed, her arm bent, and her head resting on her hand as she watched me undress. "I like hanging out with you," she said, and my heartbeat skipped, giving emphasis to what she was saying—painting the words in bold type.

I wanted it to mean more.

I wanted her to feel more.

"I like hanging out with you, too."

I peeled off the last of my clothes and took her in, naked and waiting for me. I couldn't rush this. I wanted to breathe in every curve, every dip and arc of her. To map her body with my tongue and then try to explain how fucking insatiable she made me. I stepped forward and trailed my fingers up her body like a blind man reading the secrets of eternal life. I wanted to make sure I didn't miss anything, that I'd taken in every last word she told me.

"You okay?" she asked. "You seem intense. You want to talk about Henry?"

She didn't think it was possible that I was intensely fascinated by her. "I'm not thinking about Henry. I'm thinking about how sensational your body is."

She slid her hand over mine. "Really?" she asked.

"Is that so difficult to believe?" I supposed when the man you thought you were going to spend the rest of your life with ended up cheating on you, it was easy to believe you weren't worthy of . . . admiration? Worship.

She didn't answer and I continued my exploration.

I wasn't sure I'd ever taken my time with a woman the way I did with Stella. I never liked to rush things, but that was so the end result was intensified. I liked to take my time with Stella because I wanted to savor the moment—not just build up to orgasm. I needed to squeeze out every last drop of being with her, soak myself in her. I'd never experienced anything like it before.

"Flip onto your stomach," I said, guiding her over.

I swallowed as the lines and curves changed, her skin highlighted by the hazy, setting sun coming through the windows. "Let's skip dinner," I said. "We have all day tomorrow to spend with these people. Tonight, we should do this."

She glanced over her shoulder at me, as if checking she'd heard me right. A small smile turned up the corners of her mouth—part suspicion, part unease. I got the uneasy part. The feelings Stella stirred in me were unfamiliar. I'd never spent much time fully clothed with the women I dated. But it was more than just knowing her well that set her apart. It was because Stella was Stella.

Unselfish.

Thoughtful.

Sexy.

There were a thousand things I liked about her.

I lifted her hips and pulled her back so her legs hit the floor. "Like this, I think." She went up onto her forearms, her breasts grazing the mattress, and I growled at the memory of how they felt in my mouth.

Later.

I reached for a condom. I needed to fuck Stella hard and quickly tonight. Needed to claim her—to make her see what I saw in her.

Leaning over her, I whispered in her ear, "I'm going to make you come so hard, you're going to forget everything bad and only remember the good stuff." I wanted her to forget her suspicions and bruised heart. I wanted her to know what being able to trust someone felt like. I slipped my hands over her shoulders, stroking my thumb over the dip at the top of her neck with one hand and then I trailed down the valley of her spine with my other. When I reached the base of her back, I kept going down between her arse cheeks, over her arsehole and into her opening.

She was soaked; her wetness fueling my lust. I was done just feeling her on the outside. I needed to be inside.

I put my thumb in her mouth, had her suck it clean, and then positioned my cock. Instead of taking it slow, I entered her in one hard, fast thrust, pulling her onto me as I pushed forward, getting deep, deep, deep.

She cried out so loud anyone on the lawns outside our window would hear. Hell, most people within a half-mile radius would.

"You're going to break me in two," she cried out, her hands bunched full of sheets.

"Never," I growled.

I pulled back and thrust in again, hard and fast. She let out the same desperate moan, one melting into the next. My balls tightened, and I anchored my hand around her waist. I had to steady her, keep her still, and I needed to be close to her, to feel every vibration across her skin.

"More," she cried out as I stilled.

I thrust again, not stopping this time before I pulled out and plowed into her over and over. I couldn't tell who was making which sounds as they bounced off the walls of the room.

Her back arched. "I'm . . . Please. Beck, please let me come."

This wasn't the time to make her wait. Our lust and desire had pushed us into a different state of consciousness and orgasm was the only route out. I wasn't going to be able to hold back anymore than she was.

But the way she asked my permission, the way she had waited for me to say yes before she fully let herself go—it was too much. She was too much.

"Come, baby." The words scorched my throat, and before the command had fully left my lips, she began to quiver under my fingers. My climax pushed from the base of my spine, spinning, circling, and pressing out and up. It went on and on until I was bursting out of my skin.

I wrapped my arms around Stella's waist, holding her tight as she bucked underneath me, her orgasm combining with mine as we cried out in unison.

I fell onto the bed, still holding her. Our jagged breathing settled as we found our rhythm.

"Beck . . ."

I waited for her to finish her thought. What would she say? Would she comment on how intense it was? But she left the sentence unfinished, almost as if she expected me to fill the gap.

She twisted in my arms so we were facing each other and placed her palms on my chest. "Far more relaxing than the spa."

I laughed. "Did you enjoy your day?"

She tilted her head, nuzzling into my body with a sigh. Wanting to commit her contentment to memory, I closed my eyes at the sensation of her breath on my skin. After fucking, my mind was usually elsewhere, either on fucking again or on my emails as I reached for my phone, ready to chase the next development, close the next deal. All I wanted to do with Stella was to be right here. With her in my arms.

"I can't remember my day," she replied. "But you need to tell me about Henry. You said you bonded."

"Over you. I get the impression he's not too impressed with Karen's behavior."

She didn't respond.

"You might be right about him. He might be one of the good ones."

"I'm looking forward to hearing you say that I'm right a lot when we start the design process."

"Don't bet on it. I'm a tough client to please."

"Oh yeah?" she asked, pulling out of my arms and wriggling down the bed as she grabbed the base of my cock.

I chuckled and then groaned as she kneeled between my thighs. I glanced across to the bedside table then handed her a hair clip. There was no chance I was missing the visuals.

She grinned and pulled her hair back, exposing her high, tight breasts and flat stomach. Sophie's choice: My dick in her mouth, which was likely to be epic, or her skin sliding against mine as I fucked her again, this time face-to-face.

I wanted both options immediately.

Stella was teaching me a lot about patience.

Her hair tied back, she bent, fisting my cock in her hand. Her grip was perfect—confident and strong. She glanced up, wet her lips, and swallowed. I could have come right there, all over that perfectly smooth neck, and it would have been the best blow job I'd ever had.

It would be all over far too quickly if I watched right away, so I shifted so I was staring at the ceiling when I felt her tongue connect to the underside of my cock. It was like a starting pistol had been fired. I clenched my hands and tried to take a steadying breath as she licked long, steady strokes up to my crown. This was a marathon, not a sprint . . . I hoped.

As she took my tip in her mouth and started to suck, I had to focus on keeping my hips on the bed and not ramming deep into her throat. Then she pulled back, licking up one side then down the other. Every millimeter of skin she touched buzzed and intensified the growl underneath my skin. She circled my crown with her tongue, and I willed her to take me into her mouth, but she was making me wait. Paying me back. It was pure, delicious torture, and I was going to have to live with it.

Impossibly slowly, she took me deeper and deeper, tighter and tighter and tighter, and then she pulled back and used just a little teeth.

At that moment I would have signed over my entire fortune to her if she let me flip her over onto her back and fuck her mouth into the mattress. But I held still, paralyzed with need and lust until she groaned, and I couldn't hold back anymore. Some women made noises when they gave blow jobs, and it always filled me with suspicion—was that what they thought men wanted? Had they seen that when watching porn or reading *Cosmo*? But with Stella, her sounds were so uninhibited, so real and needy, that there was no doubt she loved sucking my dick.

I'd never wanted a woman so much in my life.

"I have to come," I announced.

"In my mouth?" she asked.

I didn't have time for a discussion. I pulled her onto the bed and flipped her to her back. "Lie there." I took my dick in my hands. I wanted to see her as I came. To watch every naked part of her. She brought one leg up as if to hide herself, and I shook my head and pulled her knee wide, opening her pussy and revealing her wetness.

Fuck, yes. My dick in her mouth had done that to her.

I pushed into my hand, once, twice, and when she lifted the back of her hand to her mouth, wiping herself clean of me, I erupted all over my stomach, her name booming through the room.

"You're fucking amazing," I said, collapsing back onto the bed.

"I barely touched you," she replied, pressing her hot palm against my chest.

"And look what you did. I'm a fucking mess. Your body . . . Your . . . everything."

I was skirting too close to saying something before I knew what it was I wanted to say. I had to reel in my confessions, how these feelings were pushing up and breaking the surface of my soul. I wanted to be a man Stella wanted, craved, and deserved.

TWENTY-EIGHT

Stella

I should have been dreading a day trip with the people who'd hurt me most in the world, but with Beck by my side, I was actually looking forward to it. "Have you done many coach trips before?" I squeezed his hand as we strode across the courtyard toward the bus waiting to take us to Fort William.

"Do I look eighty to you?"

I squinted, trying to get a good look at him. "Maybe on a bad day," I replied.

He glared at me.

"Oh right, you don't have bad days. That's what Tom Ford does for you. The rest of us put up with Zara and plenty of days looking like we haven't slept in a week."

"Zara or not, I've never seen you looking anything other than fucking phenomenal."

My stomach dived to my knees. There was no one to overhear us, no need to pretend, yet the things Beck said when we were in public or private . . . He was nicer to me, more complimentary than Matt had ever been.

"The Scottish weather must be getting to you," I replied. Beck was the kind of guy who could get up at five in the morning and scrape his hands through his hair and be catwalk ready. Most of us weren't so lucky.

Raised voices by the door to the coach caught my attention and a man with a clipboard and hair as orange as a traffic cone smiled at Karen through gritted teeth.

"I don't know what to tell you," the driver said. "The booking is on the system for forty-four."

"We made it for forty-eight. There are still four more passengers than seats available."

"We could drive," Beck told Karen. "That way I can subject Stella to easy listening music."

"You do *not* like easy listening," I said, pulling on his arm.

"I'm not going to confess stuff like that when we first start dating, am I? I have to save the dodgy taste and bad habits until it's too late. I guess now is as good a time as any to confess . . ." He took a deep breath. "I love the Carpenters."

I collapsed into laughter. In some ways Beck had a gigantic ego—mainly wrapped up with his work and his lack of family money—but he threw me a curveball every now and then by not giving a shit what people thought about him.

"Let's drive—we can sing along in peace," I suggested.

We turned back to Karen and she rolled her eyes. "So that's two people down. Matt and I will drive too to give us some alone time."

A week ago, a comment like that would have hurt, brought

her betrayal back with a vengeance. But now her comments slid off me like oil to my water—she'd lost the power to hurt me. She wasn't working for my forgiveness. She seemed determined to only care about herself. I'd always been envious of her independence, of the way she charged through life, fearless and determined. But she wasn't so much fearless as careless. She wasn't so much determined as detached from people's feelings.

I'd been looking through dirty glass for years and suddenly someone had come along with some white vinegar and a cleaning cloth. But just because I could see her clearly didn't mean it didn't hurt. It also meant I was always looking around, wondering where the other dirty windows were. Who else was I seeing the way I wanted to see them rather than the way they really were?

I didn't trust my judgement.

"Is that okay?" Beck asked as we headed toward the car. "Are you worried the rental is too new money?"

I laughed. "How come you wanted to drive?" I asked.

"Rather than sit on a bus and play eye spy? I'd definitely rather drive." He aimed the key fob at the car and the lights flashed before he opened the passenger door. "We can hang out, you can give me shit, and make me laugh. And I wasn't joking about the Carpenters either."

I climbed into the car, fiddling with my phone. Bringing up their greatest hits on Spotify, I nestled the phone into the holder on the dash, connecting it to the Bluetooth. "What do you want first?" I asked as he slid into the driver's seat. "*Close To You? Superstar?*"

"I don't mind. Start at the top."

The first song was *Superstar*. The intro played, and the first line rang out. "I thought you were going to sing?" I said.

"I'm not good at multitasking," he said as he made a sharp left turn onto the drive, heading out of the hotel grounds. "Given how anxious you get in the car, I would have thought you would want me to concentrate."

"Just when it's rain—"

Before I could finish my sentence, he launched into a word-perfect sing-along, complete with intonation and emphasis.

"You not joining in?" he asked at a break between verses.

"Oh, I'm appreciating it as a spectator rather than a member of the band." I tried to swallow down a laugh, though it wasn't at his singing. It was more that this super cool, sometimes surly, Tom Ford-wearing gazillionaire was happily singing along to easy listening.

He fiddled with the steering wheel and the music faded into the background. "So, tell me a bit about Fort William. Is that where the secrets of the upper classes are buried? Am I going to commit social suicide if I don't know that Matt's grandfather founded the place in fourteen fifty-seven?"

Beck might think that buying the Dawnay building was going to lay to rest some ghosts, but something told me it wasn't the building that was going to heal the hurt Beck still held.

"Well, from what Florence told me, today is just a lunch overlooking Loch Linne."

"I can't believe we're not hiking here. We're a stone's throw away from Ben Nevis. The area's beautiful. I looked it up and the hiking is really just a walk through the grounds." He shook his head. "I suppose they have to cater to the majority. It just seems such a waste of the landscape around here."

"I've never hiked in Scotland, but from what I've seen, it looks like it would be gorgeous."

"You've been up here and never hiked? You've got to be kidding me. The boys and I practically lived up here doing our Duke of Edinburgh gold award."

"I guess I've only ever been up with Matt and he never wanted to hike. Didn't like the rain."

"Well, I'm going to bring you back and we're going to hike."

I held my breath, waiting for him to follow up his comment. Had he meant to suggest future plans? It was just the two of us in the car. There was no need to put on a show, so why was he suggesting we come back here? I'd seen Beck and I as a temporary thing—a holiday romance—but was he thinking that we might be more? My heartbeat began to boom in my ears, like a siren blasting—warning me—but of what? I wasn't going to let myself think about it. I was determined just to enjoy the moment with Beck and be grateful he was healing the wounds Matt had created.

"No camping though, right?" It was as noncommittal a reply as I could come up with.

"I'm not making any promises. Waking up in the middle of nature—it's . . . That kinda shit's important."

I laughed. "That kinda shit? You're a regular philosopher. You should write a book, offer counseling."

"I might say it badly, but it doesn't make it any less true."

"Well make sure you don't say it badly with Henry today. Are you going to talk to him about the Mayfair property?"

"I've got to. I can't chance it and wait until the ceremony when there might be a chance I miss him. I've got to find my opportunity today. I got the papers he requested ready to send through. I just hope he looks at them fast. We don't have a lot of time."

"Florence emailed me the table plan—we're at the opposite end of the room from Henry," I said. "So I think you should try to speak to him before everyone sits down. I'll just be a distraction, but you can get down to business if it's just the two of you. I'll find Florence and Gordy or head to the bar or something."

It might not be up to me to close the deal on the Dawnay building, but this was maybe even more my future than it was Beck's. After weeks of licking my wounds, the trip here had woken something in me, or perhaps it had closed the door on something. Now I was impatient to get started on my future—whether or not that future included Beck.

AFTER SEARCHING HIGH and low for Florence, I'd spotted her and Gordy in the car park, having a heated conversation, and I'd decided it wasn't my place to interrupt just because I didn't want to be wandering around the restaurant trying to avoid Matt and Karen and their families. Just a few weeks ago, I considered many people in this room *my* family, yet here we were avoiding each other's eyelines and pretending each other didn't exist.

I might not know exactly where my future lay, but I knew it wasn't among the people here.

"A gin and tonic, please," I asked the barman as I faced toward the bar, so as not to catch anyone's eye.

"You okay?" the barman asked, and I realized I was staring at him.

"Yes, completely fine. How are you?" I was being an idiot. I was a confident, capable woman in her prime, and I wasn't the one who should be avoiding anyone. I'd done nothing wrong. I took my drink and turned slightly to admire the view, grinning as I saw Beck talking to Henry. He was totally going to get the Dawnay building. I was sure of it. He could convince anyone of anything.

"Stella," a familiar voice came from behind me and I froze.

This couldn't be happening.

This was why I'd been hiding.

As much as I hadn't wanted to spend time with Karen, the very last thing I wanted to do was to speak to my ex-boyfriend.

"Matt?" I turned and looked at him, trying to fix my face with some kind of neutral expression.

His eyes were wide and red and the tendons in his neck bulging as if he were ready to hit someone. "What are you doing here?" he hissed, glancing around to check that no one was watching.

"At Fort William?" I asked, not quite understanding the question. "It was part of the itinerary, I—"

"This entire week? Why did you come?" He reached to grab my wrist, but I moved my arm and stepped out of his way just in time.

"What do you mean? You invited me," I said.

How was he angry with *me*?

"You weren't supposed to say yes, Stella. You're making a complete fool of yourself. Can't you see?"

As though a tide was turning in my stomach, nausea mixed with confusion and the sense of being cornered by an enemy.

There was so much anger and blame in his expression.

Anger at *me*. Yet it was me who was supposed to be angry. *He* was to blame. He'd run off with my best friend.

What had I done?

"If you hadn't wanted me here, you shouldn't have invited me," I said, trying to keep my voice steady despite feeling like I was trying to keep afloat on choppy waters.

The injustice of the situation was tempered by the shame that Matt always managed to sprinkle over me. Like when he told me I was being pretentious whenever I showed him a piece of furniture I'd found that would look good in our flat. Like the look he gave me when I won the pitch to redesign the interior of a local hotel up in Manchester. I'd never noticed before, but now that I thought about it, Matt made me feel ashamed of many things I was excited about.

"This is so typical of you, Stella. Needy. Desperate."

Matt and I had gone to India the summer of our graduation. On our first night in Delhi, on the way back from dinner, we came across an elephant and its owner in the middle of the city. The owner was charging tourists to take pictures with the elephant. I didn't understand how such a powerful animal was so easily led with a simple chain around its thick ankle. It could run his owner down and escape back to family and friends. How had the owner trained it to follow him?

It was only now, standing in front of Matt, that I realized.

The elephant had been conditioned to expect pain if it stepped out of line. It was the *fear* of hurt that stopped it from trying to flee.

The elephant's pain was physical. The pain Matt inflicted on me over the years was mental. But both the elephant and I had been cowed.

Diminished.

We'd both had our power taken away.

And standing in front of him, I could still feel the pull

of the chain, the rub of his ire, and I wasn't sure if I had the strength left to charge over him and free myself.

"Karen wanted to be nice. I told her you'd pull a stunt like this. You're completely oblivious to reality, Stella."

I didn't know what to say. This was a man I loved for seven years. A man I'd trusted, thought I'd have a family with, yet he looked at me with a mixture of contempt, anger, and irritation as if we were almost strangers. "You invited me," I repeated. I could hardly tell him it was the last place I wanted to be.

"What did you expect when you came up here? That I'd change my mind? You should have realized years ago that we were only a temporary thing. I never proposed, Stella. I thought you'd take the hint. Things were hardly good between us, but you seemed to carry on regardless, not reading the signs, thinking we were going to be together forever. I thought moving to London would finally put an end to things. But you went ahead and followed me. Christ —wake up."

I was a deer stuck in the headlights. Okay, Matt didn't love me. Okay, Matt was marrying my best friend—but he was trying to say it was all my fault. I felt myself weakening under the cold determination in his stare. He was determined to hurt me. Determined to break me. Matt acted as if he'd cut the chain from my ankle years ago and had been trying to shoo me away ever since. Had I been so naïve? When he'd told me about the job in London, it had been a shock, but he'd never said anything about splitting up. Just that it wasn't an opportunity he could turn down. He never suggested going on his own. Up until the night he told me he was moving out, I'd never had any indication things weren't working. But maybe they'd never been good from his perspective. He had me questioning everything.

Had I missed him trying to end things? Clearly, I'd been working toward a shared future he didn't want, but why hadn't he just said he didn't love me anymore? Why hadn't he left sooner? And if he hadn't wanted me to move to London with him, he should have just told me.

"This isn't my fault," I said. I felt pathetic that I couldn't put together a more coherent defense to his accusations.

He sighed, rolling his eyes. "You only ever see what you want to see. You've always been the same—it's like you have some kind of tunnel vision and you only see the Stella version of reality. No doubt you've done it with this new guy too." He nodded toward the window where Beck was sitting with Henry.

Perhaps I had missed signs with Matt. Maybe I should have pushed him more about our future, but I loved him and I thought that he loved me. It didn't occur to me not to trust him with my heart.

It wouldn't happen again. My heart wouldn't ever be given away so easily. Despite what Matt thought, in future I wouldn't assume someone's feelings matched mine. I wouldn't expect people to be honest, and straightforward, and loyal. I was done being the woman that men took advantage of.

I'd learned my lesson, and I wouldn't repeat the same mistakes again.

TWENTY-NINE

Beck

Thank God for Stella. I couldn't have handled the endless lunches, drinks, and dinners or inane small talk if it wasn't for her. But today I needed to nail down Henry, get him to agree in principle to a sale of the Dawnay building, and it would have all been worth it. I wasn't leaving Scotland without that victory, and I had work to do. I was running out of time.

I glanced over at Stella at the bar. There was so much riding on this conversation. But when she looked at me, I didn't doubt myself for a second. *I* wanted this. Of course I did, but I also wanted this for her—so she could do the design, get her business back on track, and move on from her idiot ex. She might have needed this win even more than I did.

I headed over toward Henry and the large picture window that overlooked the loch and the mountains behind it. The landscape matched the colors of the shop we'd visited the other day. Browns, heathers, and greens. I'd never taken much notice of the landscape when the boys and I had come up when we were teenagers. Yeah, we liked the views, but we'd been focused on the goal of getting to the top of the mountain, the end of the trail, and our gold award. I wasn't sure I'd appreciated everything that got me to that point.

"Henry," I said as he turned away from the window. "You taking in this fantastic view?"

"I certainly am. I've been coming up here most of my life, but it still holds my attention."

"I was eighteen on my first trip up here. Before I'd started my first business, before I knew what I was going to do with my life. But nothing's changed."

"And we can take comfort in that."

Though I'd rather chat to Henry than most of the other people here, I didn't want to just make small talk with him. "I've put together a pack of papers to send you on email if you have an address," I said. I pulled out my phone as Henry relayed his address to me and I typed it in. I'd made sure that the lawyers had everything ready, so if Henry was so minded, he could sign everything and get the deal done right away.

Not that I was expecting him to do that. I just didn't want there to be any reason from my end why the deal wasn't signature ready.

"Okay, I've sent that across to you," I said, tucking the phone back in my pocket.

"I'll take a look. But give me a little background, why do you want the property?" Henry asked.

I tried to swallow down the lump that formed in my throat that appeared every time I thought about my mother and the way she was treated. "I think I mentioned that I own others in the block. I want to make it the premier residential site in Mayfair."

"So a complete transformation of the entire block?"

"Exactly." I nodded.

"That property has held our family name since it was built in the mid-eighteenth century. Even if I was to sell, I'd want that name retained in relation to the building."

Despite being related by blood, I'd never borne the Dawnay name. It had never been an option for me, having been disowned by my father. I was damn sure that as soon as I bought the building, its name would be the first thing to go.

I didn't need constant reminders of who I wasn't.

"The entire block will be one large complex that will have a brand-new name," I said.

"Well perhaps you can work the Dawnay name into a wing or something?" Henry asked.

"I'd definitely look at doing something," I replied, deliberately being noncommittal.

"We'd have to agree on what exactly it was that would carry the name," Henry said. "Perhaps a plaque in the lobby explaining the family connection would work?"

Over my dead body.

"What do you think?" Henry continued.

"You want this incorporated into the contract?" I asked.

"Absolutely," Henry replied. "Selling the building is not . . . Liquidating assets is not something I generally like to do. And that building has been part of our family estate for generations."

I could tell him, explain how I might not have the Dawnay name but I had the Dawnay blood in my veins.

But there was no way I'd use my connection to my biological father to get anything in my life. He'd never given anything to me. And I wasn't going to take anything. I'd worked hard for everything I'd ever had and that wasn't about to change.

"I understand that it might be easier to transfer it to a family member. But in my experience, Henry—and forgive me if I speak out of turn—sometimes family members aren't the best people to take care of a property like the Dawnay building. I want to tend to it, nurture it—bring it to life for another generation." I glanced over at Stella, maybe hoping to feel some of the confidence she had in me and recharge myself. This was clearly important to Henry, and I didn't want to misstep.

She was facing me, but she wasn't talking to Florence. Stella's head was bowed and her eyes were fixed on the floor as she spoke to a man whose back was to me. It almost looked like she was going to cry. Was it Gordy speaking to her?

Before I could figure out who was with her, Henry replied. "I see what you're saying but—and you'll have to forgive *me* this time if I speak out of turn—I don't know you. I'm sure you're a completely honest person who does what they say they'll do . . ."

My attention should have been one hundred percent focused on Henry, but all I could see was the way Stella flinched when the man she was standing with tried to grab her wrist.

"Is that Matt with Stella?" I asked without thinking. I was interrupting when Henry should have all my attention.

"I believe so," Henry replied.

What the fuck was he doing, grabbing her? She took a step back and then he stepped toward her, menacing and threatening, and his voice was starting to increase in volume.

I half stood, hovering over my chair. Should I go over

there? Stella wasn't mine to protect, but she didn't deserve anything Matt was dishing out.

I should be closing this deal with Henry, fulfilling a lifetime's ambition but— "Henry, I'm sorry, but please excuse me."

All I could think about was making sure that Matt had hurt Stella for the last time. He didn't deserve her time, her conversation, or anymore of her tears.

I might have walked away from closing a deal I'd been working toward my entire life.

But some things were more important.

I'd never moved so quickly, and my hand was on the small of Stella's back in a second. Two at the most. She gasped as I touched her, and when she looked up at me, I saw a sadness in her eyes that I remembered from the first time we'd ever met.

I glanced at Matt. He'd done that.

I wanted to kill him. But I'd made Stella a promise that I wouldn't even *say* anything to Matt, not hold him to account or tell him how worthless he was for treating a woman so valuable with such contempt—let alone bury him.

It was a good job that a promise to Stella overrode my desire to give Matt what was coming to him.

"I'm sorry to interrupt, but I need to speak to my girlfriend," I said, and with that I led Stella out of the room.

Away from the man who'd thrown her aside.

Away from the man who stood between me and the Dawnay building, and the ending I so desperately wanted.

THIRTY

Stella

Even after a run, the man looked beautiful. Beck's glistening face, his heaving chest. It was almost too much. No wonder I'd managed to stay distracted these last few days.

"You look gorgeous," Beck said as he stood at the entrance to the hotel room.

Even the view wasn't enough to distract me from the guilt that still covered me like a fine layer of sweat on a muggy August day in London. "You think you'll see Henry today?" I asked.

Beck shrugged and pulled off his shirt. He'd whisked me out of the restaurant the day before yesterday, making some excuse about needing to speak to me. I'd never been so pleased to see anyone, but at the same time, Beck had been so close to closing the deal. And yesterday Henry had been visiting family and hadn't joined the hike. Beck could have missed his shot.

"I should have sent you back to speak to Henry. I could have waited in the car."

"You said that already. And there was no way I was leaving you."

"Also, did I say thank you?"

He turned to me and smiled. "You did. Many times." He toed off his shoes and headed into the bathroom, keeping the door open.

I could barely keep my hands off Beck on the car ride back to the hotel. At one point along the way, we'd pulled over and I'd crawled onto his lap on the back seat. I don't know what it was, but Beck interrupting Matt and me, walking away from Henry to come to my rescue was . . . I'd never had anyone do anything like that for me.

"I'd do it again," he added. "He was lucky I didn't punch him out, and if I hadn't made that promise to you, I probably would have. Are you still not going to tell me what he said to you?"

I couldn't tell him. It was too embarrassing to admit that Matt had said I looked desperate by coming to the wedding. And that I should have realized he was never going to marry me. "You know. He was just trying to justify running off with my best friend." I tried to dismiss what he'd said but just thinking about his accusations was like pouring vinegar onto a wound.

Had I been desperate? Had I missed the signs? It was true that I never thought Matt or Karen capable of so much deception, of such a lack of loyalty. I thought they loved me. But I couldn't have been more wrong.

"Typical coward. Trying to make you feel bad."

"It doesn't matter," I lied. "I'm more concerned about Henry." Focusing on the future was my only option now.

All I could do was move on, keep my heart safe, and not make the same mistake again. I had to focus on work. "He might have signed the paperwork if you hadn't come to save me."

"Maybe. Although, he seems stuck on keeping the Dawnay name attached to the building in some way."

I'd been so wrapped up in my own drama, we'd not talked about what he and Henry had spoken about. "In what way?"

"Like a wing or the lobby or something."

"And that's a big no no for you, given, your background, I guess."

He snapped his head around. "Yeah. Exactly."

"I get that," I said. He was treating this development as therapy of some kind. Having to keep the Dawnay name as part of it would undermine that in his eyes. But all the same, it seemed a small price to pay. "You have to ask yourself whether you're prepared to walk away if it's a sticking point with Henry."

"I need to shower but come and talk to me," he said.

I tried to think back to when Matt and I had first been together. Had we ever had conversations in the bathroom? Life was always so busy—I couldn't remember the last time we'd properly talked.

"You think I'm being an idiot about the name? Am I cutting my nose off to spite my face?"

"I didn't say that," I replied.

Beck continued to strip off with the bathroom door open. He was so unselfconscious. We'd only known each other a few weeks, but I knew his body better than I knew my own. That small scar on his jaw that I couldn't see unless I was just a few centimeters away—the result of falling and hitting the rocks on a trip up Snowden. The dimples just above his arse cheeks that were the reason I liked to watch him from bed as he walked naked across the room. The way his hands were twice the size of mine and wrapped around my waist, my hips, my breasts as if they owned them. I'd miss all those things about him.

I'd miss him.

"Yeah but I've gotten to know that little twitch of your mouth and the way you look away—it means you don't agree. Tell me what you think, Stella. I want to hear it."

We hadn't known each other long, but in many ways he seemed to know me better than some of my oldest friends. "It sounds like there might be a bit of nose cutting off."

"I've been known to do it before," he confessed.

"Well, I'm hardly one to talk. Florence had to talk me into coming to this wedding."

"I can understand why you wouldn't want to come. What Matt and Karen did? It's awful."

"And I understand why you don't want the Dawnay name anywhere near your building."

He stepped into the shower and looked at me. "Don't ever let a guy tell you you're not a fucking prize, Stella."

He said it as if he thought I was the best thing ever to happen to any man, and his gaze created a tingle across my skin as if his lips were on mine.

"I'm not sure if that means you're going to accept Henry's condition or not."

He sighed like it was an impossible situation. "What would you do if you were me?"

"Wrong question," I replied. "You want to know what Warren Buffet would do or Jeff Bezos."

"You're telling me not to let sentiment get in the way."

"Actually, I'm not. I think that if your aim is to make the best business deal, then agree to let Henry keep the name. That's what Warren or Jeff would do."

"Of course I want to make the best deal," he said.

That might be partly true but there were other reasons why he wanted the Dawnay building. "Or you want to lay ghosts to rest," I replied. "And if that's the case, then buying that building is never going to fulfil you in the way you need it to if you have to keep the Dawnay name attached to it."

"So walk away?"

I shook my head. "I'm saying, decide what's more important—putting the past to bed or getting that building. If this is about your father and Henry insists on keeping the name, then maybe you should walk away."

Beck got out of the shower, and I padded back to the bedroom and dressed quickly in a Zara knockoff of a Prada skirt and blouse.

"As well as being a prize, you're right," Beck said, toweling himself off. "It's more than a building or a deal. I can't live with the name being a part of the building in the future. I want to move forward and for so many years, owning that building—having my thumbprint on it and not my father's—has been the only thing holding me back."

I knew the feeling about wanting to get on with my life. I couldn't help but think I'd just shot myself in the foot. If Beck didn't buy the Dawnay building, where did that leave me? In a crappy job that I hated and a flat I'd shared with Matt.

"Then I guess you have your answer," I said.

"Maybe," he replied. "If I can't convince Henry to drop the name. But it's worth another shot."

"Hopefully you'll get to see him at the ceremony today."

Beck pulled on his trousers and pulled a shirt from the hanger in the wardrobe.

"And then we'll be done," I said. After today I could move on with my life. The Matt chapter of my life that I thought would last the entire book would be over. But with

Beck and the Dawnay building still uncertain, I had no idea what would be over the page.

He grabbed his suitcase from behind the door, reached onto the bed for a t-shirt, and pulled it over his head. "Let's pack," he said.

"Now?" I glanced at my watch. "We can't be late for the ceremony." We could pack later. There was no way I was going to be late to the church and risk having to grab a pew when everyone else was seated and turned to watch me.

"No, let's go today. Now. I have Henry's details. I can call him. Email him."

My heart started to thunder, excitement and relief mixing in my stomach. Although the thought wasn't vomit-inducing like it had been at the beginning of the week, watching Matt and Karen get married wasn't exactly first on my list of things to do today. "Wouldn't it be better for you to speak to him face-to-face?"

"I think I need to let him stew." He pulled his clothes from the wardrobe and threw them in the case. "Unless you want to be there for some reason? Closure or something?"

"It's the last place I'd want to be."

"So, come on then, get those sexy shoes off and packed." He grabbed his phone off the bedside table, and I sat like a stone on the mattress. "I'm going to call for the plane, but if you want to stay, we'll stay."

Did I care if there was a two-person gap at the reception? People would probably say I couldn't face it and they wouldn't be wrong. I wouldn't even be here if it wasn't for Beck and the design job. If Beck was offering me a get out of jail free card, why shouldn't I grab it? "Are you sure? You're so close with Henry?"

"I think we both need to escape right now."

"If you're sure, then—"

"Stella, it's almost as if you're waiting for me to change my mind. You never know—walking away might be the push that Henry needs." He held the phone up. "Say the word."

I didn't want to stay here. I didn't want to watch Matt marry Karen. I wanted to be in the air, and on the way back to London. I wasn't sure I wanted to go back to the flat Matt and I had shared or the job I'd taken to pay the mortgage, but I knew being here was worse. "Let's go."

I jumped up, adrenaline licking at my skin, and began to strip out of my wedding-appropriate outfit as I scanned the room for my jeans. "Are we really doing this? It feels wrong somehow."

Beck picked up the phone. "Joe, I'm going to need the plane today. We're going to be leaving the hotel in about ten minutes, so we should be at the airfield in half an hour." Beck hung up and turned to me. "Yes, we're doing this. Finally, you're going to do what's best for you, rather than what's best for Matt, your friends, and even me." He grinned at me and then pulled me toward him, placing a kiss on the top of my head. "It's about time."

THIRTY-ONE

Out of the back window of the car, I watched the hotel disappear and fade away into the gray, Scottish skies. I had to be sure we had gone. "It's like I'm leaving my past behind," I said. "Literally. Figuratively. It's all back there."

"Are you okay with that?" Beck asked.

I turned back to face forward in the passenger seat next to Beck. "It's a relief. To get it done. And to not have to go to the ceremony. I doubt I'll ever see Matt and Karen again."

"But you'll see Florence and Gordy?"

"Sure. Florence has been amazing through all this."

Beck stayed silent.

"She's been a great friend," I added. "I don't know what I would have done without her."

He shrugged.

It was weird because I knew Beck well enough to know he wasn't just disinterested in what I was saying. He was disagreeing with me but trying to hold himself back from saying so.

"You don't like Florence?"

He tapped his thumbs on the steering wheel. "I don't like the fact that she's still friends with Karen after what she did to you."

I reached for his arm. It was sweet that he seemed invested, but he'd gotten it wrong about Florence. "Florence isn't friends with Karen."

"She's at her wedding. And honestly, I don't know Gordy very well, but he seems like a nice bloke. I don't understand why he didn't put his foot down and refuse to come."

I had to push down a giggle. "Put his foot down? I'd like to see him try and tell Florence what to do. But for your information, Florence promised to come to Scotland if I came. She didn't want me to go through it alone. She wouldn't have come if I hadn't needed her here."

Beck took a long, slow breath. "Good," he said. "That makes more sense. And Gordy just went along with it?"

"He'll do anything to make Florence happy. You can stop judging them now. Even though it's kinda nice that you're being so protective."

"The character of a person is important to me. You know that."

In many ways I knew a lot about Beck, considering the short amount of time we'd spent in each other's company. But these days I knew better than to assume I knew anyone. After my conversation with Matt, the lack of confidence I had in my own judgement of people was reaching boiling point.

"I don't understand why you were with Matt for so long, or friends with Karen since you were five. The pair of them deserve each other from what I've seen. Neither of them merit a friend like you."

It was easy to look on as an outsider and see things that weren't right. But when you were in the middle of them, they were easier to overlook. "No one is ever entirely one hundred percent to blame," I replied.

We turned onto the main road, Beck revved up the engine and we picked up speed. "If that tool successfully made you feel like him running off with your best friend was somehow your fault—"

"No, it's not that. More that when you're in a relationship, the aim is to be happy and that means compromising and accepting you're not right all the time."

"And that's what Matt did?"

I'm not sure I understood Matt's aims at all, which made me feel all the more stupid. I'd been blindly trundling along, expecting everyone to have good hearts and me to be granted my happily ever after at some point. "They weren't Matt's core skills while we were together," I said. "But that doesn't mean I can't have good intentions."

"That's the point though, isn't it? You had good intentions and he didn't give a shit."

Matt cared about me. At one point. He must have done. "We were happy for a long time."

"And when you stopped being happy," he said. "Did you walk away?"

My stomach roiled. I hadn't stopped being happy. Even when he'd ended things, I'd loved him and thought it would work.

I'd been such a fool.

Even with a little distance from Matt, it was clear that our relationship was far from perfect. Looking back, he was controlling and demanding and more than a bit of a snob.

Beck was right. I'd seen what I'd wanted to see—ignored

the bad and created the good in our relationship. My rose-tinted glasses had been lasered on.

My fear now was that my twisted vision wasn't limited to Matt and Karen but that I wasn't capable of seeing reality. Was I only seeing the good things about Beck? It seemed real between us; it seemed like he'd do anything for me. But I'd been wrong before.

"I'm not looking back. I'm focused on the future. On the Mayfair project."

"If we get it," Beck said.

"You'll get it."

He grinned and grabbed my hand, linking his fingers through mine. Was this just pretend? "Thank you for your confidence. But I've decided. I want it without the name or not at all."

At that moment, a call came through on the Bluetooth and Henry's name flashed up. He should have been at the ceremony.

"Henry," Beck answered.

"If you've got any sense, you've whisked the lovely Stella away from this ridiculous parade. The dear girl shouldn't have to sit through such a palaver."

"Agreed. We're headed to the airfield now, and we're going to make our way back to London."

"Very good," he said. "Anyway, I called because we didn't finish our conversation back at Fort William."

Beck cleared his throat. "Yes, sorry about that. I—"

"No need to apologize. You did quite the right thing," he replied. "It actually got me thinking about family and loyalty. There have been plenty of Dawnays who haven't displayed the character you did to me in that moment when you intervened in the situation between dear Stella and Matt. In fact, between you and me, the cousin I inherited the building from wasn't the best man I've ever met. I'm thinking that perhaps the Wilde name deserves to be the only one on your development."

I squeezed my hands into fists in the hope it would hold in the squeal of delight pushing to get out.

"I appreciate that." Beck shot me a grin—it was the look of a man who knew a victory when he won one.

"You said fourteen fifty a square foot?" Henry asked.

"That's right," Beck replied.

It seemed like a lot of money, but Beck had said it was fair for the location, and after doing some research I'd worked out Beck could put over hundreds per square foot on that if I did my job properly.

"If you can go to fifteen hundred, then I'll sign," Henry said.

"If we get documents executed by Thursday, I can do that price."

"Then I suggest we light a fire under our lawyers," Henry said, chuckling. "And you and Stella will come to dinner a week on Saturday to celebrate."

Beck turned to me and without thinking about it, I nodded enthusiastically. Henry's agreement couldn't have come at a more perfect time. I had something to look forward to, to work toward.

"We'd be delighted," Beck said. "I'll let you go and get straight on to your lawyers. Enjoy the wedding, sir."

"You got your building," I said, beaming at Beck. "I knew you would."

"And you got your project," he replied.

"My future."

He reached across and cupped my face, sweeping his thumb over my cheekbone. "We should celebrate when we get back to London."

My stomach swooped and slid down to my knees. I'd deliberately not allowed myself to think about Beck and me on the other side of the Scottish border. But we were about an hour away from being back in England.

If he *was* suggesting a date, then I wasn't sure what to say—Matt had taught me I had to be more careful with my heart.

"That's the idea of Henry's dinner," I replied.

"Yes, but I'd like to celebrate just with you."

He removed any doubt to what he was saying. My pulse began to thud in my wrists. I wasn't sure if it was excitement or fear that was the cause. "It's certainly something to celebrate," I said.

Beck getting the Dawnay building was something to celebrate.

Standing up to Karen was something to celebrate.

Escaping the wedding was something to celebrate.

There were plenty of good things happening in my life I could raise a glass to. But doing that with Beck?

Was I brave enough to trust myself? Was it possible for me to see how things really were rather than how I wanted them to be?

The last week with Beck had been wonderful. But the two of us had been living a lie. Just like Matt and I had been doing. At least I was in on the deception with Beck, but it was still not the truth. It was still messy and complicated.

Matt showing me how different reality was to the life I thought I was living had pulled the rug from under me, and I needed to dust myself off and learn to walk again.

"You want to still pretend we're dating for this dinner with Henry?" I asked. We hadn't discussed what we were doing. We were pretending to be dating and sleeping together. Did that mean that we were really dating?

Beck shot me a look, his eyes narrowed. "You're pretending? It didn't seem that way last night in bed." A wide grin curled around his lips. "Or this morning in the shower or—"

"Okay, I get it. It's just, you know, Scotland was . . . Scotland."

"I don't know what 'Scotland was Scotland' means."

I didn't know what I was saying either. The fact was we hadn't discussed dating in real life. I guess that's what we were doing now—discussing what happened when we got back to London.

"You want to call it quits when we get back to London?" he asked, his voice a little colder and more distant than it had been just seconds before.

I gnawed at the inside of my cheek. Did I?

I liked Beck. I *really* liked having sex with Beck. And he was funny. And cute when he was serious. And seriously cute when he was in work mode.

He'd rescued me from Matt and suggested we didn't attend the ceremony today.

Beck seemed like a good guy. But so had Matt.

I needed to figure out if I had some fundamental flaw that only allowed me to see the good things in people.

Florence had pointed out how selfish Matt had been and how I'd given in to him all the time, but I'd never seen it like that.

I needed time to let my focus readjust. Or retrain my instincts or something. I needed to fix the part of me that was broken and didn't see things how they really were.

What I didn't want to do was jump from the frying pan into the fire.

My stomach churned as I realized that Beck and I were probably a horrible idea. History showed that my instincts were off. If it felt right, it must be wrong. Surely he would agree when he thought about it. "We're going to be working together. Maybe it's not a good idea to be mixing business with . . ." I wasn't sure what he was suggesting. I was half hoping he'd agree, half hoping he'd talk me around. No doubt he'd talk me into whatever he had in mind. "You know, sex."

Beck turned away from me and stared straight ahead. "Okay, we'll keep it professional."

That was it?

I'd expected him to present a counterargument. That was his MO, right? I'd assumed I'd have to at least put up a fight. I'd seen Beck in action. When he wanted something, he didn't stop at anything.

Looked like he didn't want me. Enough.

I guess my judgement wasn't so wonky after all. My doubts around him were well founded.

THIRTY-TWO

Beck

All I'd wanted to do was focus on my work, but since leaving Scotland, it was as if my brain had been dunked in a black fog which I just couldn't find my way out of. It had only been days but it felt like weeks—months.

I drummed my fingers on the black, glossy table, skirting the edge of my pint glass.

"Is that water?" Dexter asked as he arrived, wincing as if I were nursing a pint of battery acid.

"With a wedge of lime. Got a problem with that?" Alcohol was the last thing I needed. I wanted my head to be less fuzzy not more.

He slipped his jacket onto the back of his chair and nodded at the barman. "Where did you develop your mood? A car crash?"

"Fuck off, nothing's wrong with my mood," I snapped.

"Right," he said, leaning back and thanking the barman as they slid a glass of whiskey in front of him.

"You're a tit for paying for this place." I never understood why people paid memberships to get into what was essentially a bar and restaurant. I glanced around Dexter's club—the ceiling was a reflection of the table we were sitting around, and gold streaks shot out from the circle of dark glass like the sun trying to escape an eclipse. It looked like the kind of thing Stella would point out to me. "There are a thousand bars like this in London." That wasn't quite true. This place was nice, but I expected Dexter to be more frugal.

"Okaaay," he replied. "Are you going to tell me why you look like your dog just died?"

"Nothing wrong with me. I've just been waiting for you lot to arrive." I hadn't been able to focus in the office, which wasn't like me, so I'd taken myself off to the gym, then come straight here. I'd been hoping the exercise would clear my head, but nothing was working. All I could think about was Stella. Where was she? What was she doing? What was she thinking about? Who was she with?

"And you're not flirting with the waitresses, which means you either lost a shitload of money or you didn't get your own way on something important. Which is it?" he asked.

Jesus, did this guy think he was my therapist? "Neither, Madame Zelda. Stop trying to read my mind or fortune or whatever."

"So, how was Scotland?"

What was with the twenty questions? "You want me to fill in a questionnaire for you about my life?" I asked.

Dexter burst out laughing. "I take it you have your period."

"Don't be a sexist fucker," I said. I might go. Dexter was irritating me tonight. Everything was irritating me tonight.

"Oh sorry, I forgot you were the bastion of political correctness."

"Not being a dick isn't being politically correct—it's not being a dick."

Dexter raised his eyebrows. "Fair enough. So, you don't have your period because you're not a woman, not that being a woman is a bad thing and having a period must be great, but seriously, mate, what the fuck is the matter with you?"

I slumped back in my chair. "Just got some stuff on my mind, that's all."

Over at the hostess's table, Tristan was chatting up a member of staff. "That guy needs to get laid," Dexter said.

"Clearly," I replied as Tristan approached our table.

"Christy," he said by way of explanation. "Hot, right?"

"Doesn't mean you have to bang her," Dexter said, as if he were telling a four-year-old not to go near the fire.

"Doesn't mean that I *shouldn't* shag her either."

Tristan was going through a phase. It was just a phase that had lasted about five years.

"Is it just the three of us tonight?" he said.

"Gabriel might join us later but he's working late," Dexter said.

"How was Scotland?" Tristan asked. "Did you get the building?"

I exhaled. It should feel like more of a victory than it did. Perhaps it would be different when the documents were finally signed. "Price is agreed. Survey done. Just waiting for the contracts to catch up."

"Wow, that's great news . . . isn't it?" Tristan said.

"So what?" I barked. Without Stella, the Dawnay building didn't seem so important.

"His dog died," Dexter said, trying to explain why my

expression didn't match up to the news that the deal I'd been waiting so long for and working so hard toward was finally about to happen.

"My dog is fine." I shook my head. What was I talking about? "I don't have a fucking dog. No one died. No one's sick. I'm just . . . pre-occupied."

I didn't miss the look Tristan shot Dexter, one that said I was teetering on the brink of mental failure. Which I might just be.

"With what?" Tristan asked.

"Just stuff. Work and things. And then Dexter was being a dick and irritating me."

"Apparently, I'm sexist," Dexter said.

"That goes without saying," Tristan said. "But it's not news." He took a sip of the drink that had just been put in front of him. Clearly flirting with the hostess hadn't been just about getting her number. "Scotland worked out. Work's good. No one's dog died. How's Stella?"

Fuck him. I hated Tristan at times. He was a nosey parker. How was he still a member of our circle? "Fine."

Dexter and Tristan both sucked in a breath at the same time.

"What?" I asked.

"This bad mood is Stella related." Dexter said.

"Don't be ridiculous." If I could just stop thinking about her everything could get back to normal.

"Yup, it's definitely Stella related. Did she say no to your *very* weak game?" Tristan asked.

"My game isn't weak. And of course, she didn't say no." I groaned inwardly. I'd just given them an in.

"Ahhh," they both chorused.

"I thought by that hangdog expression it was women

trouble," Tristan said. "Not that I've ever seen it on you. This is interesting."

I didn't have women trouble. Stella and I weren't dating. We weren't even talking.

"You slept with her," Dexter said. "Then what happened?"

"Nothing. I don't want to talk about it."

"But there's an *it* that you don't want to talk about," Tristan said. He was really getting on my nerves.

"Shut up," I said.

"You two need to stop it before a fight breaks out," Dexter said. "But seriously, what happened with Stella? I've never seen you like this. You're defensive and bad-tempered. We're not laughing at you—we're laughing with you."

"I'm laughing at him," Tristan said. "But you can have Christy's number if it will help."

I needed to leave, or Tristan and I were going to end up at the end of each other's fists. I might be in a bad mood, but he was unnaturally chirpy.

"Shut up, Tristan," Dexter said.

"Sorry," he mumbled. "I just ordered a new car and I'm feeling pretty pleased with myself. I'll shut up." He waved his hand over his face and resumed a normal expression. "I was being a dick. Tell us what happened?"

"Nothing's up. I just . . ." I just wasn't sure what had gone wrong. "I suggested she and I celebrate getting the Dawnay building, and she didn't seem that keen. Said it was best to keep it professional. That's all." I didn't get it. We'd had a completely great week. Amazing. Why wouldn't she want to celebrate? But whatever. I was over it. Not that there was anything to get over.

"You like her, Beck," Dexter said. "I'm not sure what

they're putting in the air up there in Scotland, but whatever it is has you brooding over a woman."

"I am not brooding." I was just irritated.

"You wouldn't normally care what anyone thought of you, but Stella's opinion obviously matters," Dexter said. "If it makes you feel any better, I thought she was great. Gave as good as she got. And she was hot, wasn't she, Tristan?"

"I'd bang her," Tristan replied.

"Hey," I warned. I didn't like the idea of Tristan thinking of Stella like that.

"That's not saying a lot coming from Tristan—it would mean more if he wouldn't bang her," Dexter said.

"Well, the point is moot," I replied. "Even if I did like her, which I'm not saying I do, we haven't spoken since we got back."

Tristan rolled his eyes. "Persistence pays off. Look at me and Christy. I've been trying to get her number for three months. You just gotta work at it."

"I don't work at getting women," I replied. I didn't work at having people like me. Not for anyone. And especially not Stella. She was too used to just going along with what other people wanted. She needed to figure out what made her happy.

"Sometimes it's worth it," Dexter said. "You don't want to regret anything. And from your mood, it seems like Stella is important."

"I liked her. That's all." I thought she'd liked me too. But, I guess that's how it went. It just needled. I'd thought we were on the same page.

"That's all?" Tristan asked. "I've never heard you say you like a woman. I rarely hear you *mention* a woman."

Tristan was exaggerating. As usual.

"I just don't get it. We were having a great time. I read the situation all wrong."

"From what you told me on the phone from Scotland, her very serious boyfriend married her best friend. The girl's going to assume that everyone's trying to screw her over for a while. That kind of stuff messes you up."

I took in a deep breath and tried to process what Dexter had said. I wouldn't describe Stella as messed up, but he had a point. It can't have been easy for her to watch Matt and Karen play the happy couple, even if Matt seemed like a bit of a cock. "Yeah well, I get that." She must have been concerned that I couldn't be trusted. "But I'm not wasting my energy on a woman who was happy to walk away."

"She'll come around. Stella's a sensible girl," Dexter said.

"Funny, too," Tristan said. "If you're going to fuck things up with her, then can you let me have her number?"

Christ, Tristan was annoying me tonight. "What's the matter with you? You can't find your own woman, so you have to try for mine?"

He fixed me with a stare. "Your woman? Sounds serious. Sort it out. Because if it's not me, some other guy will swoop in and this mood of yours will be permanent."

A cold shiver ran through my body. Tristan was right— some other guy would swoop in. Stella was a fucking prize. The same swirl of dread that I had when I thought I was going to have to give up the Mayfair project gathered in my stomach, except this time it was sharper, more pressing and urgent.

"Yeah, well there's nothing to be done. She doesn't want me. So, that's the end of it."

The corner turned up on Dexter's mouth. "She's probably afraid. It won't be that she doesn't want you. You get that, right?"

It was Dexter who didn't get it. She *didn't* want me. There might be a reason, but it all boiled down to the same thing.

Dexter drained his whiskey. "Tristan, will you go and get me another drink?"

"It's waitress service. And for your information, I'm not the waitress," he replied, all the while his gaze fixed on his phone.

Dexter sighed. "Okay, will you fuck off for a few minutes so I can talk to Beck privately?"

Tristan looked up and grinned. "You just had to say." He slid out of the booth and inevitably headed toward Christy.

I sat back, ready for whatever it was that Dexter was about to tell me. He'd been through a lot in the last few years. Losing his parents. The shit his brother put him through. Building his business from scratch. But he always kept a clear head, and I admired him for it. He never for a moment doubted his destiny.

"I don't want to go all deep and shit on you," he said. "But have you considered that you don't get close to people because of what happened with your biological father?" It was a testament to how well Dexter knew me that he didn't refer to the man who'd gotten my mother pregnant as my dad or ever just my father. He knew me better than that.

"You think I don't get close to people because I never knew my biological father?"

"You experienced a fundamental rejection from the moment you were born and it's bound to take its toll."

"I'm not as naïve as you think I am," I said. "It's definitely affected me. I've just spent God knows how long chasing down the Dawnay property."

"I'd hate to see that be the reason you lose someone who could make you happy," he said.

I wasn't sure what Dexter was trying to say but he had my attention.

"Your biological father was an arsehole," he continued.

"Clearly," I replied. "But what's that got to do with Stella?"

"Stella is running because she's scared. Not because she's an arsehole."

"I don't think she's an arsehole." I thought she was wonderful. Special. All those things they wrote about in poetry and love songs. I felt them all when I looked at Stella.

"Sometimes you have to chase after the things that are important."

Stella had nothing to be afraid of with me. She knew that. Dexter had this wrong. "She's not afraid of me."

"No, I bet she's afraid of being hurt. Look what she went through. This isn't about her not wanting you, it's about her not wanting to let *anyone* in."

Dexter had a point. I could definitely see that Stella would be reticent about getting involved with someone again after Matt, but I wasn't proposing or suggesting we move in together. "I just suggested a drink. If she's not interested, then—"

"Mate, she's interested. I saw it when she was in the pub with us that night."

"In the pub? We hardly knew each other then."

"Trust me. I know what a woman looks like when she's into a guy. And you were taken with her as well. There was something about the two of you. You just fit together."

Dexter described exactly how I felt—it was like we were

two sides of the same coin. But the feeling clearly wasn't mutual. I shrugged. "You know what I'm like. I'm not a good boyfriend anyway."

"You know what I'm going to say to that," he warned. "You're not a good boyfriend because you don't care about the women you spend time with."

"So, if your theories are correct, if Stella had been the right woman, I'd have chased after her."

"No, you'd be sitting in the pub, nursing a pint of water, brooding because you got knocked back and it's the first time it's ever happened."

I picked up my pint, hoping he'd continue but not wanting to ask him to explain further.

"I've never seen you in a bad mood because a woman turned down an invitation to dinner or drinks or whatever."

I couldn't remember it ever happening.

"It's bound to have happened before, but I bet you don't remember because you never gave a shit before. But with Stella, it's different. I can tell."

I didn't want to say he was right, but Dexter *was* right— she was different. Stella seemed to get me. Know me. Not just because she knew my mother's occupation and how I liked my steak—she knew my soul. "I can't make her date me, Dexter. She said no."

"She doesn't trust herself. Doesn't trust you. You need to woo her. Keep showing her what a good man you are, and she'll come around."

"I shouldn't have to convince someone to date me." I'd seen how Stella could go along with things to make other people happy. I wanted her to really want me. To actively choose to be with me. I didn't want to have to persuade her.

"This isn't about how she feels about you. It's all about how she feels about the world. Be the guy who makes the world safe for her. If Stella's the woman for you, then it's your job to give her what she needs. And she needs to know she's safe with you. She needs to understand you're not going to fuck her over. And take it from me, every woman needs to know that she's worth fighting for."

She definitely deserved all of those things.

"If she's as important to you as I think she is," Dexter continued. "Don't let anything stand in your way. The man who sired you turned his back on you, but that's not what Stella is doing. She's not rejecting you—she's protecting herself."

I let Dexter's words settle. When something was important to me, I worked to get what I wanted, to prove that I was worthy. I tapped the edge of my pint glass. But I hadn't fought for Stella. Hadn't even stated my case. Dexter was right—it was because I didn't want to risk being rejected. Again.

I knew I didn't want to lose someone as important as Stella was, just because *I* was scared. I wasn't going to let my past dictate my future. Henry selling me the Dawnay building was the end of that chapter in my life.

And Stella London was in my future. Of that I was certain.

THIRTY-THREE

I was going to show Beck Wilde. The interiors of the Mayfair project were going to be the talk of London. They would win awards and have people whispering at parties about how fabulous they were. I just needed to be inspired, find suppliers, and hunt down things that had never been seen in London before.

"That's the third time you've yawned in the last seven minutes," Florence said, tipping her head to the side and staring at the underside of a table. The cute interiors shop just off Marylebone High Street was one of my favorites. It had a mixture of antiques and new pieces—furniture, art, vases, pots, rugs. It was like visiting an overstuffed London mansion owned by someone who had great taste but not enough space. "Why are you so tired? Has Beck been keeping you up?"

"I think I'm going to have to make a few trips abroad," I said, swerving around her questions. I'd taken the week off in Scotland so there was no way my dragon of a boss would let me take more holiday. My job was next on my to-do list—after *forget about Beck* and before *sort my life out.*

"For what? With Beck?"

"For suppliers." I wished she'd stop bringing him up. "Unless I go for an entirely British interior. Make it a feature that everything has been crafted by artisans in this country. It could be a selling point." But would it be luxurious enough? I wanted some kind of theme other than opulence and luxury. I needed to find an edge. I was going to do whatever it took to impress the hell out of Beck. Maybe then he'd realize what he'd let slip through his fingers.

"It feels like you've got your mojo back a little," Florence said. "Do you think you got some closure last week?"

I flopped down on a green damask settee. "I'm not sure if closure is the way to describe it." Beck being there had pulled my focus. He'd been a complete distraction.

"It does seem like you've moved on. Hopefully, you can get your design business back up and running, leave that recruitment consultancy, and forget about Matt and Karen. Especially now you're seeing someone else."

"I'm not seeing someone else," I said. "Beck and I . . . It's nothing. And now we're back in London, so . . ."

"What?" Florence asked, finally pulling herself away from the Chinese basin she'd been eyeing up and joining me on the settee. "What happened? You both seemed so into each other."

I'd been into him. Too into him. I'd gotten so caught up in it—the sex, the way he held my hand as if he wouldn't let go for anything. The way he looked at me when he thought I wasn't looking. We'd been fast-forwarded into the honeymoon stages of a relationship and all of a sudden we were home and our relationship had been annulled. "I guess we put on a good show."

She nudged me. "Come on, we both know it was more than that. What happened?"

"I've just learned that I'm way too trusting. I've got to toughen up. Assume the worst. See things how they are and not how I want them to be." I stood and started scanning the room for more inspiration.

"Stella, what on earth went wrong?"

"Nothing. But Beck—I barely knew him. And one thing's for certain. I'm not jumping from the frying pan into the fire."

"No, there should be no jumping into any fires. Did he end things between you?"

"Things? There were no things to end. It was just casual—something to pass the time."

"So he didn't bring up seeing you again in London?" she asked.

"Kind of. I mean, hardly." I swallowed, trying to get rid of the disappointment I'd felt when he hadn't even tried to convince me we could combine the professional and the personal.

"So he did?" she asked.

"He said something about celebrating him getting the building."

"Right," Florence said. "And what did you say?"

"Nothing much. He didn't seem too bothered. I said something about how because we'd be working together, we should be professional."

"He asked to see you again and you said no." Florence rolled her eyes and pushed herself up from the settee.

"No. This wasn't me. I . . . When Beck wants something, he goes for it. Fights for it. And I just wasn't ultra-enthusiastic about his idea of a celebration, and he agreed and went cold. He clearly wasn't that bothered. I gave him an easy out."

"Are you sure?" she asked. "He seemed pretty smitten to me."

"Yeah, well I thought Matt was smitten." I shrugged. "People can't be trusted. No, wait—*men* can't be trusted."

When she didn't respond, I glanced over at her. Her nose wrinkled like someone was making her sniff sour milk. "We're friends, right? And friends tell each other when they're being idiots, agreed?"

My stomach sank to my knees.

"Matt couldn't be trusted. He was an arsehole. Doesn't mean Beck will be. Keep Matt behind you. Don't let him ruin your future. Don't let him take what you and Beck have."

My heart spluttered in that same way it did when I thought I'd fucked up at work or when I'd inadvertently made a friend cry. "Wait, no," I said. This wasn't me. "Beck didn't want me. It was obvious. I might not have jumped at his idea of a celebration, but he didn't seem bothered. Not at all. I know what he looks like when he's determined he wants something."

"You've seen what he looks like when he wants to buy a building," Florence said. "Not when he's asking a woman on a date. The biggest egos are the ones most easily crushed."

The idea that I'd crushed Beck's ego was ludicrous. "I'm sure he has plenty of women willing to kiss him and make him feel better."

"Maybe not the one he wants, though," she replied.

I folded my arms and headed over to the window. I needed to think—get my head straight.

"I don't want to make the same mistake again," I said as Florence came up beside me. "I don't want to be the fool who thinks her boyfriend's in love with her and is the last to know I'm not the person he wants to marry."

"You weren't the last person to know. Everyone thought you and Matt would get married."

"I didn't want to read the signs wrong—think Beck was into me and then figure out it was just about sex. I need to be moving on, not having history repeat itself."

"I get it. When Beck came along . . . You were still—"

"Reeling. From shock, betrayal, pain. I can't go through it again. It's time to move on," I said, pulling back and nodding resolutely.

"I think that sounds perfect. And having seen you two together last week, I'd say Beck Wilde is the man to move on with."

I rolled my eyes. "Just because I'm moving on doesn't mean I have to jump the first guy who comes along."

"Agreed. But don't run away from a guy who might just be perfect for you because you're scared. It's understandable that you're suspicious of him, but if you like him, you should give him a chance."

"And what? Wait until he hurts me? Matt was right, looking back, there were signs he wasn't thinking long term with me. I mean, why in the hell did he talk about marriage so much but always say it wasn't the right time? I wasn't even putting pressure on him to marry me and he always—"

"Don't torture yourself by looking back. Just because you didn't spot any so-called signs doesn't mean you have joint culpability."

"Matt thought it was more than joint. He thought the entire thing was my fault."

"Well of course he did. He's a spoiled, selfish child who doesn't want to have to be accountable for his own actions."

"But if I hadn't been so clueless, I could have avoided being hurt."

She tilted her head, challenging me without saying a word.

"Okay, maybe I was always going to get hurt," I said. "But at least I wouldn't have felt so freaking stupid."

"I get that. But the only way to not risk being hurt is not to fall in love again. Beck, or whoever it is, won't come with a cast-iron guarantee."

"True," I replied. "But at the same time, if the warning bells go off—"

"Your warning bells are on a hair-trigger at the moment."

Maybe she was right. Perhaps I'd overreacted, but the fact was Beck wasn't tearing down my front door, telling me how desperate he was to be with me.

"I want a man who really wants me. Who sees me as a prize. A guy who wants to convince me that we should be together."

"Do you feel that way about Beck? Do you really want *him*? See *him* as a prize? It's not just up to Beck. You need to decide what you want, and it can't just be someone who likes you. I swear, you never asked yourself if you were happy when you were with Matt. You just carried on because that's what he wanted. You're always so focused on everyone else, you never stop to ask yourself what you want."

It wasn't the first time someone had described our relationship along those lines. "I did love Matt," I said. "I would have left him if I hadn't."

"Really?" she asked. "Or were you just used to him, didn't know any better and making the best of it?"

"I wanted to marry him," I said. I wouldn't have stayed with someone for seven years making the best of it. I'd thought we had a future together.

"You wanted to be married to him or you thought that's what was next?"

"I loved him, Florence."

She sighed. "I know I'm being harsh. I just want you to be happy. The next man in your life should be so special you can't live without him. I don't want you ending up with someone just because they pick you."

Maybe Matt and I were no Anthony and Cleopatra, but I was happy. I took a breath, thinking back, trying to remember what being with Matt had been like. It was only months we'd been apart, but the memories were so hazy now. I had been happy but there was something missing. Being with Beck had showed me that. Beck listened to me, trusted me, took my advice. And I believed in him and thought he felt the same.

"There were things that weren't right with Matt. And I probably did just go along with things. I wanted to make him happy."

"But what will make you happy, Stella?" she asked.

I tried to hold back a grin as I thought about Beck slowing down in the rain for me, holding my hand, whisking me away from Matt but not making a scene because he'd promised not to. And then that body and the things that it could do to my body. "I do like him," I said in a small voice.

"Beck?" she asked.

"I just don't understand why he wasn't more persistent," I said. "And although I like him, want him, think he could make me happy—I can't be with a man who doesn't want me enough to fight for me."

"I get it. But something tells me that Beck's relationships have been all about his dick up until you. He's probably as confused as you are. Maybe you need to let him know you're ready to be fought for."

"Maybe," I replied. Now that I'd let myself think about him, I couldn't wait to see him.

"Weren't you meant to have dinner with Karen's godfather?" she asked me.

I nodded. That was this Saturday. Just two days away.

"Maybe that's a good time to let him know."

"Let him know what?" I asked.

"That you're ready. To be fought for."

Maybe I'd been too quick to label our relationship a holiday romance, as something that couldn't be real. Because it felt more than real to me. I'd tried to convince myself I wasn't the right woman for him, but the longer I spent without him, the more I couldn't shake the feeling he was who I was meant to be with.

THIRTY-FOUR

Stella

As I knocked on my boss's door, I couldn't decide if I was the world's biggest idiot or just a fool pursuing my dreams.

"What is it?" she barked.

I opened the door.

"What now, Stella? I have a lot to get through and unless you've made this month's target, so do you."

At least she hadn't suddenly become pleasant or I might have felt a little bad. I wondered whether she was always a bitch or if this awful job had made her that way.

"I won't take up much of your time. I just wanted to hand you this in person." The nerves in my stomach sloshed as I placed the sealed envelope on her desk. I was doing the right thing—I knew it. It was time to take a leap of faith.

"What is this?" she asked, as if I'd just delivered up a turd on a spade.

"My resignation. Let me know if you want me to work my notice." Instantly it was as if someone had tied balloons to my body and I was ten tons lighter. I turned and headed out.

"Your resignation? What the hell are you talking about?"

At the door I turned and grinned. "I'm leaving." I wasn't a recruitment consultant. Not in my heart.

"Who are you going to? Whitman and Jones? They are complete bastards to work—"

"I haven't got a job to go to. I'm going to concentrate on establishing my own design business."

"No job?" She rose to her feet and leaned across her desk. If I were a little closer, I might be worried she'd lunge at me. "Haven't you got bills to pay?"

Paying the mortgage wasn't enough anymore—I wanted to be happy.

"I'm selling my place." I didn't want to be in the flat that Matt and I had moved into together, surrounded by broken promises and bloody awful taste. "In this market, the agent said they'd have a buyer for me by the end of the week." I was planning to use the equity in the flat to tide me over until my business got up and running. If it took longer than my money lasted, I'd get a part-time job—one that didn't consume my soul.

"Well, good luck to you," she spat as if she was wishing a tropical disease on me rather than luck. "Clear your desk. I don't want to see you in the office again."

My grin hadn't faded one bit as I headed out, my balloons leading the way.

I was free. And at the start of a new life.

THIRTY-FIVE

Stella

I rotated my ankle, looking at my new shoes from every angle. The red satin straps hugged my foot and perfectly matched my nail polish. They were the highest heels I'd ever seen and beyond sexy. If these heels didn't hint that I was ready to be fought for, then nothing would.

I figured Florence was right—I was guarded and still a little bruised, so Beck needed to know I was ready. For him. Because I was. He might not be able to give me what I needed, but I owed it to myself to find out.

I'd decided I'd lay my cards on the table, tell him how I felt and what I needed from him. He'd have to be all in or all out. I wasn't going to just be one of a pack of girls he was dating. Beck might say no, but I knew I couldn't date him knowing he wasn't as committed to me as I was to him.

I needed a man who wanted me and no one else. If I was giving away my heart, I wanted another in return.

The door buzzed and my breath caught. This was it. I'd missed him. The echo of his absence had been getting louder. Knowing he was on the other side of the door was like the tide had rushed in and filled up my heart.

I hitched up my bra—off the shoulder was the perfect blend of demure and sexy but strapless bras and I would never be friends—and turned to the side to check that the bottom of my long, black dress wasn't stuck in my knickers, then grabbed my clutch and headed out.

A wave of heat chased up my body as I answered the door and came eye to eye with Beck.

Even in a few days his hair seemed to have grown, and I wanted to push my fingers through it so I could see his pretty eyes more clearly.

"Hi," I said, my pulse vibrating across my skin.

His gaze didn't leave my face. "You look beautiful."

Perhaps I didn't need to spend so much time on the dress, shoes, or perfect shade of nail polish.

"You too," I replied, trying to resist the urge to slide my hands up his chest and lay my cheek against his heart.

"Are you ready?" he asked, knocking me out of my own head.

I nodded, and he slid his hand into mine and squeezed just like we were back in Scotland. I bit down on my bottom lip as we headed to the car.

"We should talk," he said as he got into the driver's seat and started the engine.

"Talk?" I asked as if that wasn't exactly what I'd been about to suggest.

"Yeah," he replied. "I have things I need to say. A lot of things, actually."

"Me too."

He shot me a glance.

Anticipation and impatience tickled at my fingertips.

"We'll discuss everything later," he said. "But first we'll have dinner."

"This is just Henry and us, right?" I asked. "You'd tell me if it were a welcome back from honeymoon party for Karen and Matt, right?"

"No, I would have declined the invitation."

Beck didn't look at me, just pinched his eyebrows together, making his frown sterner.

"I never should have been invited to the wedding—they should have been too ashamed, and they should have been worried I'd turn up and burn the place to the ground. Not that I ever would, but I shouldn't have been so predictably polite about it. You know what I mean?"

"I do," he said, his expression neutral as he navigated the heavy traffic.

"I'm done with being polite to people who hurt me." I exhaled as I stared out of the window. London had so many amazing things to offer. Life had so much to grab. I wasn't willing to sit by anymore. "Do you mind if we turn the air conditioning down and open the window?"

"Not at all," he said, pressing a button on the steering wheel. The fans stopped whirring and the windows opened.

"That's better," I said.

He glanced at me and grinned as if he knew something I didn't.

"What?" I asked, wanting to be in on the secret, too.

"Nothing," he replied. "Later."

"We're going to talk about me wanting the window open later?"

He paused as if he was considering whether he was going to elaborate. He nodded. "Later. Let's do dinner. Then after that, our deal is done."

Later felt like a long way away.

We passed endless streets of wrought-iron railings. Gazing out the window, I wanted to get behind them and discover what was inside. I couldn't wait to get back to designing. To sourcing materials, researching suppliers. "I resigned this week," I announced as we continued to drive toward Henry's townhouse.

"Permanently?" he asked.

"Yeah. Handed my notice in on Tuesday."

"That's amazing, Stella. How do you feel?"

Warmth settled in my belly at his enthusiasm. "Nervous but relieved, I think. I don't have many savings, but the flat is on the market and there are five viewings set up for this weekend. I'm hoping I can use the equity to live while I'm getting back on my feet."

"You're going to focus solely on interior design?"

"Absolutely. I don't know how I stayed doing recruitment for as long as I did."

"So you're figuring out what you want and going for it," he said, almost to himself. "Good for you."

With every word I'd spoken, Beck's grin got bigger and bigger. Was he just happy for me? Was that how this worked? I wanted to dip inside his brain and figure out what he was thinking. Was he seeing us as colleagues, friends, boss and employee? Or did he want me to join his little black book of women that he leafed through whenever he wanted company?

I didn't like any of those options.

"I know you said later, Beck. But—"

"Here we are," he said, pulling into a gated driveway. "They must have been expecting us."

"Can we just have five minutes before we go in?"

"Let's get this Henry thing done. And then everything after that's real. If it hasn't been already."

Before I could ask him what he meant, he'd switched the engine off and climbed out of the car.

Everything after this dinner was real? How much had he been pretending?

Later better bloody hurry up.

THIRTY-SIX

Beck

I'd had the builders work overnight to make sure everything was ready. I'd never had to talk about my feelings, and I wasn't convinced that me *just* talking was going to change her mind. I wanted something tangible I could show Stella —to demonstrate how I felt.

Stella was a once-in-a-lifetime woman and this was my one chance to convince her I was the man for her. I had to get it right.

"Dinner was nice," Stella said from the passenger seat. "Henry's so charming." I was so on edge, so amped up over what I was going to say that I'd almost forgotten she was next to me.

"Yes. Nice."

"Are you okay?" she asked.

I wasn't sure I was. My palms were sweaty. I couldn't sit still. I thought I'd wanted Henry's signature on the contract for the Dawnay building badly, but it didn't compare to the need that coursed through me knowing Stella wasn't mine.

"Fine," I replied. I'd feel better when we got to my office and I showed her what I'd done.

"You're heading east," she said. "I can get the tube home if—"

"I'll take you. Just need to pick up something from the office." *Wooing* women, as Dexter put it, wasn't something I was practiced in. I'd never had to convince a woman to give me a chance. Never had to explain how I felt. And now, without any experience, I had my one shot.

I'd make it work. I had to.

I drew up outside my building.

"The City's always so quiet at the weekend," she said, glancing around. The streetlights highlighted her cheekbones and her full, soft lips. It had been too long since I'd been able to properly touch her.

"Will you come up?" I asked.

"To your office?" She raised her eyebrows as if she didn't understand, but without further questions, she unclicked her seatbelt and opened the door. That was the thing with Stella—yes, her ex had left her mistrustful, but underneath that, when the people unworthy of her were cleaned away, there was an open, beautiful woman who would do anything to please someone she cared about. She just needed the right man to care about.

I took her hand as I joined her on the pavement, and she tipped her head back and smiled.

"We are due a conversation," she said. "I have things I need to say and you said you did, too."

I led her through the sliding doors and inside toward the lifts.

"You're right," I replied. "I'd like to go first if you don't mind."

She nodded, and I squeezed her hand, silently thanking her for her patience.

"It seems like an age since I was last here," she said as the lift doors opened onto my office floor.

It felt like a different lifetime to me. I led her toward the glass wall with the view of St. Paul's.

"It looks great lit up at night," she said, gazing up at the cathedral that had stood there for nearly four hundred years. "Did you know that in order to get such an audacious design built, Sir Christopher Wren pretended he was building a more modest church and then he whipped off the scaffolds and surprised everyone?"

I grinned. Perhaps subconsciously I'd taken inspiration from the architect of St. Paul's. I'd gotten Stella up to my office under false pretenses. "Is that right? There must be something in the air around here," I replied.

"What do you mean?" she asked.

Without answering her, I headed away from my office to the other side of the floor and came to a standstill outside the second glass office on the floor that I'd just had created.

"What?" Stella asked.

I nodded toward the pink neon sign behind the desk. "I think your new business needs an office."

She stepped closer and peered inside, her nose almost pressed up against the glass.

"We can go in—I kinda own the building." I pulled open the door and led her inside.

"I don't get it. The sign says London Designs." She let my hand drop and made her way toward the desk.

Jesus, I knew I'd be bad at this. "Yeah. I didn't know how else to—I wanted to show you how—I need you to know . . ."

Bollocks. Dexter said I had charm, but it had all escaped me now.

"Stella, I know you're worried about us working together and mixing business with pleasure—but we've done that from the start. And we do it so well together."

"I don't get it. You want me to work from your office?" she asked.

"I want us to be partners."

"Business partners?" she asked.

"No." Christ. How could I be so bad at this? "When we made our deal, I had no idea that pretending to be your boyfriend would result in what we have—what I feel for you. It might have started off as pretend but what I feel for you is as real as it gets."

She blushed and leaned against the desk I hoped she would accept as hers. My heartbeat thumped in my chest like a clenched fist pounding on a door, waiting for her response.

She didn't speak. Had it been enough?

"If you still have to work through your feelings for Matt, I'm prepared to be patient. To win you over. To make you see that he never deserved you. If you have doubts about us being able to work and be together then I'll erase them for you. Give me a chance and I'll prove to you how much I'm in love with you."

Stella gasped as the strength of my feelings hit me like a fist to my throat.

I loved her.

She was all I wanted.

She stepped toward me. Close enough for me to touch her but somehow, I held back. I wanted to hear clearly, and I wasn't sure I could concentrate if I was touching her.

"I don't have feelings for Matt that I need to work through. And yes, I'm a little nervous about working together if we're in a relationship. But really, most of all, I'm scared."

"Of me?"

She pressed her hand to my chest and I relaxed instantly. Her warmth was like coming home—it was belonging. Wherever she was, I was meant to be.

"I'm terrified of being hurt," she replied. "Of being made a fool of. But most of all I'm afraid of how I feel about you. It's so powerful that even after a few weeks, I know you could devastate me forever. You're capable of hurting me far more than Matt ever could have because of what I feel for you. I wouldn't be able to live through you breaking my heart."

I slid my hands around her waist. "You won't ever have to."

"But after Scotland, you didn't seem bothered if we saw each other again—I said about us working together and you sort of shrugged as if it didn't matter."

"Stella, I was floored. I'd assumed that things would continue between us and when you seemed so unsure, I was on the back foot. Unprepared."

She nodded, fiddling with the button on my shirt. "I thought you'd convince me. I'd seen you when you want something, and you gave in so easily I thought I wasn't important. And after what's happened—I need to be important to someone."

Of course she needed that—deserved it. She needed me to have fought for her—and I hadn't. I just hoped it wasn't too late. "No one's ever been *more* important to me," I said.

She looked up at me as if she was trying to gauge if I was telling the truth.

A thousand words clambered up my throat, fighting to get out. "It's why I brought you here," I said. "I want us to be together—whether we're at home or in the office. I want you to do what you love—to be happy—and if I can help then I'll do whatever I can. I want to support you and your business."

She glanced around. "Twenty-four hours a day?" She giggled, and it was such a delicious sound, I knew I'd be working to hear it as often as I could for as long as I lived.

"You don't realize how different you are for me. I've never felt . . . The idea of losing you causes me actual, physical pain. I didn't realize that was a thing, but I've been walking around with a tightness in my jaw and a headache that won't go away but disappeared the moment I laid eyes on you tonight." She reached up for my face. "I want to wake up with you every morning, not just when we're in some castle in Scotland. I want us to work together so we don't have to spend the day apart. We can talk all day. Discuss business projects. Jesus, I want to know what color underwear you're wearing every morning and why you're pissed off after a phone call.

"I want it all.

"I want to love you. If you'll let me."

I took a breath. It was all I had. I just hoped it was enough.

She paused and it was as if every nanosecond was strung out and had become an hour. Finally she spoke. "Being with you in Scotland shifted things for me," she said. "I came back, and I knew what I wanted. I handed my notice in, put the flat on the market—I just knew."

"And do you know about us?" I asked, impatient as ever. But she was so resolute about everything, why hadn't she reached out? I'd not heard from her at all since Scotland.

"That's the final piece of the puzzle. You say you want me, and I know I want you. I came here to give you a speech about how I wasn't prepared to be just some girl you're dating."

"You'll never be just some girl I'm dating. You're the woman I want to spend every waking hour with, want to tell every thought in my head to. You're the only person I'll take sartorial advice from and the only human being on this planet I'd let share my office. You'll never be some girl. You're my woman. Fuck Matt, fuck every other man on the planet."

She placed her finger over my lips. "I need to be clear with you now—I was hurt by what Matt did. Devastated even. But he never made me feel like you do. I feel strong, not weak, with you, like my opinion matters, like I'm smart and sexy and cared for when I'm with you. Don't ever compare yourself to anyone and especially not Matt."

The tension in my muscles eased. I'd needed to hear that from her more than I'd let myself believe. For me it was simple—I'd never had a relationship with a woman worth mentioning—but she'd thought she would spend the rest of her life with Matt. I hated him for having that part of her before I could, but I also wanted to shake the prick's hand for being stupid enough to let her go. Because that meant I got her.

"You're incomparable to anyone," I said.

"So, we're doing this?" she asked.

I chuckled. "We are. But you might need to use your pumice stone on me as we go on our journey. I have some rough edges and I'm pretty sure I'm going to fuck up left and right. You'll have to tell me."

"Oh, I will, don't worry."

I cupped her face in my hands. "I know you will." And I'd enjoy every second of her setting me straight and explaining exactly how I should love her.

I'd love her any way she needed and every way I could.

THIRTY-SEVEN

Beck

I slid my hands up her thighs, taking her skirt with me. "You know what this calls for."

"I know you're trying to get into my knickers," she replied leaning back on the desk and opening her legs.

I was trying. And I wasn't hearing any complaints.

"But I don't know what occasion you're referring to."

"You mean apart from the fact I just told you I loved you and you apparently love me back, apart from the fact we're alone for the first time in days, and apart from the fact I've dreamt about the feel of your skin under my fingertips every night since we left Scotland?"

She grinned in response. This woman's smile had the power to end me. I felt it deep in my gut—like I needed it to function. I'd never stop yearning for, working for, dreaming of it.

"Apart from all those things," she said, tipping her head back as I pressed more and more urgent kisses up her throat.

"We have to christen your new office. That way, every

meeting, every telephone call, every thought you have in here, will have me as a backdrop."

I started to unbutton her blouse but she stopped me. "Beck, the whole of London can see us."

"Not unless they're standing on the dome of St Paul's—" She went to interrupt me but my amusement must have shown on my face and she stopped. "Before you say something about people watching from the Golden Gallery or the Stone Gallery—the place is closed."

I finished unbuttoning her blouse. "And if there was some private function or an interloper, hidden away after closing . . ." I dipped and placed a kiss between her breasts. "Then I think they deserve a show."

I reached up between her legs, pulled off her knickers, and she gasped as I trailed my fingers across her pussy. "Wow, you're sensitive."

"Don't tease me," she pleaded. "Not tonight."

I plunged two fingers deep into her and she groaned. "I promise. There will be no teasing."

Not teasing exactly. But the things for which you work hardest, taste the sweetest.

I withdrew my hand and straightened out, tasting her as I licked my fingers clean. "Just like honey," I said.

She sat up, reaching for my belt, and I took a step back, took off my jacket, and hung it on the coat stand behind the door.

"Beck," she implored.

I took a breath. I didn't need to rush. We had the rest of our lives to do this—for me to . . .

Make her beg.

Make her come.

Make her happy.

I was going to savor every moment.

Undoing the cufflinks on my shirt, I slid them onto a glass side table and rolled up my sleeves. Stella's groan suggested to me that, despite her protestations, she liked a little bit of torture.

She was my perfect woman in every way.

"You're so impatient. What *am* I going to do with you?" I asked.

"Anything you like," she replied.

Like I said—my *perfect* woman.

I didn't reply and just stood watching her, watching her beautiful bare pussy, ripe and ready for my fingers, lips, and cock. She groaned and reached to touch herself.

In a flash, I had circled her wrist with my fingers. "Not unless you ask me first. That's mine to play with."

I took her hand and placed it over my fabric-covered cock. "And this is yours."

She fumbled to undo my zip and then wrapped her fingers around it.

So fucking eager.

So fucking perfect.

And mine.

I gritted my teeth, but I couldn't resist and I pushed into her hand. Fuck, even her fingers were better than the best I'd ever had until Stella.

"I don't think you'd be able to hold back," she said. "Even if you wanted to."

"You want to test that theory?" I asked, stepping away from her.

She shook her head, panic slicing across her face.

"Yeah, I didn't think so." I pushed her down onto her desk, one side of her lit up by the streetlights, the other shadowed but all beautiful.

I spread her knees apart, bending to inspect her pussy.

Talk about beautiful—all curves, contours, and softness but hot and needy at the same time. And it belonged to me now.

She squirmed under my inspection, not out of embarrassment but desire. Fuck, how did I get so lucky? "Please, Beck."

She was right. I couldn't hold back—didn't want to. I pressed the head of my cock at her entrance and tried not to explode at the searing heat of her. Fuck, I'd missed this. Missed us. Missed feeling that I had everything I needed.

It was only when she left that I realized she was so much more than I could ever have imagined.

She was everything.

I took a deep breath and slid into her, watching her as she watched me. And it was just as I remembered and more. Being as close to another person as it's possible to be seemed to take on meaning with Stella, like our union had been foretold a millennium ago by an omniscient god or was written in the stars when the universe exploded into existence.

We were meant to be.

I'd never been surer about anything than I was about her. About us.

"I didn't know it was possible to feel this way about anyone. It feels like more than love," she whispered, echoing my thoughts.

I folded my body over hers. "I know." I began to move in and out, feeling our fate surrounding us, binding us stronger. The push and pull of our bodies sinking me further into our destiny.

She caught my jaw in her hand, her fingers pressing into my stubble, and brought my lips to hers. She plunged her tongue into my mouth, her groans shooting vibrations of pleasure down my spine.

Breaking our kiss, I braced myself, hands flat on the desk either side of her and took a breath. It was too much. This woman was too fucking much for me.

Her hair splayed on the glass desk, the reflection of her body everywhere I looked from the glass windows to the chrome legs of the table, she surrounded me and it was overwhelming and perfect and I wanted it to last forever.

But I needed to fuck her. I needed to come. And when we were done, I needed to do it again and again and again.

A lifetime of this woman wouldn't ever be enough.

I was two seconds away from giving up, from surrendering to my orgasm, but I wanted her pleasure more than my own, and by some force of will, adrenaline seared through my limbs, giving me the strength to keep going, to keep chasing away the ache in me that she created. For it was only her who held the cure.

"Beck!" she cried out.

The desperation in her eyes told me she couldn't take anymore, and I understood.

"Come, Stella. Come for me."

She sighed, thankful and longing, and her body silently erupted beneath me. It was the most beautiful thing I'd ever seen and I was gone. I was lost to her and I pushed in again, gasping at the fierce rumble of my orgasm that gathered into a roar when it reached my chest and exploded.

I wasn't sure I could withstand the power of my climax, the pleasure I got from being with her.

After a moment of blackness, I opened my eyes to find her gazing up at me. Panting, I lay my head on her chest and tried to find my voice. "Tell me what you want?" I asked, my breath heavy against her skin.

"You," she whispered. "I want you. I need you. It's only you. Ever."

Since I met her, whether I'd known it or not, those were the words I'd been waiting to hear from Stella. Hearing it calmed me. As if the final piece of the jigsaw had been found. And I needed nothing but her—not buildings or developments, not acceptance from a section of society that had so resolutely rejected me. I didn't need anything but to be with the woman who had changed how I saw myself. She was the woman who healed my wounds, faded my scars, and showed me my future.

EPILOGUE

Stella

Was it wrong to feel a sexual connection toward a slab of stone? I took in the thin, gray veins of the white Statuario marble and shivered. *So beautiful.*

"Stella? Are you drooling?" Florence appeared at my side.

"Maybe. What are you doing here?" Had I been too engrossed in fixtures and missed a lunch date?

"I called by the office and they said you were down here."

The last time she'd called by my office, it had been a different office, a different job—an entirely different life that I was leading.

"Is everything okay?" I asked, sweeping my hand down the cold, smooth surface and turning away in case I got tempted to lick it.

Florence winced and I guided her out of the penthouse unit we were working on and toward the lift. "Let's get out of here."

"I wanted you to hear this from me," Florence said as she stepped inside.

"Oh God, will you stop starting sentences like that?" I laughed. "At least this time, I know you're not about to tell me that Karen's running off with Beck." There was never a day that went by that I doubted Beck's love for me. He was a man who believed that love was a verb and found every way he could to show me how he felt.

He'd taught me what real love was.

"Well, no, but you won't believe it when I tell you what she's done now."

The goods lift hit the floor with a thump.

"What?" I asked.

"Well, she's walked out on Matt. Left him."

For all Karen's faults, I didn't think she'd walk on a marriage that was only six month's old.

"Apparently she found him with his hand up one of her mother's friends' skirts at their housewarming. And they were snogging each other's faces off. Of course, he blamed it on the booze."

I laughed although it wasn't funny. I'd never thought Matt was a cheater. He might have cheated on me, but I didn't think that's who he was in his DNA. But perhaps that's how he was wired. "Are you sure that's not just the story Karen made up to deflect from something she'd done?"

Florence shrugged. "I heard it from Bea who heard it from Karen."

"Are they trying to make it work or is that it? The D word?" I asked.

"From what I heard, Karen's already moved on."

We headed across the road to the bench where Beck and I sat and had our lunch on days we were on site.

Beck was right—those two really did deserve each other.

"How do you feel?" Florence asked. "I wondered if you'd be a bit upset."

"Upset?" I asked. "I don't feel anything other than relief that I'm not part of the drama. And grateful it wasn't me that found him. That he ended things when he did and he didn't come back to me in the months before the wedding when I might have taken him back. Him marrying Karen was awful but it led me to Beck, and I can't be sad about that."

I grinned as Beck waved from the entrance to One Park Street. He strode over to us.

"Christ, he's so good looking, Stella."

"He is. But it's his heart and his humor that make me love him more every day."

"What are you two gossiping about?" Beck asked as he bounded over.

"I was just telling Florence how much I love you," I said and that grin he wore when things went his way crept across his face.

"Not as much as I love you," he said, dropping a kiss on the top of my head.

"You two are ridiculously perfect for each other," Florence said.

"Just as you and Gordy are."

"Which is the other reason I'm here," Florence said. "Gordy proposed and I said yes."

I jumped up and threw myself at Florence. "Yes! I'm so happy for you."

"I want you to be maid of honor. Gordy wants a huge

wedding. I'd prefer to elope but, you know, he doesn't often put his foot down."

"I'm excited." I turned to Beck. "Isn't this great?"

"I wish you were this excited when I propose to you." He rolled his eyes.

I had to stifle a giggle. Beck proposed on an almost monthly basis. And each time, I said maybe or no or not yet. He took it in his stride, but I could understand why me being so excited smarted a little. "It's different. Florence and Gordy have been together forever."

"Just like we will be," he replied.

"Right. So who cares if we get married?" I'd been so sure that I'd marry Matt, that somehow I didn't want to cheapen what Beck and I had by wanting to get married. A ceremony that everyone else could have wasn't enough somehow. I didn't see the point.

"I'll wear you down eventually," he said.

I laughed. If it was important to Beck, then one of these times he proposed, I'd say yes. But I knew he loved me and that was all I needed. Beck's love, adoration, respect, and time was more than I could ever have hoped for and I had it all. He was all I'd ever need.

Twelve months later

Beck

I stared up at the newly renovated, soon-to-launch, One Park Street. The red brickwork had been cleaned, repointed, and repaired and looked as good as it no doubt did when it was built over a hundred and fifty years ago. The arched windows were lit up, hiding the beautiful interiors Stella had completely transformed. Tonight, we launched the sales of the first units on a strictly invitation-only basis.

"You did it," Stella said as she stood next to me.

I slid my arm around her waist. "We did it."

"But this for you . . . It's more than just another development. How does it feel?"

"Different to how I expected," I replied. "Looking back, I was a maniac—giving you the interiors on this job was insane. But I was desperate."

"Hey." Stella thwacked me in the stomach and laughed.

"You did a more than amazing job—far better than any designer I've ever worked with. But seriously, I didn't know you from Adam. I should never have agreed to you leading this. I wanted the Dawnay building whatever the cost."

"Do you feel free now? Like you've conquered your past?" she asked.

I couldn't remember the last time I'd given my biological father a second thought. "Yeah, but I'm not sure that's got anything to do with the building. I think that's about you and the life we have together—the future we're going to have." I loved that I could still make her blush. I hoped that never went away, even when we were ninety and hitting each other with our walking sticks. "The thought of five baby Wildes in our new place makes everything else seem ridiculous."

"Less of the five," Stella said. "And less of the Wildes. They will be London babies."

"But after we're married, they'll be Wildes."

"No, after we're married, I'll still be Stella London. You'll still be Beck Wilde. Our babies will be London-Wildes or Wilde-Londons."

"That's ridiculous. We're not having kids with a double-barreled name."

"Then they'll be Londons," she said.

I grinned—partly because she knew I'd give in to just about anything she wanted. But mainly because she hadn't told me how she had no intention of marrying me.

Because she usually did. Every time I asked her. And I asked her a lot. Stella was a prize I'd never give up fighting for.

A familiar hand gripped my shoulder. "Not bad, mate. Not bad at all," Dexter said as he came up behind us.

"Not bad? You want to see the interior," I said.

"It's incredible," Stella said. "It's the real estate equivalent of a diamond."

"You got that wrong," Dexter said and the gleam in his eye meant only one thing—he'd found a stone he'd been chasing.

"You deal in coal," I said. "I prefer bricks and mortar."

"Stop teasing Dexter," Stella said.

"You keep hold of this one," Dexter said. "She's special. Women like Stella don't come along more than once in a lifetime."

"I know, mate. It hasn't happened for you, yet. But it will."

Dexter smiled and nodded—clearly not wanting to get into it but not believing me either.

"I have a feeling that this time next year, we'll be double dating," Stella said. "I mean, any girl would be lucky to have you—funny, handsome, and millions of pounds worth of diamonds at your fingertips on a daily basis." She turned to me. "If this guy hadn't tricked me into falling in love with him, I'd be first in the queue."

My heart almost stopped every time she told me she loved me. Even now. Over a year since we met.

"I shouldn't complain," Dexter said. "It's not like I've never had what you guys have. I was just stupid enough to fuck it up. Just this once, don't follow my example."

Dexter believed in love but that it only happened once a lifetime. But being with Stella had shifted my perspective on a lot of things. Dexter was right. Loving a woman was important and I wouldn't believe that my mate was going to go the rest of his life on his own.

"I'll try," I said, for once not wanting to mock him. "As soon as she finally says yes, you'll be my first call. We're going to need a rock of a ring."

"I don't need a rock," Stella said and I bit back a grin. So she'd thought about the ring she wanted. Interesting.

I bent and pressed a kiss on her lips. "You deserve a rock."

"Can't you two keep your hands off each other for even a second?" an annoying voice said from behind me.

I turned to find Tristan and Gabriel coming toward us. Gabriel was supposed to be in Miami. He must have just stepped off the flight. He knew tonight was important to me —so it was important to him to be here.

How did I get so fucking lucky? Friends who would stand in front of a bullet for me and a woman I'd stand in front of a bullet for. No wonder my past had dissolved into the air. Life didn't get any better than right now.

"You boys are looking gorgeous," Stella said to the two of them and I tightened my grip. She was now a regular at our Sunday night drinks and the guys adored her. It was like a woman had been initiated into our group.

"Not as beautiful as you," Tristan said, taking her arm and placing a kiss on the back of her hand.

"Knock it off," I said, pulling Stella back, and she laughed.

"Now I know Stella's taken, I think I can safely say, I'll never marry," Tristan said.

He was full of shit. But it was exactly how I would feel if Tristan was with Stella—there wouldn't be any point looking for anyone else when the woman who was meant for me was already taken.

"So this is One Park Street," Tristan said. "Looks decent enough but if it's that nice, then why aren't you two moving in?"

Stella had suggested we take one of the two penthouses, but I'd been a bit reticent. I wasn't sure how I'd feel living somewhere with such a strong connection with the Dawnay family. But now, after the block's transformation, after being with Stella and working so closely with her on this building, I couldn't think of a better place to live.

"Actually," I said, pulling the keys to the penthouse from my trouser pocket. "I've been thinking about that. As it's launch night, maybe we should take a tour and look at it from a buyer's perspective."

Stella lifted up on her tiptoes and her eyes lit up. "Really? I've been hoping against hope that you might have a change of heart when you saw the place."

"Excuse us, gentleman, go help yourself to champagne. We're going to go and look at the flat where we're going to bring my first son home from hospital," I said, guiding Stella into the building and toward the private lift for Penthouse A.

"Are you serious about this?" she asked.

"Which bit? The son thing? The hospital or the penthouse?"

She grinned. "I meant the penthouse but all of it, I guess."

We stepped out of the lift and directly into the lobby of the best apartment in W_1. The marble floors, the crystal chandelier, the inlaid brass detailing on the door frames. It all looked perfect.

"I'm serious about everything to do with our future," I replied, striding toward the entrance to the living space, but Stella didn't move and when I turned, she was biting the inside of her cheek like she did when she was nervous.

"Well, if that's the case, then I have a question," she said.

"Ask me anything," I replied.

She fumbled in her handbag and pulled something out. "How about we wear these?" she said, presenting a black velvet box to me. I recognized it as one of the jewelry boxes Dexter used for his clients.

Was my woman proposing to me? After all these months of me asking her to marry me—she was finally saying yes? I couldn't take my eyes off her. Tonight was the perfect night—just when I thought life couldn't get any better. But that was life with Stella. Just as I thought we reached the pinnacle, she went and set a new standard in happiness.

When I didn't take the box from her, tentatively she opened it to reveal two rings, side by side—one a band of diamonds and one plain platinum.

I hoped this woman would never stop surprising me.

I grinned and she rolled her eyes.

"So what do you say?" she asked.

Okay so it might not be the most romantic proposal I'd ever heard, but I wouldn't want it any other way.

"Sure, I'll wear the ring."

"Beck!" she said.

"What? I can't answer a question you haven't asked me."

She laughed. "You're impossible. But I love you. Will you marry me?"

"You're perfect. And I love you too, and I'll marry you every day of the week for the rest of your life."

I took the box from her and pulled the diamond ring out and got on one knee. "You're the most gracious, kind, funny, sexy woman I've ever met, and I love you so much sometimes it frightens me. My entire life, I've been searching for something, needing to fill a missing void in my life. For years I thought the Dawnay building was the answer. But all along it was you I was waiting for."

Stella stepped forward, tilted her head to the side, and pushed her fingers through my hair.

"Marry me," I said. "And I'll never stop working to make you happy."

She sat on my bended knee and clasped her arms around my neck. "I love you, Beck Wilde. Now. Tomorrow. Forever. It's as if my life didn't really begin until I met you. And you've got a deal."

Being with Stella London wasn't just a one-off, deal of a lifetime. It was a daily win, and nothing would ever compare. It didn't matter what happened in life—good or bad—as long as Stella was by my side, everything was perfect. Searching for a closed door on my past had opened the heavens and brought me Stella, and I'd never look back.

***

Thank you for reading Mr. Mayfair.

Have you read Dexter and Hollie's story in **Mr. Knightsbridge**?

Love fake relationship romances? You'll love **Duke of Manhattan**

Loved Beck Wilde? You'll love Dylan James from **Indigo Nights**

To sign up to my newsletter and receive all my latest news, book updates, giveaways and freebies go to www.louisebay.com/newsletter

All books are stand alone

The Doctors Series

Dr. Off Limits

Dr. Perfect

The Mister Series

Mr. Mayfair

Mr. Knightsbridge

Mr. Smithfield

Mr. Park Lane

Mr. Bloomsbury

Mr. Notting Hill

The Christmas Collection

14 Days of Christmas

The Player Series

International Player

Private Player

Dr. Off Limits

Standalones

Hollywood Scandal

Love Unexpected

Hopeful

The Empire State Series

The Gentleman Series

The Ruthless Gentleman

The Wrong Gentleman

The Royals Series

King of Wall Street

Park Avenue Prince

Duke of Manhattan

The British Knight

The Earl of London

The Nights Series

Indigo Nights

Promised Nights

Parisian Nights

Faithful

What kind of books do you like?

Friends to lovers

Mr. Mayfair

Promised Nights

International Player

Fake relationship (marriage of convenience)

Duke of Manhattan

Mr. Mayfair

Mr. Notting Hill

Enemies to Lovers

King of Wall Street

The British Knight

The Earl of London

Hollywood Scandal

Parisian Nights

14 Days of Christmas

Mr. Bloomsbury

Office Romance/ Workplace romance

Mr. Knightsbridge

King of Wall Street

The British Knight

The Ruthless Gentleman

Mr. Bloomsbury

Second Chance

International Player

Hopeful

Best Friend's Brother

Promised Nights

Vacation/Holiday Romance

The Empire State Series

Indigo Nights

The Ruthless Gentleman

The Wrong Gentleman

Love Unexpected

14 Days of Christmas

Holiday/Christmas Romance

14 Days of Christmas

This Christmas

British Hero

Promised Nights (British heroine)

Indigo Nights (American heroine)

Hopeful (British heroine)

Duke of Manhattan (American heroine)

The British Knight (American heroine)

The Earl of London (British heroine)

The Wrong Gentleman (American heroine)

The Ruthless Gentleman (American heroine)

International Player (British heroine)

Mr. Mayfair (British heroine)

Mr. Knightsbridge (American heroine)

Mr. Smithfield (American heroine)

Private Player (British heroine)

Mr. Bloomsbury (American heroine)

14 Days of Christmas (British heroine)

Mr. Notting Hill (British heroine)

Single Dad

King of Wall Street

Mr. Smithfield

Sign up to the Louise Bay mailing list www.louisebay/newsletter

Read more at www.louisebay.com